WHERE THE LIGHT ENTERS

Version 12

"Trust your wound...
Don't turn your head. Keep looking
At the bandaged place. That's where
the light enters you.
– Rumi

Where the Light Enters
Copyright © 2016 by Nick Kaufman

Published by Piscataqua Press
An imprint of RiverRun Bookstore
142 Fleet Street | Portsmouth, NH | 03801
www.riverrunbookstore.com
www.piscataquapress.com
ISBN: 978-1-944393-13-7
Printed in the United States of America

Dedicated to
Peggy, Sashi, and Noah
who set me free.

Hey Sonny Boy,
Having a good time on the hippy dippy Antioch campus in the middle of the cow field? What do you do in Yellow Springs Ohio? Just kidding. I know you like folk dancing and all that civil rights shit. I finally graduated from this loony bin. Walked out is more like it, like I walked out of Harvard and the Peace Corps. Fucking shitholes. My headmaster thought I'd be a good fit at the big H but nobody asked me. Anyway I'm still at loose ends but glad I'm away from the shrinks and in my own apartment. My shrinks said I wasn't done, but I was done with him. Nine months in a locked room was enough and the pansy groups talking about their feelings, a bunch of crazies, not for me sonny boy. I'm bound for somewhere, maybe not college or the Peace Corps, but somewhere. Hey, see you home soon. I'll make you dinner when you're in town. Love you little bro. Paul

Dearest Joshua,
Just a note to let you know I will meet you at the airport. Even your Father might show up. Please tell me your airline, flight number, day and time of arrival, and terminal. I'll meet you by the baggage gate. I don't want to repeat the Holiday fiasco - looking for you all over the airport. Can't wait to see your smiling face. Love, Mother

CHAPTER 1

The front door sprung open and Paul walked briskly down the hall toward my room.

"Hey there, Viking Voyager," he said. His six foot frame and broad shoulders filled my bedroom doorway. I'd hardly unpacked my bags and was browsing through my National Geographics, looking for pictures of Norwegian beauties. He'd gained back some weight since he'd left the hospital after his episode in the Peace Corps - he almost looked healthy again.

I jumped from bed and gripped his shoulders. He gave me a slug in the arm. It hurt but felt good at the same time.

"Checking out the Scandinavian chicks?" he asked.

"Yeah."

"*Land of Free Love.* I hear they're cuter than Guatemalans."

I was about to leave for a year in Norway after my sophomore year.

"How's things with Manny?" I asked. Dad had fixed Paul up in Manny's second hand furniture store after he left the hospital.

"A pain in the ass. When I started, he said, 'Don't worry. I take care of you.' So after two months I ask for a raise. You know what I get? A fucking quarter. What the hell is a quarter after Dad took care of his family?" He grew red in the face.

"You know Manny. He's a kook," I said reaching for my football shirt.

"He's a cheap son of a bitch!"

"Hey, want to throw the ball around?" I asked.

Mother intercepted us on the stairs on our way out, cradling a mixing bowl. "Hi there, stranger. Aren't you going to say hello?" Her complexion had paled since the holidays. Her brown hair was graying and shadows had deepened under her eyes. She waited to be kissed.

"Hi, Mother." Paul leaned over and kissed her on the forehead.

"That's better. Where're you going? Dinner's almost ready."

"I just got here for Christ sakes!" Paul said.

"We'll be just a few minutes," I said, grabbing the ball from Paul and moving him out the door.

"Well, don't be tardy. You don't want the food to spoil."

Paul and I walked into a small clearing, the only place where we could see the sky in our 7-acre pine grove. We lived at the end of a road on Lake Okonowauki. Mother had built our split-level house in the 1950's when Dad's medical practice boomed and I was in elementary school. With large picture windows and redwood sides, it looked right out of House Beautiful. It was filled with paintings and sculptures that you couldn't touch, *objets d'art*, as Mother said.

"Fuck the food," Paul said.

"Hey, *boobalah*. Throw me a deep one." I hiked the ball and ran into the meadow. When I looked over my shoulder, it fell into my hands. I returned to the huddle, breathing hard, grateful that he'd reclaimed his touch. We ran through his high school plays when

2

he captained the team - buttonhooks, slants, and fly patterns - until the dinner bell rang, a soft oriental chime.

"Shit!" Paul slammed the ball into the ground. "I'm not even hungry."

"No big deal," I said, as we scrambled to pick up the ball. Although he'd dropped a lot of pounds in the jungle, he'd trimmed down to muscle and bone with lots of edges. He stiff-armed me in the chest and grabbed it one-handed.

"Nice try, sonny boy," he said, grinning fiercely. He tucked it into his stomach and, arm in arm, we left for the dining room.

Mother was waiting at the head of the table with her hands folded over her plate. Dad had returned from the office, distinguished as usual in his custom wool suit. He'd unbuttoned his collar and loosened his tie and was reading the financials at his end of the table. I unfolded my cloth napkin and waited to hear the menu.

"I got everything from the Star Market today," Mother said.

"The brussel sprouts are fresh, the roast was only 1.49 a pound, the challah came from the Delitizer, and I mashed the potatoes with butter and salt. It's good to be together again."

The recitation over, Dad carved the rib roast with an electric knife and sequestered the garlic cloves on his plate. Mother had set out the Wedgwood china edged with floral touches, Tiffany glasses, and heirloom silverware with decorated handles, the artifacts of Sunday dinners for 20 years.

"Would you like soup?" she asked, poising the ladle over the steaming tureen of chicken soup.

"Sure, Mother," I said.

"Chicken, carrots, parsley, and a package of Lipton cubes for the base."

"Looks good, Mom." I gazed at the parsley bits

3

sinking to the bottom of my bowl.

"*Et toi*, Paul?"

"Nope. Don't feel like it."

"It's the first course."

"It's 90 degrees."

"The soup will cool you off. Like taking a hot shower on a hot night."

"I take cold showers on hot nights."

"Mira, he doesn't want it," Dad said. He set his paper aside.

"How about you, Jacob?"

"I'll have a little. I'm not that hungry myself."

Mother asked about my thoughts for the week and when my passport expired, but my mind was half way between Ohio and Norway and I had nothing planned.

"How about the Red Sox tonight?" Paul asked, popping a crouton into his mouth.

"Sounds great," I said.

"Maybe Father will join you."

"I have patients, Mira. You know that." He added an ice cube to cool his soup.

"Well, since we're all together," Mother said, clearing her throat, "I'd like to have a family party."

"Not another party," Paul said. "Every time we're together you plan a party." He tore off a piece of French bread, scattering the crumbs over the table.

"I just thought, it's been a while. And Josh is leaving next week."

"So what?" Paul said.

"You don't have to raise your voice." She patted her mouth with her napkin. "I can hear you fine."

"I'm not raising my voice."

"Well, maybe it's your tone."

He threw his napkin on the table. Mother's fingers trembled as she took a sip of soup. Crows were cawing in the woods, short staccato bursts followed by silence.

4

"I think I need a breath of fresh air. Anybody care to join me?" Mother asked, looking in my direction.

"No thanks, Mother. I'm okay."

She left and I could hear her rattled through the kitchen cabinet looking for her pills, then I heard her walk to her room and close the door. "She's not herself yet," Dad said. "You can't talk to her like that." He buried his head in his hands. It had been a year since her last episode. Paul and I never knew how many pills she'd swallowed, just that she went to the hospital and didn't come back for three months. Dad pushed his soup aside and I heard him walk up to her room.

"Home sweet home!" Paul declared. "Yesiree, let's have another family soiree. 'Tell us about your time in the Peace Corps, Paul, how you went cuckoo in the jungle. And now Joshua's flying to the Artic. I wonder how long he'll last in the dark for 24 hours?'"

My breathing halted, I put my spoon down. I figured he was sick of my nightmares. I'd wake up yelling and stumbling around, looking for someone to stop me and tell me I was all right. I'd had so many my family stopped coming, except for Paul. He'd come and tell me Red Sox stories, like how Yastrzemski had hit a walk-off home run to beat the Yankees. Anything to keep me from thinking about what I didn't want to think about.

"I'm kidding, Josh. You'll be okay. Only one failure per family, according to David Riesman. We doubled our quota a long time ago. At least I learned something at fucking Harvard."

We went down to the den to watch the game. The Sox were tied in the fifth with Conigliaro at bat. I heard Mother's door open and Dad coming down the back stairs. His face was drawn and tired.

"I'd like you boys to come back to the table. I

want to see if we can finish the meal. Is that too much to ask?"

"No, Dad," we said.

"We only have a few days together. Let's make the best of them. I don't know what else to say."

We returned to the table. Mother was back in her seat, her face puffy from crying. She had freshened her rouge and mascara.

"So," She spread her hands on the table, "Are we ready for the roast?"

"Sure, Mother," we said.

"I hope it hasn't spoiled. I put in lots of garlic, Jacob, just the way you like it. Maybe you boys can clear the soup."

We dabbled with the roast and mashed potatoes, keeping the conversation on the weather and agendas for the week. Mother looked quietly out the window, her mouth stuck in a tight smile. After dinner Paul and I returned to the den, but after the Sox fell behind in the ninth, he left quickly. He asked me to come into town for dinner later in the week. A few seconds later I heard his car jerk into gear and speed up the driveway.

Dad joined me as the game ended, dressed for the office. "Paul leave already?" He sagged into a chair. "Who's playing?"

"The Orioles."

"Sox good this year?"

"Nine games out."

"Semester go well?"

I told him about the C in sociology and B in literature and left out the D's in biology and anatomy. I was supposedly pre-med and the D's would be another disappointment. I'd already busted one expectation by going to Norway instead of France. But living on a Norwegian farm near the Arctic Circle during a summer student exchange had whetted my appetite for more Norwegian adventure.

"Your plane leaves when?" he asked.

"Next Monday. Patients tonight?"

"Just rounds at the hospital. I'll stop at Brighams on the way home, pick up some sundaes?"

"No thanks, Dad. I don't know what I'm doing tonight."

He fingered his black beret, a gift Mother had brought from Paris. Not a good fit for a Russian immigrant who liked to dig in the garden in his Bermudas and T-shirt.

"How are you fixed for cash?" He asked.

"I've got a little." In fact, I was broke, having bought a Gibson J-50 guitar with my semester's spending money.

Dad pulled out a wad of bills wedged in a silver money clip and peeled off five twenties.

"Will that tide you over?"

"Sure, thanks." The bills were smooth and crisp. He always gave me more than I needed.

"Maybe I'll see you later," he said and left.

But I wouldn't see him when he returned, only hear the front door open at midnight and his footsteps in the hall, walking away from their bedroom. He'd been sleeping on the couch since Mother had complained about his snoring.

I turned off the TV and came up for a snack. The refrigerator was filled with leftovers, mummified in double wrapped plastic.

"Joshua? Found your appetite?" Mother asked from the living room.

"No. Just looking. Seen the paper?"

"It's here on the table."

Mother sat on the couch next to her baby black Steinway surrounded by textbooks for her classes at the Harvard Extension. She was buttoned to the chin in a cotton smock that flowed to her ankles. "I'm glad you haven't left, too."

7

I scanned the movie listings.

"Going out?" she asked.

"Might as well."

"I thought we'd catch up."

"How about tomorrow?"

"I've got classes. There's a movie in Boston, *Lust For Life*, about Paul Gauguin." She sounded excited.

"I was thinking of *The Great Escape*. Steve McQueen."

"A war movie? Maybe this week we'll find some time to visit Grandfather together. He wants to see you before you go."

"Sure." I winced at the thought of a nursing home visit. "How's your program?"

"Challenging. Baudelaire and Sartre. Only twenty credits left for my BA. Maybe Paul and I will graduate together!"

"Oh, great." I got up to leave.

"I'll leave the front light on," I heard her say as I shut the door.

I jumped in my car, a VW bug from high school that I stored in the driveway. It was barely dusk as I drove away, but darkness always gathered first in our woods. Out on the lake the water was still light. I wasn't sure where I wanted to go. I'd already watched *The Great Escape*, but there was nothing else I wanted to see. I always looked forward to coming home, but once I got there wanted to leave. So I'd drive around, looking for something to do. Sometimes just staying in motion led to a destination.

CHAPTER 2

Mother had left for class, Dad for the hospital when I woke in the morning. My feet dangled over the bed I'd outgrown in high school. I found my passport in a bottom drawer, expired, and headed for the post office in town to renew it.

Twenty thousand Catholics and three Jewish families lived in Quinnipiac, an Indian name that nobody knew the meaning of. It was an old mill town famous for football, hockey, and not much else. Dad had moved to the suburbs in the Depression because he couldn't make a living in Boston. Although his mother, Ida, didn't like him living so far away, his practice prospered.

I stopped by Jones Drugstore for film and a coke. To Don Jones, Dad was 'Doc' and he filled all his prescriptions. He'd served me ice cream since I could smile. Retreating behind his prescription counter after I filled him in on our news, he asked his daughter Cindy to serve me.

The last time I saw Cindy was when she was cartwheeling across the stage to Sousa marches at a Friday afternoon pep rally in high school. I played clarinet in the band pit where the sightlines were perfect for looking up her skirt. Although I'd had a crush on her for years and frequently passed her in hallways between classes, I'd never said a word to her until I asked for a coke.

"Excuse me?" she said.

"Coke," I said, louder.

"Plain?"

"Vanilla."

Her short white uniform hiked up her thigh as she bent for a glass. She hadn't changed: straight red hair down to her waist, freckles like the Milky Way, and eyes so green you thought they were painted. She still wore white tennis sneakers with pink laces.

"Aren't you Paul Volken's little brother?" she asked.

"Yeah."

"God! You were this high the last time I saw you." She leveled her hand at her breasts. "How's your brother?" Her eyes softened and she came a step closer.

"Good!"

"I heard he was in the Peace Corps."

"He's back."

She looked confused. "So quick?"

"Going back to Harvard this fall."

"Smart guy."

I'd heard the same thing from every teacher from first grade through high school.

"Funny how I lost track of him." She looked wistfully out the door while she squirted two globs of vanilla syrup into my drink. I drank the coke, leaving the intense vanilla in the bottom for last.

"Tell Paul hello," she said, as I got up to leave.

"Sure." I felt honored to deliver the message. Beautiful girls always fell for him.

I put the bill on Dad's tab as I did with all of my charges in town: gas at Slamins and hardware at O'Connor's. I felt like royalty; able to walk into stores and buy what I wanted and be talked to with the respect Dad had earned. I walked across the town green, a peaceful square bordered by a Church, police station, post office, and a bandstand in the middle. The postmaster told me that quick passport renewals were only done in Boston. By the time I'd driven to Sculley Square and got my renewal, my stomach was growling for my grand mother's corned beef and *kreplah*.

Ida's apartment in Brighton was a third floor walk-up near Commonwealth Avenue, the fifth and nicest place Dad's extended family had lived in since their arrival from Russia in 1913.

"Who rings the bell?"Ida squawked through the intercom.

"It's me, Joshua."

"Joshua? You home. Thanks God." Every time I flew home from school she thanked God for my safe arrival. I entered a marble foyer through a wrought iron glass door. Although it was early afternoon, I could smell meat in the oven. From the scent of garlic it had to be roast beef.

Ida and her sister Bertha peered over the banister, neither one taller than five feet. Ida was dressed in a baggy smock, slippers, apron, and hairnet and Bertha was clothed in a fancy skirt and blouse from Lord & Taylor.

"Bring the mail and news, Joshua," Ida said, tossing her mail key over the banister. "*Mein* legs are too old for ups and downs." Her key pinged on the marble floor. I gathered her mail and newspaper. Neither read English; they ordered the newspaper so that their neighbors thought they could.

"Such a *ponem* you have," Ida said, pinching my cheek hard when I arrived on her floor.

"You got tall, *schloyma*?" Bertha asked.

"Not really. You got short."

"Short and *forklempt*. But you, Joshua, a foot. Yah?" Ida asked.

I opened my hands. "Two feet, Ma."

"Ha! Just like your father." She stroked my

cheek. Ida put on an apron when she woke in the morning and cooked all day while Bertha sewed. She did piece work for tailors and Ida prepared corn beef, brisket, kreplah, rolled beef, coffee rolls, and bread. Ida stored her daily cooking in plastic bags that filled a freezer in her bedroom closet. When Dad's sisters, nieces, and nephews arrived for Sunday brunch, they devoured it, *kibitzing* about family woes, temple gossip, and the best buys at Filene's Basement.

"So, how's things?" Ida asked, as she and Bertha settled onto the living room couch by the television that was always on the *fritz*.

"Mother's having a party Sunday," I said.

"*Oih veys meer.* More *borsht*," Bertha grumbled.

"I hate *borsht*," Ida said.

"Why don't you tell her?" I said. Ida shrugged.

"College you like?" Bertha asked.

"I hate labs and dissecting frogs."

"You make good doctor," Ida said. "You *guthartsik*." Ida held her hand on her heart.

"Even if I pass out?"

"Your father hates blood too," Ida said.

"You will do what you do, Joshua," Bertha said.

"Hungry?" Ida asked.

"Sure. You have enough?"

"Enough? Ha!" Ida chuckled and left.

"Can you fix TV?" Bertha asked.

I fiddled with the aerial as Ida set out platters of roast beef, potatoes, candied carrots, and *challah*, a Sunday feast on a Tuesday afternoon. Mother once tried to pry out her recipe for cinnamon rolls. But Ida cooked with a pinch of this and that and didn't like to divulge her secrets. She gave her the recipe, omitting to tell my mother to let the dough rise before putting them in the oven. The rolls emerged in neat little rows, hard as rocks.

"Nothing like eating light, Ma," I said, sitting

down at the kitchen table for a plate of steaming food.

"*Schloyma*, you need meat on the bones," Bertha said. Ida stuck a fork in the roast and sliced three pieces, lean and tender. I mixed mouthfuls of beef with potatoes and washed it down with seltzer.

"How's Pauly?" Ida asked.

"Fine."

"Still working?" Bertha asked.

"I worry, Joshua," Ida said. "Harvard, Peace Corps. Heat in the woods not good. *Nishtan kopp.*" She tapped her forehead.

"He's going back to school, Ma. It'll take time."

"Time, *schmine*. Who has time?" The veins of her hands stood out like a road map. She glanced at the picture of Abe on the wall, taken just before he died. Short and balding, with thick glasses that made him look lost. He'd never found his way after leaving the ship, stripped of his possessions and savings. Sometimes he never even left his room.

"More meat?" Ida asked.

"NO! I'll explode."

"But you have room..."

"For brownies?"

"You know about sweets, *schloyma*?" I knew, but loved hearing Ida's expressions. "Man has two stomachs. One for meat and one for sweet."

She brought me a tray of brownies cut in squares, half with nuts, half without, the way Paul and I liked it. Bertha quickly sampled both while I bit into a moist, fudgy piece. No wonder Dad had chocolate ice cream sodas with his lunch. She wrapped up the brownies with nuts for Paul and asked me to give her a ride to Temple. Bertha had stopped going to services after Moishe, her husband, died and the Rabbi mispronounced his name at the graveside service.

"You still going every day, Ma?" I asked. She

gripped my arm tightly as we walked into the Temple.

"In afternoons, I go and sit. Went with *mein* father. He was Orthodox. I sat upstairs *mid* women. Countries change, but *Shul* is *Shul*, *yah*? When we come to Boston, Abe and I do Reform cause we want to sit *tsuzamen*." She linked her weathered hands together.

I liked hearing Ida's stories, even the repetitions, hoping to learn a new fragment, a different Yiddish word, since my father told little about his past. With his sixteen-hour days, he was a man of the moment with little time for the past.

"You miss Russia, Ma?"

"*Nein*. They try to kill Jacob when he was baby. I hid him in pickle barrel. No one look there! But I miss living with *meine mishpoche*."

"*Mishpoche*?"

"Cousins, uncles, *mishpoche*."

"But Ma, we live in Brookline and Quinnipiac."

"Not close enough."

As we arrived at the Temple she grabbed my hand. "You good boy, Joshua. The day you born, your eyes, brown like Jacob."

"My eyes are hazel, Ma."

"Good enough, *schmendrik*. You make a girl happy. *Farshtain?* Easy to marry rich girl as poor one."

I'd never been to the Brighton *shul*, hadn't been to services since our annual appearance last September for the High Holidays. The Temple was empty except for a few older people in the front rows. Sunlight streamed through the stained glass windows onto a dark wooden altar. She nudged me toward the front, nodding at acquaintances before settling in.

The organ started as I was leaving, a swirling dirge, rising and falling into silence only to emerge in a higher key, a restless moan looking for

14

peace. It spilled onto the street and into the tenements where thousands of Jewish immigrants had come to live.

I drove to Manny's to deliver Paul's brownies. He ran a used furniture warehouse on the edge of East Boston, a large brick building with boarded up windows on a dingy, treeless street. Manny had hired Paul because Dad had treated his kids, as well as everyone else in his family. I walked through the aisles of discarded furniture stacked on metal shelves thirty feet high - desks, chairs, tables and cabinets, tarnished and moldy.

Manny's tiny office was crowded with dark green filing cabinets and a gray metal desk overflowing with folders. Next to the desk was a Belmont Springs water cooler. Dad said Manny hated paying $2.95 for refills, so he filled it with water from the tap. The water was so murky, even goldfish couldn't have survived.

Manny was pawing through a stack of bills as I came through the door. His shirt was unbuttoned, revealing a chest of dark hair and a heavy golden chain. I hadn't seen him since Mother's last *bon voyage* party when Paul left for the Peace Corps.

"*Oy vayes shmir.* Joshua. You back? Don't tell me you need job, too?"

"No, Manny. I came to see my brother."

"Pauly, *mein* sales *boychik*?" He shook his head. "You know, every year you look more like your father."

"Thanks, Manny," I said, hoping Dad's charisma would show up in me. When he entered a room, people noticed.

"Manny!" Someone yelled from the warehouse. He swung open the door with a yard stick. "Pardon *mein* intercom, Joshua. What?" Manny screamed.

"You want what for box springs?" the voice yelled

back.

"I'm coming. Come Joshua."

Two college students were haggling with the manager, Jose, over the price of second hand box springs. Manny conferred privately with Jose. "Tell them, $10 for one, $19.50 for two," he said.

"Business is tough, Joshua. Everyone wants a bargain," he said, as Jose left to negotiate. "Especially Hahvahd *boychiks*!"

The students handed their money to Manny who counted it to the dime. "And three bucks to deliver," he added. As Jose hoisted the box springs onto the truck, Manny said, "We deliver Monday, *boychicks*. No delivery on the Sabbath, right Jose?" Jose shook his head emphatically no.

I followed Manny to the back of the warehouse. "College kids, they got money, Joshua. If they pay two thousand for Hahvahd, they pay twenty bucks for bed, *yah*? You find Pauly there." He pointed at a pair of battered swinging doors.

I walked into a showroom of new desks, chairs, and cabinets. At the end of the room a few tired salesmen sat in brown cubicles, dressed in slacks, white shirts, and ties, writing orders and talking on the phone. One of them directed me to wait while he looked for Paul. I sat down in a plush swivel chair like the seat in Dad's office. When Paul returned from the warehouse, dressed in his own suit and tie, clipboard in hand, he looked like a real businessman.

"Hey, Josh. What are you up to?"

"I ordered a passport and went to Ida's."

"Oh God!"

"She says you haven't been over but sent you a present." I showed him the brownies.

"Great. Come to my office." He pulled up a chair and sat down at his desk. He had a phone, file cabinet, in and out box cluttered with orders, and one of Dad's Schaeffer pen & pencil sets.

"I have a few things to finish up but then we'll have dinner. Help yourself to coffee, although it's a little dodgy." I flipped through the latest *Sports Illustrated* magazines on his desk, reviewing the standings and predictions. A radio played golden oldies the way it did when we were kids, doing our homework together at the kitchen table listening to the top twenty.

A salesman came by with a batch of pink messages. "Hey, Paul, these came when you were out. Mac needs those 45 blue Morton swivels soon. Nice piece of change!" He grinned.

When the clock hit five, Paul filed his unfilled orders and put his pen set away. "I got to drop something at Manny's," he said. We walked through the shelves of piled furniture and Paul knocked gingerly on his door.

"Yah, who knocks? *Oye*, the *boychicks*."

"You asked for Mac's order."

Manny frowned. "It's not delivered?"

"I tried. He didn't call back."

Manny's eyes narrowed into slits. "It's been two days."

Paul turned ashen, looked at his shoes. "I'll take care of it."

"Tomorrow or I give it to Sol. Even Hahvahd *boychiks* have to do their job."

My neck stiffened when he said it. Like the days when Paul missed a tackle and someone scored. We left his office in silence. "He's a pain," I said, as we emerged from the furniture bunker into the light of an early summer evening.

"Fuck him. Let's go to my place," he said.

Paul lived on the ground floor of a gray Gothic mansion on Beacon Street that had been converted into rentals. We walked through a spacious foyer until we came to a door in the back that looked like an

17

entrance to a closet. A large black lab jumped out as he opened it and licked his hands.

"That's a nice Molly, yes, sweet little girl," Paul cooed in a baby voice and patted her gently. He lowered her to the floor amid Molly's squeals of delight.

"When did you get a dog?" I asked.

"A couple of months ago. I found her on the street."

There wasn't much in the apartment. Two narrow rooms, railcar style - a kitchen/bathroom in back, living room/bedroom in front, furnished with a drop leaf table without chairs, wooden dresser from our basement, thread bare couch, and mattress/box spring bed neatly dressed with hospital corners.

"What do you think?" he asked.

"Terrific!" I opened a window to let in some air.

"It's a great neighborhood. Two blocks from Coolidge Corner and ner the trolley. First place I saw after the hospital."

"Nice and cozy."

"I don't need much right now. Throw your things on the couch."

It was covered with dog hair, so I hung my jacket on a chair. A small patch of worn yellow foam lay next to his bed with a bowl of water beside it.

"Molly likes to sleep close. I hope you like kosher hot dogs because that's what we're having."

"Sounds great."

"I love Hebrew National. They're thick and tasty." He put up water to boil and opened a can of Boston Baked Beans.

"Don't forget dessert," I said, putting Ida's brownies beside his six-packs.

"Help yourself to the booze," Paul said. He opened a Bud and drained half. "When do you leave?"

"Monday, after the party."

"Oh, Christ, the party!" He turned on the radio,

tapping his fingers to the music.

"Want another?" He asked, opening a new Bud for himself while prodding the boiling hot dogs with a fork. "I wish they'd had hot dogs in Guatemala. Nothing but rice and beans until I was ready to puke."

"No food in the town?"

"Town? I was in the boonies." No one around for miles. I leaned back on the wall on the makeshift bed and nursed my beer.

It was quiet in the back of the house, no sounds of traffic, trolleys, cars or anything else.

"Let's go to the Sox. The Orioles are playing. Got any plans?" he asked.

"Not really."

"Whatever happened to that girl, the good looker you took out on the lake on the sailfish one night."

"Jenny? She's around," I said.

"Have a crush on her?"

"No, just a friend."

"So give me her number," he teased.

"No way." I tensed, set my beer aside.

He spilled the hot dogs and beans onto the plates and tore off paper towels for napkins. We sat on the bed, cradling the food on our laps. "Know what I like about Hebrew National?" he asked.

"Nope."

"All beef. No pork." He sliced his frank into five hefty chunks. I forked in a mouthful. The sugary beans tempered the brine of the beef.

"What do you think?" he asked.

"Just like Mother's," I teased.

"Yeah, right! Fuck you." He tossed his empty beer into the trash and belched. He'd begun to move slower, his eyes slightly glazed.

"When does school start?" I asked.

"Who the hell knows."

"You're not going back? It's only a year."

"Yeah, a fucking long year." He stood up. "Let's get out of here. We'll sit in the bleachers."

He took off his shirt and hung it in the closet next to a skimpy collection of clothes. He turned his back while he changed. Everyone in my house turned their backs when they changed. Paul was still thin from Guatemala, though not as emaciated as he was last summer when Dad and I saw him in the Washington hospital, his face gaunt, his eyes vacant, staring at the floor, unable to speak.

"Ready?" he asked. "We'll do a quick rinse around." He washed, I dried; some routines never change. I poured the last half of my beer into the sink and tossed it into a pile of empties next to his bed.

We rode the Beacon Street trolley to Kenmore Square. People were streaming up Brookline Avenue, students with time to kill, fathers holding their children close by their side. "Souvenirs, heah," barkers yelled. The smell of grilled sausage, roasted peanuts, and popcorn permeated the air. With its lights ablaze and banners flying, the green stadium looked like a ship ready to sail.

We walked through the ground floor of the stadium where you could smell the disinfectant from the bathrooms and emerged onto a brightly lit field. Dark fingered base paths parted the Day-Glo green grass bordered by grand stands from 1911. As the players finished their warm-ups, the reds of the sunset bruised into purple. Paul snagged a beer and popcorn and settled into his seat.

"McNally's pitching," he grumbled. "He's 10-1."

"Who's pitching for the Sox?"

"Lamabe, 2-7. We need runs or forget it."

The Sox fell behind by five in the third; by the sixth there was nothing to do but eat. I filled up on ice cream and cracker jacks. Paul stayed with the Bud.

"Want to get going?" I asked as the crowd started to thin in the sixth inning.

"Sure. This game is fucked."

He steadied himself and inched down the row, leaning heavily on the railing. He walked like an old man, uncertain where to put his next foot down. I helped him down the steps, worried how we'd get home.

Lansdowne Street had emptied, leaving the sidewalks strewn with candy wrappers and programs. Hawkers were cleaning their grills and stowing their food. Even the banners had died on the poles.

"Shitty game," Paul said. "They need pitching for Christ's sake!" As we crossed into Kenmore Square, a roar erupted from the stadium. I looked back at the blazing lights, but Paul stared ahead, saying miracles didn't happen at Fenway.

The Kenmore Station was deserted. Paul walked to the dim end of the platform, braced himself on a girder, and pissed on the tracks. I replayed the game inning-by-inning, out by out, as my stomach tightened, like I used to do when he took bad hits in football and he couldn't get up from the field, hoping he'd finish before the train or passengers arrived. I turned my head, waiting for the trolley's piercing light, the rumble and screech of wheels, the blast of hot wind that preceded the train. He staggered back as the train came in, adjusting his trousers. "There, that's better," he mumbled.

I helped him to our seats. He leaned his head against the window, swaying to the clickity-clack of the tracks. Within seconds his eyes had closed and his head had begun to droop, searching for a place to rest. He found my shoulder and stayed there until we reached his apartment.

CHAPTER 3

The bell jingled as I entered Sal's barbershop in the morning.

Mother had left a reminder about my haircut and our lunch with Grandfather at Green Acres.

"What do you want?" Sal asked, looking at my hair as if it was infested. Barely five feet tall and graying, he owned a one-room barbershop in Quinnipiac that had two barber chairs, a Chinese calendar on the wall from the previous year, and no customers.

"The regular," I said. He always asked what I wanted, but cut it the way he liked. His stale breath was hot on my neck as I watched a semester's growth litter the floor and checked the box scores in the Globe.

"How's you father? he asked. "I read he's president of Rotary."

"Really?"

"They elect him last week. He raise money for kids. He's a good man."

"Could you leave more on top?" I asked, alarmed at a two-inch furrow burrowed into my scalp.

"You don't wanna the butch?"

"No wanna the butch," I confirmed.

He evened out the furrow and I departed, afraid to look at the damage in the rear view mirror. By the time I'd reached Green Acres, the day had clouded over, bleaching the variegated summer greens into a monochrome.

Green Acres was built on a Dorchester hill. One side overlooked Boston, the other stared at rocky ledges tangled with weeds and litter. Grandfather had lived in the home since he'd developed Parkinson's five years before. He shared a room with three other patients. After one roommate went to the hospital and never returned, I stopped asking about his replacement. Although Green Acres was billed as a Recuperative Center, no one ever left or got better.

I met Mother on the main floor. She had brought Chinese food and a birthday cake from Okemo's, Grandfather's favorite bakery because of its fluffy, vanilla frosting and dark heavy cake. The hallway was permeated with the odor of fried food and urine.

Grandfather always demanded to know our arrival time so the nurses could dress him in his best clothes. He prided himself on his seven suits, one for every day of the week. He was waiting alone in the common room and, although it was Wednesday, he wore his Sunday suit, a blue striped wool blend with a maroon tie. He had an imposing, Mt. Rushmore head on a diminutive body that had shriveled with time. He'd dyed his white hair black and gripped the wheelchair fiercely to keep his hands from shaking.

"Why, don't you look good today, Father!" Mother said, tying a red balloon on his chair. Grandfather stared at the wall clock as if in a trance.

"Look who I brought, Father," Mother said, as she unpacked the picnic basket. He eyed me suspiciously.

"Happy Birthday, Grandfather." I slid a birthday present across the table that Mother had bought. I was eager to get to the cake.

"Will you tell me what hour it is, Mira?" he asked.

Mira looked at the clock. "Why Father, it's one o'clock."

"Do you know what time lunch is served here?"

"Twelve."

"Correct. So why were you not here at twelve?" His clenched hands had turned white.

"Because I couldn't come at twelve. Remember? I told you yesterday on the phone."

"You are mistaken. I never eat at one. I've been waiting for one hour."

"I'm sorry Father. You misunderstood. I did tell you."

"Grandfather, look what I brought." I pulled out a paper on Hemingway, written for the only course I'd enjoyed in the last semester. His club-like hands fisted the paper across the table. After steadying his thin arms on the wheelchair, he lifted it to his face where it trembled as if caught in a stiff wind. Grandfather had taught literature at the University of Dresden. But anti-Semitism had forced him into tailoring when he'd come to Boston.

Mother opened the food and set out paper plates and plastic silverware. Her cheeks beaded with perspiration.

"Joshua. How do you spell *separate*?" Grandfather asked.

"Separate?" His stare bored a hole in me. "S,E,P,E,R,A,T,E."

He shook his head sorrowfully. "There's no E after P. S,E,P,A,R,A,T,E. Do they teach spelling at uh...."

"Antioch, Grandfather. They don't teach spelling. What do you think of the arguments?"

He shrugged. "You're better off studying someone who can write. He's a war correspondent. Have you read Flaubert?"

"Hemingway writes about love, Grandfather."

He waved his hand dismissively. "Love, you say?

I'll tell you about love. *Let me not to the marriage of true minds admit impediments. Love is not love which alters when it alteration finds.*" He continued but his voice cracked and stopped at *the edge of doom.* Tears dripped down his cheeks, making dark splotches on the red tissue wrapping.

"You know who wrote it?"

I shook my head.

"Shakespeare," Mother whispered. "Sonnet 116."

"You remembered that at least," Grandfather said.

The odor of egg foo yung was making me nauseous.

"Let's eat, Father," Mother implored, "before the food gets cold."

Grandfather surveyed the cartons of wonton soup, egg rolls, beef and chicken lo mein.

"What do you want?" I asked, rising to serve him.

"You eat," he said.

"But your food will spoil," Mother said.

"I'm not hungry. I ate when we were supposed to eat."

Mother spilled fried wontons and rice on my plate. The balloon bobbled in the breezes of a rotating fan. A passing nurse paused at our table.

"Boy, that smells good. Aren't you a lucky guy, Billy!"

"I'm not eating."

"Why not, Honey? The food will get cold."

"We were supposed to eat at twelve."

"Well, the food's here now."

"Why don't you eat it then?"

"Because it's your birthday, Hon." She shook her head and left.

The Andy Griffith show fired bursts of laughter from an overhanging television. Mother and I started to eat without looking up. Then Mother dimmed the lights, lit the candles, and we sang Happy Birthday as the final credits ended. Grandfather stared at the flickering candles, composing a wish. It took him three wheezing breaths to blow them out.

"Would you like a piece with a rose, Grandfather?" Mother asked, slicing the cake.

"What's it made of?" Grandfather poked his knife into a flower.

"Frosting," Mother replied.

He lifted it to his mouth. "Ach! Too sweet."

"Eat the cake then," Mother said.

He shook his head. "Give it to the nurses. They never have anything good to eat."

"The whole cake?" Mother asked. "Don't you want a piece?"

"Why? I'm not hungry."

Mother rose and closed the flaps on the coagulating food.

"I'm tired," Grandfather said. "Would you ask the nurse to put me to bed?"

"At one thirty?"

"So?" He slid my paper across the table.

"Would you like to read it later, Grandfather?" I asked.

"Maybe a different paper. Have you studied Balzac?"

"We studied American writers," I said, scanning the page for other mistakes.

A nurse wheeled Grandfather back to his room. I regretted leaving the cake, but had lost my appetite. We left the dinner at the nurse's station in a grease-stained bag.

"Grandfather wasn't himself today," Mother said as we walked through the parking lot.

"No, he wasn't," I said, although he didn't seem different from other visits.

"Will you be home for dinner?"

"I don't know. Might go to the movies."

"Again? I'll make you a steak. Sirloin's on sale."

"I don't feel like it, Mother."

27

Her hands trembled as she opened her alligator purse and removed a vial of pills with red warning labels. "Well then, maybe I'll take an afternoon nap. I didn't sleep well last night." She put two white pills on her tongue and swallowed. "Will you call me later?"

"Sure."

"Give me a kiss."

I leaned over, shied away from her mouth, and gave her a loose hug goodbye.

She got in the car, powdered her face and combed her hair, and left.

I thought about the frosted flowers all the way to Tuler's, a diner with the best coffee rolls in Boston. It was run by an old Russian couple who always argued behind the counter. I ordered a warm pastry and savored the deep pockets of cinnamon and sugar. A black lab with a sizable paunch sauntered out of the back and sat at my feet. I fed him part of my pastry. "*Schloyma*!" Bessie yelled. "Such a pest!" Ruth said.

Schloyma looked up and licked my hand. His tongue was warm and rough. Once we had dogs, three of them. They were fun to play with while they lasted. Gretel was run over, even our cats Mikey and Ikey ran away. Then we got a bag of goldfish - less trouble, Mother had said. But three weeks later we discovered their small orange bodies floating like flower petals over the white sand and undersea plants. I started to worry that no pets could survive in our house.

I gave the last of my roll to *Schloyma*, bought an extra pastry for dad and headed for home and found a message from Paul asking if I wanted some help buying clothes for Norway. We met at Copley Square and walked through the Public Garden where people sat on benches, reading the news and feeding the ducks. We used to feed them, too, when we were kids. We'd come with Mother's wicker picnic basket packed with food to ride the swan boats and look for landmarks from *Make Way For Ducklings*, one of the bedtime stories she used to read us. Wigglely Pigglely Adventures, Mother had called them. She'd steady our hands when the ducks swam over to pluck the peanuts from our palms.

Filene's Basement, Dad's favorite clothing store, was jammed with shoppers, searching the counters for bargains piled three feet high. Paul poked through the sweaters for something thick and warm. I'd never chosen my clothes growing up. If he and Dad had liked something, I'd agreed. But two years at Antioch had made long hair and sandals more appealing than Ivy League crew cuts and penny loafers.

He held up a maroon Shetland sweater. "You like it? Saks Fifth Avenue," he grinned. "Only three bucks here."

I shrugged but acquiesced, adding a gray sweatshirt for folk dancing which I remembered from my last time in Norway. We emerged hours later onto a deserted Washington Street and went for a burger in the North End, one of Paul's favorite haunts. Tourists strolled through the waterfront streets, looking for tables in crowded restaurants and pastry shops. Across the harbor at Logan, planes rumbled into the sky.

"Norway's going to be great," he said. "No fucking heat, rain, or people who say *manana* when you say *pronto*. You excited, kiddo?"

"Yeah."

"Lots of nookey there. And blonds are the best." He put an arm around my neck. I was afraid he'd squeeze too hard.

We walked into the Rusty Scupper, an old brick pub set on a rotting wooden pier. It was dim and packed with people hovering around a bar and thick with cigarette smoke that stung my eyes. A waitress walked by.

"Heyah, Paul. How you doing?" she said.

"Hi Tammy. Not bad. This is my brother, Josh."

"The better half?" she snickered. "Just kidding."

"How about a table?"

She disappeared without a reply, carrying a tray of soiled dishes. We anchored ourselves at the bar.

"Hey, Paul. The regular?" a barman asked.

"Sure, Phil. And one for my brother."

He filled two glasses with foaming amber beer. Paul took a swig, keeping his eye on Tammy as she moved about. She pushed the make up hard: face powder, eye liner, hair spray, and lashes that almost clicked when she blinked. I hated to think what would happen if she got caught in the rain.

"Tammy's great," Paul said. "Been here for years. Maybe she'll come to Mother's gala." He howled with laughter, a high-pitched squeal, half laugh, half scream.

The smell of hamburgers and French fries made me hungry. I picked at a bowl of peanuts and nursed my beer. Tammy rushed by with a tray of fried chicken fingers.

"How's the table coming, Tammy?" Paul asked.

"Hold your horses, Paul."

"You can't rattle Tammy. You hungry?"

"I'm starved." I studied the wall of colored bottles, 10 kinds of whiskey, 5 of gin, 7 of vodka, 4 of tequila, a foreign country to me. A stocky guy with a stubby neck and massive shoulders tapped Paul on the back.

"What do you know? Another gentleman from Wigglesworth."

"Hey, Stanley," Paul said. "I thought you'd gone home for the summer."

"Home? There are alternatives."

"This is my brother, Josh. Stanley's my old roommate."

"Is this the guy at the hippy school in Indiana?"

"Ohio," I said.

"Don't mind Stanley. He's a snot."

"I prefer jaded. I heard you returned from the jungle, prematurely."

"Yeah, I guess."

"Tired of saving the world?"

"It just didn't work out." Paul stared down at his beer.

"You wouldn't catch me in the boonies. No amenities. What was it like?"

"Hot and rainy."

"That's it? Did you amuse yourself with the natives?"

Paul shrugged.

"He's run out of words. What do you do, Josh?"

"I'm heading for Norway."

"Really? A bit off the beaten track." He looked at me as if he had discovered an interesting specimen in a jar. "I like that."

"Thanks."

"Well, gentlemen, I must be off. The evening's young and I'm horny."

"See you Stanley," Paul said. Stanley moved down the bar and stopped by two coeds cradling beers.

"He's a fucking bear of a wrestler. Hasn't lost a match in two years," Paul said.

"What's with his neck?"

He laughed. "He works out a lot. A hundred chin-ups a day, ten one-handed."

We waited for a table to open. But after a while the pretzels and peanuts had filled us up. Paul made a final trip to the bathroom and we left. An evening breeze had blown away the heat. Paul was up for walking so we started over Beacon Hill to his apartment.

"Remember the nights on the Cape when the fog rolled in?" Paul said. "You'd see it coming over the

31

ocean at sunset. Then a breeze would hit and boom, you couldn't see a thing. Weird, huh?"

I remembered those nights when everything disappeared. Those were the weekends we spent with Mother because Dad wouldn't leave his practice. We spent our days on the beach playing in the waves while Mother read on the beach.

"Remember the blueberry ice cream with little blue specks at Seven Seas?" I said.

"God, I could go for a cone," Paul said. "Want to stop at Bailey's around the corner?"

Bailey's was a throwback to an era when an ice cream parlor was a fancy destination. With dark wood interiors, full-length mirrors, overhead fans, and glass cases filled with candy and fudge, you inhaled sugar when you entered. We sat down at a marble counter.

"I wonder why Dad likes Bailey's better than Brigham's," I said.

"He had a girlfriend there when he was in medical school."

"You're kidding."

"The Bailey's by Tufts. She gave him free cones. He was in love but couldn't marry because she was a *schikza*. They saw each other until Mother came along."

"And that was that?"

"Not really. He continued to see her, after hours. I remember the fights."

"Christ, I don't remember that." I half admired Dad for having another woman. After all, he and mother had separate bedrooms.

"You were in kindergarten, sonny boy." He gave me a belt in the arm. A waitress came and took our order.

"My treat," Paul said, "I screwed up dinner."

"What happened to her?"

"I don't know. They stopped arguing about it when

I was in junior high. But he still prefers Bailey's."

Bailey's used a triangular scoop that made pointy headed cones. I licked the side of my ice cream while Paul gulped his in chunks. I was always the last to finish my cone, the last to do everything: dress, brush my teeth, get out of the shower, do my homework, finish my meal. They'd wait in the car, ready to go, car door open and motor running, while I tried to part my hair.

"Seven Seas had a lot of flavors," Paul said, as we started back.

"Seventeen," I said.

"I don't remember stuff like that. Like in class, I can't remember details. I take notes, study all night, and go blank on the tests. Just sit there and sweat. Fucking Stanley never cracks a book and pulls A's. Sorry about the burgers tonight."

"That's okay."

"Sometimes Tammy's a bitch. I could make you something at my place."

"I'm heading for home. See you Sunday."

Paul was silent.

"You're not coming?" I asked.

"I hate those parties!" He stopped abruptly in front of his building.

"Turning in?" I asked.

"Nope. Feel like walking. If I don't see you Sunday, I'll give you a call." I was hungry for a burger and fries but was too tired to eat and left for home.

Winter moths were fluttering around the porch light when I drove down the driveway. Dozens of dead ones lay inside the glass globe. There was a light in the living room that reminded me I'd forgotten to call Mother. I closed the front door quietly and went downstairs. A reading lamp glared on an empty sofa. It was unlike Mother to leave on a light. She'd grown up in the Depression and counted her pennies in coupons and kilowatts. I hurried up the stairs, two at a time.

Her door was closed. I listened for a sound, any sound, and cracked open the door. The curtains were rustling in the breezes. I waited for my eyes to adjust to the dark, holding my breath until I could make out her shape. She lay on her back in bed, with her arm resting next to a bottle of pills. My stomach tightened in the stillness. I waited for a quiver of her hand, a single breath. Then she coughed, rolled onto her side. I backed slowly out of the room.

CHAPTER 4

I picked up my passport in the morning and stopped by the dentist, the last item on Mother's list. A *bon voyage* could never begin without clean teeth. Her dentist, a part time travel agent, had planned all of her trips to France. He'd probably given her a package price for travel and teeth.

"You don't want Novocain, do you?" he asked, starting to drill deep into my cavity. "I'm a wee bit behind today."

"Okay," I said. I stared at his crooked incisors; for a dentist he had terrible teeth.

"I booked a new trip for Mira," he said and rattled off a list of Parisian museums, restaurants, and theaters that was difficult to understand over the drill. "I got her a room in Plaisir D'Amour, a three star hotel in the Latin Quarter. How come you're not studying in France?"

With a mouth full of his fingers and tools, I could only shrug. I examined the posters of destinations and dentures.

"You're missing a wonderful chance to learn French and read their amazing writers. You took it in high school I assume?"

A blinding pain jolted my jaw. I'd taken four years and remembered only two phrases – *bon jour* and *au revoir*.

"I prefer the modern writers to the older generation myself."

I clenched the chair and counted the gargoyles on a Notre Dame poster. I'd lost of track of time, listening to the grinding of steel into bone, when he stared into my glassy eyes and said we were done.

"That wasn't so bad, was it?" he asked.

I spat out the remains of my tooth into a bloody basin and shook my head, no.

Fatigued from pain, I drove a few blocks to Dad's office on Mass Avenue to put up my feet. Mother and Dad had fought about keeping the Boston office during the Depression. She'd only wanted him to see patients in Quinnipiac so he'd be closer to home. But for Dad, Boston was home and he continued to see people in both places.

I opened the iron-gated elevator door and slid the brass lever up. Floors of lawyers, doctors, and accountants glided by, the roster of professions approved by my parents. The lift quivered to a stop on the ninth floor.

"Joshua," exclaimed Stellina, Dad's secretary. "What a surprise." She was in her thirties, her eyes were warm and welcoming, and her dark hair flowed to her waist.

"Home for the summer?"

"No. Going to Norway," I said between clenched teeth.

Her eyebrows arched. "A strange place to study. Is something wrong with your jaw?"

"No. I had a cavity. Just had it filled."

"Oh, too bad. Is your father expecting you?"

"No. I was around the corner."

She glanced at Dad's appointment book. "He stepped out for a moment. I don't know when he'll be back. You're welcome to wait." She bent over to file a bill, displaying an outline of her pink underwear through her white uniform.

"Sure. I'll wait."

"You can sit in his office if you like. I'll get

you an aspirin."

The bracing odor of ethyl alcohol recalled dozens of office visits. The only time Dad ever held me was when I was sick, cradling my face in his hands, peering into my eyes with a pen light strapped to his head. He'd thrust a stick into my throat until I coughed and roam over my chest with a chilly metal stethoscope. But it was the touch of his hands, calloused and calm, that was the cure. I was quite a medical handful then, sick with coughs and fevers and allergies that kept me bedridden for days while Paul hardly missed a day of school.

I opened the drawers of his mahogany desk with its inlaid leather surface and shaded bronze lamp. Its contents still cast a spell - embossed stationary and business cards, silver monogrammed Parker pens, inscrutable scribbles on 3 by 5 prescription pads for pills. I spun around in his leather chair, surveying the pictures: a family portrait from Russia in which three year old Dad sat on Ida's lap - even then he was dressed in a suit; Dad surrounded by nurses at the Leonard Morse Hospital, his hair dark and full, like Rudolph Valentino Mother used to say; Abe and Ida sitting on lawn chairs by the lake, watching Paul and me play in the water; and a wall of medical degrees from Boston's finest - Tufts, Eye & Ear, Mass General, and the Beth Israel. All the mementos of our family save a picture of Mother.

Stellina appeared in the doorway in her overcoat, a handbag draped over her arm. "I'm sorry, Joshua. I guess he's not coming back . She looked nervously at her watch and blushed. You feeling better?"

"Yes, a little."

"I really have to go."

I knew she meant we; I had become a good translator listening to Mother.

She closed the exam room doors and flicked off

the lights. Her perfume filled the wrought iron cage as we rode downstairs. I studied the grill work, unable to think of something to say. Dad always had beautiful secretaries.

"What a wonderful night," Stellina said as we stepped on the sidewalk.

"Want a ride home?" I blurted.

She blushed. "Oh, Joshua. You're so sweet. It's too nice not to walk. But you have a good trip. Okay?"

Her perfume lingered after she left. I went to a phone booth and debated my options. I had many girls with whom I was friends and often called them when I'd run out of movies in Boston. Jenny had great legs but often had a boyfriend; Lacy had nice breasts but was hard to talk to; Becky wasn't my type, but I could talk with her about everything. I liked them all but never let it go further than gentle kisses until I was alone in bed. I fingered my dime, sweltering in the booth considering my choices.

"Joshua? You back in Boston?" Jenny asked. It wasn't the worst choice, just the usual.

"Yup, for a few days. What're you doing?"

"Not much. Robbie and I are going to the Atlantic Cafe tomorrow."

"What's up tonight?"

"Watching TV."

"I thought I'd stop by."

"Now?"

The last time I'd seen Jenny was the previous summer when I'd taken her out on our sailfish under a full moon. She'd worn a tiny blue bikini under a white transparent shirt. I remembered how the suit snuggled her body, how she straddled the prow, letting the water ripple into her thighs. I counted 36 steps to her third floor apartment and hoped for the best.

"Love Story's almost over, Josh," she said as we walked into her living room. Her shorts clung to her thighs as if they were wet.

"How long you around?" she asked, keeping an eye on the movie.

"A couple of days. I leave on Monday."

"Back to school?"

"Norway. A year abroad."

"Norway?" She laughed. "I'm sorry. It just seems a weird place to study. Don't they have better programs in Europe?"

"It is Europe."

She leaned back against the couch. Her legs splayed open.

"Seen Nora or Shea?" I asked.

"They're on the North Shore. Robbie's there, too, caddying at Sea Pines and living in Brighton." The movie ended with a rush of music. She looked at her watch. "Jeez, I'm hungry."

I followed her into the kitchen where she emptied a cake mix into a bowl and added water and eggs. "Thirty minutes," she read from the directions on the back and poured the mix into a pan. I grabbed a spoon to sample the chocolate lining the bowl, but before I could manage a lick, she washed it in the sink. We returned to the television where she switched channels between Sunset Strip and Paladin. I smelled the rising batter, pictured its dark crusty outside and soft interior still mushy from heat. Someone knocked at the door.

"Robbie!" She bolted down the hallway. I heard them whispering by the door ending with a barely audible, "Damn." The cake would soon be done, but not soon enough for me.

"I'm heading out," I announced, rising as they entered.

"No cake?" Jenny asked, her arm encircled around Robbie's waist.

"Another time," I said.

"Give me a call when you're back in town."

The problem was, I probably would. I grabbed one last look at her tight fitting pants and left. A group of students were ambling up the stairs, beers in hand. The hallway swelled with their laughter and the thump of the Rolling Stones spilling out of a party below. It wasn't late, but late enough for me. I stopped by a convenience store for more aspirin and slipped into the house just after ten.

Mother was singing at the piano, a lullaby she'd learned from her Grandmother who'd raised her after her mother had died. She had a beautiful voice, low and sultry from having sung the blues. Bobby Blue was her nick name in the days when she had her own band on the radio before she'd met Dad. She'd known the songs for so long, she sang from the heart, her head cocked back, her eyes closed, letting the music fill the room. Only when she was singing did she seem free.

Mother chose the trumpet for Paul and the clarinet for me before we were ten. But the forced march of daily practice drained the joy from the music, except for the times when we gathered around the piano to sing. Although our voices were disparate and we never sang in tune, singing was the only thing we did together other than eat. I wanted to head for my room, but she'd heard me enter.

"Where've you been?" she asked.

"In town. At the dentist," I said, joining her at the piano.

"How did it go?"

"Not great. He doesn't like Novocaine."

"Sydney's a very good dentist. Maybe he was busy." She played a tune from Carousel, *You Never Walk Alone*. "Remember this?"

"I don't feel like singing."

"How about a bite? It'll make you feel better."

We went to the refrigerator where she resuscitated the leftovers.

"Looks like you've been busy," I said, noticing the foil-covered dishes on the counter. "No caterer for Sunday?"

"They're coming. These are extras. We're having *toute la famille.* Aunt Frieda's bringing Grandfather, a very nice outing for him. And all of Father's sisters and brothers. Why don't you invite that nice girl from last summer?"

I nibbled at a piece of meat. "I don't think she'd fit in. I stopped by to see Dad but he wasn't around."

"Really? Probably on his rounds. And how was dinner with Paul? All he needs is a little rest until Harvard begins. Then it's clear sailing till graduation. The Peace Corps wasn't his cup of tea."

I opened a packet of dark, squishy vegetables.

"The cleaning crew arrives at nine, the caterer at eleven. It's a long time since both you boys were home. Now, you're leaving, just like Paul. Well, not like Paul. You two *are* different. And the countries, too. I'm sitting here gabbing, but we never have time to talk. Not like the old days."

I remembered the old days, too. She sat on a high stool next to the stove watching me eat, gowned head to toe in a royal blue robe, perched under the kitchen clock that I watched until I was excused.

"I was looking through the pictures trying to remember the name of the father with those two little girls at Craigville Beach," Mother said. "You played with them in the water. Wilson, Williams? One of those Christian names that sound alike. It was a delight to have someone take you into the waves. I wasn't strong enough for that. And Father, being afraid of the water. Imagine a grown man who can't swim!"

I remembered Dad in the water. Even if he was up

41

to his knees, he was afraid to let go of my hand, the only time I felt he needed me. "Wilson had a dog, a golden retriever," I said. "We played ball in the surf."

"You remember the oddest details. I thought one day we might buy a seaside cottage where the family could *rendezvous* each summer, but that didn't work out with you boys at college."

"Thanks for the snack, Mother," I said, rising. I put my plate in the sink.

"Oh, of course, time to turn in. Tomorrow's a new day." Mother wrapped up the leftovers of the leftovers.

I got into bed after eleven and slid under the thin cotton sheet. The wind had died and the heat was oppressive, the heat bugs chanting their monotonous beat. Unable to sleep, I summoned Jenny, her legs splayed on the couch, exposing a sliver of underwear. I slipped out of bed and locked the door.

CHAPTER 5

I was woken early from a deep sleep by the cleaners shampooing the carpets, buffing the floors, and washing the windows. The panes were so transparent swallows crashed into them with a sickening thud.

I rolled out of bed just as a silver Cadillac swooped down the driveway. It was Manny arriving to gorge on the appetizers. I put on my uniform for the day - Cardullo's dress shirt, Gorsiagan's tie, and Filene's sports jacket - and watched the driveway fill with the Chevys of the Samuels and the Cadillacs of the Volkens. Aunt Frieda wrestled Grandfather out of her car and into a wheelchair. Ida and Bertha emerged from Aunt Pauline's simonized Fleetwood. Pauline was the first of the Volkens to make a million from her machine shop in the South End.

The Volkens never got together with the Samuels except at Mother's parties because neither family liked each other. They had little in common; earthy Russians who liked to make and spend money trying to mix it up with Mother's Germanic cousins who tried to make a living in the arts. I slipped into the kitchen to steal a few *eclairs* and settled into a corner of the living room to enjoy them. Mother hung her abstract paintings in the living room to imitate the *salons* she loved to visit in Paris. A black tied waiter circulated through the crowd offering *hors d'oeuvres*, miniature wieners and chopped liver for the Volkens, *pate* and *brie* for the Samuels.

Dad's sisters - Pauline, Gilda, and Helen - collected around the punch bowl as he held court, offering advice about ailments and politics. They banded so closely together they seemed to be still on the ship. Grandfather and Mother's siblings - Frieda, Marion, and Joe - assembled at the piano while Mother played Rogers & Hammerstein show tunes. She sight read the melodies and filled in the harmony, singing loudly to keep everyone in tune. But nobody knew the words and they often lagged measures behind the music. They finished with a disorganized, *Oh what a beautiful morning, I got a beautiful feeling, Everything's going my way*.

"Joshua, sing a tune," Mother said, offering me a stack of song sheets. I liked singing with my guitar in college, but had not sung the show tunes since high school.

"I don't feel like it Mother."

"Don't be fussy, Joshua," Mother said.

"Anything will do," Frieda agreed.

"How about *The Water Is Wide*?" I said.

"The water is what?" Grandfather asked.

"Wide!" Frieda shouted.

"I don't know that tune," Mother said.

"It's a folk song. Joan Baez sings it."

"Joan who?" Grandfather asked.

"Buyers! A folk song." Frieda said.

"Folk song? Oih!" Grandfather started to wheel himself away.

"Don't leave, Grandfather," Mother pleaded. "Sing anything," she said. "We'll lose them."

So I sang *a cappella*, uncomfortable and hot. *The water is wide, I cannot get over, And neither have I wings to fly, Give me a boat that can carry two, And*

44

both shall row, My true love and I.

"A little gloomy," Frieda said. They drifted toward the food as Mother launched into a lively *The Surrey With The Fringe On Top*. I spotted Ida through the trees walking to the lake and made my exit.

Ida had settled on the dock under the branches of a white pine. It hovered over our swimming hole bleeding sap, its roots clinging to the shore. A dense thicket of pines muffled the music from the house. Ida grabbed my hand as I sat beside her.

"This was Abe's spot, *Schmen*. Watching you and Pauly swing into the water, over, over. You know?" she laughed.

"Yah, Ma."

"Swim he couldn't. But he watched. The lake is quiet, *nu*?"

"A lot of people are away."

"*Un* Paul, where is he?"

"Working, I guess."

"On Sunday? He never missed party before."

"Maybe he's tired of parties."

"That I know." A crow swooped over the lake, punctuating the quiet with a grating caw.

"You leave when?"

"Tomorrow."

"Why you go so far?"

"I like Norway. They have 24 hours of sunlight."

"*Un* winter?"

"I'll use a flashlight."

"Ach! Like your father. Always a joke." She ruffled my hair and fanned herself with a napkin. "It was hot, *Schmen*, when we come. Seventeen days on the boat. *Gott in himel*. No *volken* in sky."

"*Volken*, like our name," I said, knowing the story but wanting to hear it again.

"Volken not our real name. Our real name was Mesritch. But this I cannot spell. Clouds beautiful in New York, so I call us, *Volken*." She reminisced about the family in Odessa, how her kitchen filled with music on Sundays. "Remember Jacob play?"

"*Jah*, Ma. You still have his guitar?"

"*Balalaika?* Of course! One day, you play. You go long away, Joshua. I worry about Pauly. Older I get, I *farshtein* nothing."

"He'll be okay."

"You think?" She looked as if she wanted to believe me. It had been almost a year since Paul's episode and Dad was on the case. "You hungry?" I asked.

"*Jah*, hungry. But the music, *oih gevalt!*"

"You want me to get you something?"

"*Nein*, I come. In a bit." So we waited, watching small ripples nibble the shore. After a while, the music stopped and people started to leave. She leaned heavily on my arm as I escorted her over the rutted path. Her old gray dress cloaked her sagging body to the ankles. I knew from pictures that once she had been a great beauty.

Bertha was waiting at the car and helped Ida into her seat. "Take care, *Schmen*," Ida said. She grabbed my arm as tightly as Dad when he ventured into deep water. "Come back *snel*," she said.

Mother was stacking dirty plates and glasses in the dishwasher and humming *Somewhere Over the Rainbow* when I came in.

"What did you think of the party, Joshua?" she asked. "Wasn't it fun to see everyone?"

"Yeah."

"Did you like the salmon *francaise*?"

"Great."

"We don't have many *hors d'oeuvres* remaining, thanks to Manny." She began to wrap the leftovers and to squeeze them into the fridge. "I even got Frieda to sing after you left. What did you think,

Jacob?" Dad had entered with a platter of half eaten *pate.*

"Fine, Mira."

"And the borscht?"

"I wish you wouldn't make a big deal about the borscht."

"I want your family to feel at home."

"They've been here fifty years. We don't need a table for borscht and a table for salmon whatever," he muttered.

"*Francaise,*" Mother said. "Your family never likes what I serve."

"That has nothing to do with the food." They glared at each other across the kitchen.

"A fine thanks I get for having a party," she said.

"No one asked for a party."

"Joshua's leaving."

"We don't have to have a party when someone leaves."

"We did for Paul."

"Yes, we did!" He threw his dish towel on the counter and left.

Mother's hands shook as she tore the foil.

"The party was good, Mother," I said.

"I'm glad somebody liked it. Where was Paul? He said he was coming. I don't know what gets into your father. He's so unreasonable."

I offered to help put the food away, but Mother liked arranging the leftovers in the refrigerator. I went to my room to pack. My trunk felt like a gaping hole. I was used to leaving for a semester in Ohio, but a year near the Arctic Circle? I felt like I needed everything but wanted nothing.

I filled the trunk with warm clothes and a handful of paperbacks about World War II sea battles, and threw in an old sweatshirt from Paul for good luck. Mother and Dad had retired to their bedrooms by the time I'd finished. The only sound in the house was the hum of the dish washer. Nobody seemed to call us except for the answering service.

I went to the den to call Paul, letting it ring as I watched the Sox self-destruct in the ninth. Out by out, I waited for Paul to pick up. By the end of the game, the phone was still ringing. The following morning mother dropped me at the airport with a few wishes to keep in touch and come home by Christmas.

CHAPTER 6

"God, it's hot in here," Brad said, slipping into the seat beside me. "I hope this buggy gets moving." The four prop Icelandic flight shook under the assault of baggage carts dropping their loads into the hold. Brad, a college classmate, was going to Norway to study in a folk high school like me. Folk high schools were like the last step between High schools and college. He stuck his pack, jammed with climbing gear, under his seat and studied an issue of Rock Climber.

"Sorry, sir," a stewardess complained. "You'll have to stow that bag." She grabbed my pack containing my boots, foul weather gear and mother's six pot roast sandwiches that she had surprised me with at the airport and wedged it into a crevice in the overhead. I hadn't slept much the night before, but the airport bustle had revived me with its scores of chattering students leaving for overseas destinations.

The four propellers feathered into a blur of menacing blades as we jerked back from the terminal. I ground my teeth on the bumpy taxiway, looking for the rescue vehicles at their stations. Then, revved into full power, and lurched into the sky. I searched for the thread of Beacon Street, the trees of the Public Garden, the waters of Lake Okonowauki by our home, but the landscape had dwindled into smudges of brown and green. As we veered into the clouds, we shuddered and pitched. A red light flashed on. Pinned to the bulkhead, I reached for a barf bag. My head spun and a stench arose in my throat. I went over the Sox starting line up – Monbouquette, Conigliaro, Malzone, Yastrzemski – and clutched the sides of my seat.

"You okay?" Brad asked. "I guess flying is not your sport."

"Nope." I opened a spigot of fresh air from the bulkhead.

"Ever go by ship?"

"Nope."

He began to shuffle through his pack. A head taller than me, he had a muscular build with broad shoulders tapering to a trim waist. I'd seen him around campus, but he ran with the gym rats who rarely showed up in the library where I hung out. "Boy, am I hungry. Got any munchies?"

I pointed to the overhead. "Try the pot roast sandwiches. My mother's idea of a snack."

"Think you got enough?" He chuckled as he unwrapped the double layers of Saran wrap. "Sure beats P,B,& J. God it's a hike to Norway! This buggy stops everywhere."

He sat back with his pot roast and climbing magazines. I pulled out one of my World War Two paperbacks, *The Hunt For The Graf Spee*, a German battleship destroyed by the British fleet off Paraguay. The engines throbbed in the quiet cabin as the plane sped away from the sinking sun on its sixteen-hour trip to Oslo.

Most of the passengers, including Brad, fell asleep, their legs akimbo and heads resting on each other's shoulders. But I was restless and stared into the night where all the waymarks had vanished. Not a trace of clouds or the earth below, just a dark abyss. I returned to the Hunt for the Graf Spee, watched as stewardesses came by with snacks, observed the refuelings in Newfoundland and Iceland in the middle of the night in a sleepless torpor.

A light flicked on between the seats in front of me and I glimpsed someone opening a Playboy, revealing a spread-eagled woman with large breasts and a furry crotch. Never had I seen a naked body. Page after page unfolded of athletic positions I had not imagined. I was repelled but unable to stop looking until my fellow traveler turned out the light. I passed out shortly after, dreaming of naked bodies floating through the aisles of the plane.

The sun seared my window at dawn and lit up the cabin with a radiant heat. We flew over the Norwegian coastline and left the curve of the ocean behind except for the probing fingers of the fjords. There were few signs of houses or roads below, just moors and mountains, lakes and streams, and lots of rocks. Perhaps they grew them there, I thought. And the light was clear. I could see for hundreds of miles in all directions with everything etched in the sharpest detail. No more misty days for me or National Geographic pictures of girls churning cheese: the Land of Free Love was now below me.

Brad stirred and woke. "Where are we?" he groaned. A day's growth shadowed his face. His breath smelled like rancid meat.

"Norway," I said.

"It looks nippy down there. Any more pot roast doohickeys?"

He finished the last of the sandwiches as we began our descent. By the time we'd landed at Fornebu Airport my tired brain had shrunk to the size of a pea. I prattled mindlessly about food, a hot shower, bad breath, and anything to keep me awake. I was eager to meet my host family and be on my way.

Kristen and Lars were all dressed up. She was in her 40's with pretty dark eyes that sparkled when she talked. She wore a black skirt embroidered with flowers and a white blouse buttoned to the neck. Her coiled brown hair was pinned with a pewter comb. Lars stood beside her, straight as a soldier on parade, with short dark hair and a narrow weathered face that had known the sun. Red and green reindeer leapt across his cardigan sweater. I started to say hello and realized I didn't know how.

Kristen smiled. *"Jeg heter Kristen Bakken og det heter Lars. Velkommen til Norge."* Lars clicked his heels, bowed, and offered his calloused hand. His grip was strong and I clicked my heels in response and bowed, too.

"Joshua Volken," I said. I figured *Norge* meant Norway.

"Har du koffert?" Kristin asked.

I looked up *koffert* in my pocket dictionary. It meant, suitcase. and replied, *"Jahvol."*

"Ikke jahvol," she laughed. *"ikke Javol."* That's German.

"Ja," I repeated.

"Veldig godt. Kom med meg." She led me down the hall to baggage. On the way, I passed Brad who'd found his family, too. From the look on his face, he appeared as confused as me.

The road from the airport meandered through forests until we reached the crest of a valley which Kristen called Lier, a patchwork of small farms amid rolling, wooded hills. I had dozens of questions but no way to ask them so I settled for silence. We drove down the valley several miles and turned into a dirt road marked by seven mailboxes, each named Bakken. Kicking up clouds of dust, we sped by rows of fruit trees and fenced in pastures until we arrived at their farmhouse. Two stories high with a wide front porch and a patch of grass in front, it was across the yard from a barn and sheds in various stages of disrepair. A green tractor was parked by the barn, its large black tires caked with mud. Many new smells greeted me - hay, manure, cows, and flowers that surrounded their house.

"*Er du trett?*" Kristin asked. She mimed a yawn.

"*Ja, trett,*" I repeated. And hungry and in need of a bath, but with no way to say it.

I followed her up to a small, wood paneled room with bare wood floors and a pitcher and basin for washing on a dresser. I opened a window. Something was missing - screens. Nothing between me and the cool arctic twilight air uncoiling through the room. I could see hills miles away and a mist gathering over the meadows. 11:30 and the sun still above the horizon. Could I sleep in the light? I crawled under the feather eiderdown ready to embrace my new home.

CHAPTER 7

Laundry was drying on the lines in the bright morning light - overalls, shirts, and socks by the dozen. My watch said afternoon, my body morning. I wandered into a gray wooded barn that smelled of hay and manure. Dust danced in the sunlight filtering through the sideboards. A peal of laughter came from the hayloft. I climbed up a rickety ladder and found a skinny eight-year-old girl with a mop of blonde hair lying on her back in the hay playing with two worn dolls.

"Hi," I said. "I'm Josh."

"*God dag,*" she replied. "*Jeg heter Brigitta. Velkommen til Norge.*" She flicked the hair from her eyes. We stared at each other, plotting our next sentence.

"Breakfast?" I mimed eating food.

"*Frokost?*" She showed me her watch which read three in the afternoon, and giggled. She scurried down the ladder and out the barn door and into the farmhouse.

The kitchen was spacious and neat. A gas stove stood against a wall next to a cupboard with jars of preserved fruit and vegetables. An oak dinning table was in the center of the of the kitchen with a scattering of bread crumbs. White window curtains billowed in the afternoon breezes. Brigitta pointed at two canisters on the counter. *"Te eller kaffe?"*

"Kaffe," I guessed. "Thanks, I mean, *takk."*

"A ligge mor det." She went to the pantry and brought me coffee, jam, sardines, and a chunk of brown cheese. The cheese was sweet and tasted like peanut butter, the jam like raspberries fresh from the vine. I spread them on bread, homemade and dense as cake, but paused at the sardines, lying headless and embalmed in oil.

"Det smaker godt, Josh." She smirked and plucked one out of the oily can and swallowed it whole.

A living room branched off the kitchen with another dining table surrounded by stiff-backed chairs, their wicker bottoms stretched with age. A cherry cupboard overflowed with antique treasures -Delft dishes, pottery platters, and colored glasses. A wall of pictures told the family story.

Daguerreotypes of handlebar-mustached men and glassy eyed women with high-necked blouses, waiting for the camera to snap. Black and white pictures of gatherings with the family dressed in their Sunday best. And a wall of color snapshots - weddings, holidays, and aerials of the homestead. Generations of Bakkens at a glance. A pendulum clock on the blackened fireplace mantle marked time, its brass arm counting the hours in Roman numerals. On a sideboard lay a Bible printed in 1647, its frayed parchment delicate to the touch.

"Liker du ga pa tur?" Brigitta asked, setting my dishes in the sink. "Sure," I said uncertain what she meant. I followed her into the yard where chickens pecked randomly in the dirt and slack-mouthed cows munched grass in the pasture. We

entered a field with shoulder-high hedges crowded with clusters of red berries.

"*Bringebaer!*" she said. I plucked one from the vine – they were raspberries and delicious.

Kristin was kneeling on the ground between the hedges surrounded by cartons of fruit. "*Sov du godt?*" She asked. She spoke slowly, enunciating each word.

"*Ja, godt.*" I had slept long and well.

She handed Brigitta and me quart size cartons. We settled by a vine where berries fell to the ground when they were touched. Within minutes we'd filled two cartons and eaten another. My fingers turned red as blood. Four hours later we piled our boxes in a wheelbarrow and brought them home. Kristin stored some in the pantry and poured the rest into pots on the stove, adding water and sugar.

"*Liker du bringerbaer syltetoy og saft?*" Kristin asked.

I didn't get the choices but said yes to *saft.*

"*Det vil bli hyggeling.*" She began to boil the raspberries into jam which I learned was *syltetoy* and extracted the juice into a syrup for drinks, what she called *saft.* I grew hungry but had no idea when they ate.

An older couple arrived for dinner at *klokken tjue,* 20 hours. Introduced as *Bestefar* and *Bestemor,* they looked like grandparents with their halting gait and weathered faces. Whose grandparents I didn't know and spent my time trying to guess. Unable to speak English, they nodded politely, repeating America at sporadic moments with an approving smile. *Bestemor* donned an apron and tended the simmering raspberries; *Bestefar* sat at the table cracking his knuckles.

Lars pulled into the yard on the tractor. He shook off his boots in the kitchen and splashed

water on his face. As Kristen and *Bestemor* put food
on the table, I reached for the bread. Brigitta shot
me a warning glance. Then, *Bestefar* bowed his head
and murmured grace into his folded hands.

"*Fiske kakke?*" Kristen asked, handing me a
platter of something.

"Sure. *Takk.*" It looked like hamburgers but
smelled like fish. The only fish I liked was smoked
salmon. I loaded up on cauliflower and potatoes.

Bestefar talked with Lars, gesturing to the hay
fields. They had a similar look, an elongated face,
hazel eyes, and close-cropped hair. Kristin and
Bestemor teased Brigitta who smiled as she toyed
with her food. I studied their faces and gestures
and guessed at their meanings. Right or wrong didn't
matter to me as long as I was part of the family.

They talked quickly amongst themselves but slowly
to me. I learned how to say fish cakes, bread,
butter, tea, sugar, hot, thank you, pass the salt,
tired, full, bathroom, and good night, a new world
of 17 nouns and a few active tenses. Sometimes I
tracked down words in my pocket dictionary;
sometimes I let them pass. When I finally understood
a sentence, the conversation had usually shifted so
I smiled until my face hurt when asked a question. I
drifted through platters of food and a delicious
homemade cake, careful to observe the custom of
finishing everything on my plate.

Brigitta pulled me into the living room after
dinner. "*Vil du leser med meg?*" She handed me a
book, *Den Lille Prins*.

I considered the large print and colorful
pictures. "*Jeg vil…* try?" I asked.

"*Forsoker,*" she said.

I stumbled through the Norwegian. She giggled at
every mistake, repeating words until I got them
right. She spoke with a lilt that sounded like

singing. Even one syllable could swoop up and down.

"*Forstar du?*" Brigitta asked after the first chapter.

"*Jeg forstar ikke,*" I said. I didn't understand a thing.

Using the pictures she explained. A little prince had left his home, Asteroid B612, where he was in love with a thorny rose. He was exploring the universe, traveling from star to star. He met peculiar people who gave strange answers to simple questions. I got the drift but my time zone had caught up with me.

"*Kan vi leser i morgen?*" she asked.

"Sure," I yawned. I'd read in the morning.

She led me to the pantry and pointed toward a tin on the top shelf. "*Josh, hjelper meg.*"

I grabbed the canister and she pried it open, giving me a handful of cookies with a fine layer of powdered sugar.

"*Det snakker godt,*" I said.

"*Smaker godt,*" she corrected, stuffing one in her mouth.

"*Smaker godt,*" I repeated and stuck my hand in for more.

A few weeks after my first dazed meal in Lier, I took the train into Oslo to meet Kjell Svenson, my Norwegian advisor for study abroad. Throngs of tourists from all over Europe crowded Karl Johansgata; a cobble-stoned boulevard in Oslo's center. A wood sided trolley, a *trikken*, ran down the center of the avenue, clanging its bell and letting out passengers. I half expected to see horse drawn carriages on the narrow, meandering side streets with their old-fashioned gas lamps. At the end of Karl Johansgata was the Palace of Harald V surrounded by beautiful gardens.

I wandered past crowded cafes, their windows full

of pastries and open-faced sandwiches, past souvenir shops hawking trolls and sweaters, and past circular kiosks selling *Der Spiegel*, *Le Monde*, and the *Guardian*. Reaching into my pocket for a few coins to buy *Aftenbladet*, the Oslo daily, and the *International Herald Tribune*, I found only American money. I furtively scanned the *Tribune's* sports pages to check on the Red Sox and asked for directions to a bank.

"*Penger*," I said to the teller. I slipped her a twenty from Dad. I'd found the bank more by accident than design as I'd confused the words for left and right.

"American, huh?" she asked in English.

"*Ja,*" I answered, imitating the lilt I'd learned from Brigitta.

"How long you here for?" She counted out 140 *kroner*, densely decorated brown bills with a King on the front and silver coins with holes in the middle.

"*Et ar.*"

"A year? Not your average tourist." She smiled. "Here you go. Sounds like you're already fluent. That's a wictory."

"Victory," I corrected and flashed her a thumbs up sign.

I celebrated my first transaction by purchasing *Aftenbladet* and the *Tribune* and sweets in a pastry shop, *konditori,* where I ordered *kakedeig*, *mordeig*, and *tertedeig.* Downing my sampler of half moons, éclairs, and rum soaked pastrics, I studied the box scores from the sports pages. The long summer day was still young when I arrived by *trikken* at Kjell's on the outskirts of town. He was a tweed-suited man in his 40's with hair askew and reams of books lining his wood-paneled living room. He reviewed my fall courses on Undset, Kierkegaard, Munch, and Grieg. I

60

wasn't sure how much I would understand at Nansen School which started in a few months. But I was determined to leave English behind and hoped my scattering of phrases was moving me toward fluency.

With the sun still high, I started to walk to the city, crossing a grassy park decorated with sculpture gardens and fountains. People lay on the ground, reading and basking in the sun. Several girls wore skimpy bikinis, their tops removed and their bottoms barely covered. Their breasts were pressed into the steamy grass, their hair dangling freely. Nearby, two little girls, naked and barely three, played in a fountain. Their bodies, so different from what I'd glimpsed on the plane. Everyone seemed free in the park, letting the warmth invade their bodies. I wanted to take a moment to lie in the grass, too, and read a few pages of Ibsen to see how far my Norwegian would take me. But, sweltering in my clothes and afraid to miss the last train to Lier, I left.

"Train station," I said when Kristen answered the phone.

"*Hvor?*" she asked.

"The station," I repeated.

"*Hvilken?*"

"Choo choo," I said.

She paused and hung up. Confused, I wondered if I should walk home, only a couple of kilometers down the valley. But after a few minutes Brigitta ran into the station, laughing and repeating Oslo or Lier and pointing to Kristen in the car.

Oslo or Lier - they hadn't known where I was calling from.

"*Er du sulten?*" Brigitta asked.

Sulten, ja, hungry. The pastries had worn off and I was famished.

Chapter 8

I had trouble sleeping in the never-ending twilight. I'd close the curtains, pull the comforter over my head, and read until I was bleary. Sometimes I'd awake thinking it was morning; but the clock always read three A.M. Neither awake nor asleep, it was like living in a fever. I longed for the moon and the stars, the comfort of darkness that would allow me to sleep.

When I'd finally tumbled out of bed, Lars and Kristen had left for the fields and Brigitta had disappeared with her friends. I'd come downstairs to an empty kitchen with breakfast leftovers on the table. I'd munch on cheese and jam sandwiches and study my vocabulary, twenty new words every day. Then I'd wander over the farm, looking for someone to talk to or following dirt roads to see where they went.

The hardest part was the silence when no one was around and not knowing when they would be back. Or the silence at the end of one of my fractured sentences which led to confused smiles. I would have done anything to be understood. But I also tired of speaking Norwegian and often retreated to solitary places, especially the woods that began where the pastures ended. Still, no matter how much I was alone, the silence in Lier was not as empty as the silence in Quinnipiac.

—

One morning shortly after my Oslo adventure, one of my rambles took me into the barn where Lars was milking cows. "*Liker du a prover?*" He asked politely, offering me a stool and a pail. He talked quickly because he was busy and spoke in a guttural dialect that sounded like he had potatoes in his mouth.

I squatted next to a half-ton cow that smelled like she'd slept in her dung. Her tail swished ominously as she shifted on her feet. I didn't know any reassuring Norwegian to whisper in her ear as I'd observed Lars doing. I grabbed one of her pink, rubbery teats that hung from a sack bloated with milk. It was warm and slippery and felt embarrassing to touch. I yanked with two hands; she mooed and swatted me in the head.

"*Nei, nei, nei.*" Lars grabbed my thumb and forefinger and showed me how to funnel the milk down the teat and into the metal pail. "*Forstar du?*" He asked, amused but impatient.

I held the teat between my fingers and pressed, but too tightly. She lurched and kicked over the pail on my trousers. To my surprise the milk was warm and clotted with cream, so different from the cold, homogenized milk in bottles in our Quinnipiac refrigerator.

"*Nei, nei, nei,*" Lars said. He patted the cow on the shoulder. "*Jeg vil gjore det na,*" he said to me.

I needed no translation and left for greener pastures, relieved.

I found Brigitta in the apple orchard dangling from a tree. "*Morn, Josh. Liker du plukker blabaer?*"

I didn't know they had blueberries in Norway. I asked where.

"*Til fjellen.*" She pointed at the hills above the house.

We started up a switchback trail through a forest of evergreens. Brigitta kept a fast pace in the cold, moist air. Small white mushrooms sprouted like flowers over the ground. After an hour we came to a meadow on top. Blueberries, tiny and tart, grew on the low-lying bushes that flourished between the rocks. We roamed from bush to bush until we reached an escarpment with a view of the valley. Odd rectangular plots, some darkly fallow, some rich with grasses, divided the land. Farmhouses stood in the middle of the plots, surrounded by fruit trees and barns. A stream rambled through the farms and forests that covered the hillsides. The sound of Lars' tractor drifted up from below.

The pace was different in Lier, at least for Brigitta and me. I didn't feel I had to talk; our conversations came and went as needed. Despite the language barrier, I was beginning to feel at home and seldom in need of staying in motion. I was lonely, I was cut off, but it was a separateness I accepted.

We followed the ridge line to a pond where Brigitta threw off her shoes and dangled her feet in the water. Whitened tree trunks, stripped of their bark, hovered in the bottom. "*Kald,*" I said, thrusting my fingers into the frigid water. "*Ikke sa kald,*" disagreed Brigitta, and tossed a rock into the pond. I grasped a slice of slate and skipped it across the surface.

"*Hvordan gjorde du det?*" she asked.

I showed her how to cradle the slate in her fingers and fling it sidearm. We aimed at a log in the middle which I pretended to be the Graf Spee. I'd forgotten the fun of skipping stones. An hour later we descended home. I could smell fish frying on the stove as we walked into the yard.

"*Har du god tid?*" Kristen asked.

"*Mor! Josh spretter en stein pa vannen ti timer!*"

I hadn't skipped my stone ten times, but liked Brigitta's enthusiasm. I loved the way she said *mor*, mother. It rolled off her tongue in a gush ending with a trill on the 'r'.

"*Nei, si du det!*" Kristen laughed. I grabbed the plates and silverware from the cupboard and set the table, accustomed to eating at nine at night.

On Saturday night, Kristen and I drove to Lier. She'd told me about a dance in the village and handed me the keys to the car. I was finally on Norwegian time and had learned to pick strawberries without mangling the fruit. I was even used to chickens pestering my feet while I scattered their feed and milking the cows without Lars looking over my shoulder.

Kristen leaned back and closed her eyes, lulled by the hum of the Volvo wagon. She rarely took a moment for herself; she went from task to task until the day was done, which in summer meant when we had dinner at eight. We sped past dozens of farms, neat white houses and red barns surrounded by pastures and orchards, until we arrived at a few scattered buildings that hardly looked like a village.

"Where's the dance?" I asked.

"*Pa kirken.*" She pointed to a church. I'd been to the village before, but not for an evening out. "*Jeg kommer tilbake klokken tolv.*"

A dance in a church till midnight? I walked into a dark, wood building with a modest spire. The pews were empty, but music drifted from the floor below. People had gathered in the basement around an accordionist, playing a polka. They laughed as they stumbled, but everyone danced. I hadn't done polkas since sixth grade gym class.

With scarcely a break, they began a new dance, singing, "*Per Spelman han hadde ein einste ku,*" a song about a farmer and his only cow. Two girls in their late teens grabbed my arms and pulled me into the circle. They guided me with their hands, giggling when I bumped into them or stepped on their toes. I followed their leads mimicking their footsteps. We danced for a while, in circles and squares, sometimes together, sometimes not. I was soaked with sweat when the accordionist finally took a break.

"Jeg heter Solveig and denne er Johanna," one of the girls said, curtsying.

"Jeg heter Josh" I replied, returning her greeting with a bow.

"Would you like a snack?" Solveig continued in Norwegian and gestured to a punch bowl and cookies. "You're not Norwegian?"

"No, American.

"You live here?"

"I live with the Bakken's."

"Kristin and Lars?"

"Yes," I replied, surprised she would know them.

"America." She smiled approvingly. "You speak well." Her eyes sparkled with more than linguistic approval.

We talked for a few minutes before we rejoined the weave of the dance. I managed to meet all the girls in the hall, holding their hands for a few seconds of flirting, before moving on. I'd always associated accordions with dancing monkeys, but the music was beautiful, slow dances that sounded like anthems and frenzied jigs that left me breathless. I was surprised it was already twelve when it ended. I said goodbye to Solveig and helped sweep the floor and stack the chairs before they turned out the lights. Kristin was waiting in the car.

"*Var det deilig* ?" Kristen asked.

"*Deilig*?"

"Fun," she replied in English.

"You speak English?"

"I speak but… *ikke* good. You want to learn *norsk, ikke sant*?"

"*Ja.*"

"So… we speak *Norsk*," she laughed. I did miss English a little, but felt closer to her in Norwegian.

"I met Solveig," I said.

"Solveig Hamsun? She's fun. Solveig means sun path."

Kristin drove home slowly. Rings had appeared around her eyes. I wondered how early she would arise Sunday morning. Twilight had started earlier since I'd first arrived, becoming dark by eleven. But I was used to the white nights and fell asleep when my head hit the pillow.

The weather turned hot in late August. The hay withered into brittle yellow reeds that rattled in the breeze. I could speak in multi-word sentences and carry on small conversations. Pass the salt. Pick the cherries, *kirsebaer* - a beautiful word with a soft 'shish' on *kirse* that sounded like an expiring breath. I was surprised at how many words sounded like English. When I blanked on a word, I made it up. Doctor became *doktoren*. Some words sounded like poetry: butterfly was *sommerfugl*, *summer bird*. I began to enjoy talking with people, even though my accent still made them smile.

With the hot weather came the harvest. Neighboring farmers joined the Bakkens in cutting their football-sized hay fields, nestled between the hills and the creek. Farmable land was rare in mountainous Norway so every foot counted. Brigitta showed me how to swipe the hay near the ground with one sweep of the scythe. I joined a line of families cutting their way across the fields, raking hay into ten foot bales and pitch forking it into a wagon to take to storage. The work was heavy - I regretted the long daylight that pushed our labor into the evening. I'd never worked so hard at home.

I stopped counting the bales by noon and fell into a working silence, ignoring my fatigue. Muscles that I never knew existed ached and the sweat had baked into my body. At the end of the day Brigitta and I jumped on the last wagon home, transporting the hay over a rutted field to the barn.

I sank into a steaming tub and let the hot water rise and fall with my breath. My hands floated to the surface, pink as a newborn's. The family had begun to gather in the kitchen for dinner. I slid into my jeans and slipper socks and went down. I rescued Brigitta who was trapped on a ladder with too many dishes. On the table was a blue airmail envelope addressed to me; the writing was ragged and had no return address.

Hey sonny boy, how's things in the boonies? Not bad I hope. It was bad when I got to my village in Guatemalala, a hundred miles from the capital and no nookie anywhere and it was hot as hell. I had to sleep on the ground with all he bugs. Then the rains came turning every thing to mud. I was supposed to build a school. But nobody wanted it but the Peace Corps. My Spanish was lousy and I had nothing to say to anyone and what I had to say they didn't want to hear.

All that fucking time I spent in the hospital when I came back. went for nothing. Those jerks don't know what they're doing. It was bad. While You were folk dancing in fucking Ohio I was stuck in McLean. Maybe you'll be better off in the arctic. Maybe not. Fuck it's late. Don't fuck around with the babes too much kiddoo. Paul

I held my breath till I finished. We had talked as little about Paul's episode as Mother's. Learning

the details was like walking on broken glass in bare
feet. As Kristin put the finishing touches on fish
cakes and potatoes, Brigitta, having just started
school, joined me in the living room with her
homework. She propped her feet on my lap and asked
me to name the capitals of South America. I'd
memorized them in a sixth grade class which really
impressed her. She finished her capitals quickly and
gave me *Den Lille Prins to read*. Rejected by the
flower he'd loved for asking too many questions,
he'd fled on the backs of geese to an asteroid so
tiny that he was able to watch the sun set forty
times a day.

Chapter 9

The coffee house near Oslo University was packed with students on a busy Saturday night. I was meeting Brad near his workplace before he shipped off to his folk high school. As the days had darkened earlier, a chill had crept into the air. Folklora was dense with cigarette smoke and decorated with posters of Che Guevara. I ordered a beer and waited. Brad appeared with a girl on each arm and a beer in his hand. He walked as though it wasn't his first drink.

"Hey man. Meet a couple of my friends, Greta and Helga. How's life on the farm?"

"Hanging out, picking up *Norsk*."

"I'm learning idiomatically," he said, gesturing at Greta. "Damn this city's dead for a Saturday night!"

"Better than Tromso," said Helga, in British-accented English.

"They prefer folk dancing. Where're you from, Josh?"

I gathered from the way Greta hung on Brad's arm that Helga was intended for me. She had a narrow face and pale complexion with dark glasses that complemented a black turtleneck and jeans. She looked like she'd spent too much time in the dark.

"Boston," I said, relieved to speak English.

"Land of the bean and the cod," added Brad. " Refills anyone?" He drained his glass and waited for orders.

"I'll pass," I said.

"Isn't Boston known for universities?" Helga asked.

"Hahvahd, the pinnacle of learning," Brad answered. "They know everything theyah."

"Everything that's passé." Helga stubbed out her cigarette. "America's out of touch. The Avant Garde's in Europe now - Grotowski, Stockhausen, Camus. Name an American who's relevant."

"Copland," I said.

"All he writes is folk music," Helga said.

"Anneuser Busch," Brad said.

"Anneuser who?"

"Makes the best damn beer in the world!"

"You're not serious," scowled Helga.

"Hey," Brad declared, pulling out a flask of Wild Turkey and pouring a jigger in our glasses. "*Skol!*" He drained his glass and I followed. The whiskey burned a path into my stomach.

"Know the films of Wajda?" pursued Helga.

"Who?" I asked. A gauzy buzz shrouded my mind.

"Ashes and Diamonds? They show such films in America?"

"Don't know. Maybe nobody's interested." Brad nodded in agreement. "We have enough films without bothering with the fringe. There's lots of diversity."

"Fringe?" Helga ripped a cigarette out of her pack. "We have more diversity in Europe, 100 miles in every direction."

"In New York City, it's a hundred blocks in any direction,"I said.

Brad re-filled my jigger and we saluted each other, "To diversity, wherever she be found!"

72

"You can't compare a bunch of immigrants with two thousand years of European culture," she said.

I drained my glass and jammed it on the table. "What does Norway know about diversity? You're a bunch of lily white Lutherans."

Brad gave a hoot. "Two points for the U. S. of A."

"Boors! *Kom, Greta, vi ga.*" They shoved back their chairs and left.

Brad stared at the empty table. "You could have gone a little lighter on the diversity crap."

We struggled to our feet and left. My head was wobbly, like a balloon bobbing in the wind. I leaned into a black iron lamppost emitting a flickering gas light.

"You don't look too good," Brad said.

An acrid taste rose in my throat, the odor burning my nose. I looked for distractions: if Malzone played third, who filled out the infield? Bressoud, Guindon?

Too late. *Fiske kakke* and beer slid into the gutter. I bent over, my eyes jammed shut, convulsing.

"It's okay buddy," said Brad, patting my back. "You're only throwing up."

I waited for the heaving to stop.

"My Dad used to say, 'nothing like a good puke'. Want to come back to my place 'til your head clears?"

Brad's apartment, a one room, fourth floor walk-up on Karlsongata, was six blocks from the University. A foam mattress lay on the floor amid a tangle of sheets and dirty laundry. Brad kicked off his boots and heavy wool socks so stiff from wear, you could tell the left from the right.

"Ever heard of a washing machine?" I asked.

"I got Greta. She does them at her place on

Fredrikstadtgate."

"That's convenient, if she'll still talk to you."

"No worries. She pretty levelheaded."

"Who was her friend?" I sat down in his kitchenette, a bright yellow room with a harsh overhead light.

"A hellfire from the University. I'll make you some coffee. Best thing for an addled brain." He dumped two heaping tablespoons of instant into boiled water.

"Nice recipe," I said, taking a sip.

"It's like my Dad's. He can't cook either."

I felt a kick of adrenaline. Brad shook his head. "You are one hell of a double date."

We talked about the start of school in Lillehammer and Honefoss. Brad wasn't crazy about being in the middle of nowhere.

"You go stir crazy in Lier?"

"At first, but now it's okay. God, what time is it?"

"Can't find my watch. Probably tenish."

"Damn! I missed the train."

"Stay here." He pointed to a couch propped up on apple boxes. I called the Bakkens and said I'd be home in the morning.

"I never called my folks about anything," Brad said. "I snuck out the back windows and hoped I didn't get caught. My Dad's in the military; you follow orders or else. Hungry?"

He pulled out Skippy peanut butter and crackers, bought in the PX at the Oslo Nato base. His cupboard was sparsely provisioned. Handing me a sleeping bag, he cleared off the couch. I fell asleep listening to him snore, a deep, steady hum.

The night before I left for Nansen School, Kristin baked a farewell dinner. I'd helped the Bakkens harvest the last crop of strawberries and plowed the potato fields without clipping the plants turning the corners. Norwegians ate potatoes at every meal, even when they served spaghetti.

We ate in the dining room with their Sunday dinnerware. We had reindeer steaks and for dessert *blot kakke*, a multi-layer cake with raspberry filling and whipped cream topping, Brigitta's favorite. For my trip, I received gifts the Bakkens had made themselves. A pewter candleholder for the long winter nights and a boyish troll from Brigitta to remind me of *Den Lille Prins* which I'd promised to finish reading when I came back at Christmas. I packed my trunk, shedding my Quinnipiac clothes - alligator shirts, argyle socks, cashmere sweaters, and silk pajamas - replacing them with flannel shirts, leather work boots, and a coarse wool sweater that Kristen had bought at the general store.

It was a quiet ride to the train in Oslo. A mist hovered over the hills, hinting at ice. Kristin and Brigitta lingered on the platform by my window while I stowed my bag in the overhead and waited for the journey to begin, curling my Herald Tribune in ever tightening spirals. As the train lurched forward, Brigitta followed, yelling goodbye over the din of shrieking wheels.

The countryside streamed by my window: backyards filled with vegetable plots and flower gardens, meadows overgrown with sagging bushes, and deep evergreen forests split by swollen streams surging under the bridges. We sped northward blaring our horn, past empty crossings with their blinking red lights suspended in the dark.

CHAPTER 10

A hand written sign on the front door read, *Velkommen til Nansen Skolen. Forsamling: Fem Klokken* - something was happening somewhere later at school. I entered a large Victorian house. On the first floor comfy sofas and chairs filled two spacious study areas, one with a fieldstone fireplace. A dining room adjoined these rooms and a woodsy field in the back overlooked a large lake. In a secluded alcove on the second floor, which included a classroom, a tall, gangly man, dressed in a suit and topped with a beret, was reading an art book. His swept back grey hair accentuated a high forehead and mischievous eyes.

"*God dag,*" he said. "*Velkommen til skolen.*"

"*Jeg heter Joshua Volken, Amerikanske studente.*" I bowed and offered my hand.

"You speak good Norwegian, Joshua," he said in lightly accented British. "It's rare that we have an American. I'm Thorlief, director of the school."

"*Higgelig a treffig deg,*" I said, determined to speak Norwegian until I ran out.

"Nice to meet you, too. You're early. Do you know where you're staying?" Students at Nansen Skolen rented rooms in the town.

"*Ja. Det vaer godt.*"

"*Det er godt,*" he corrected. "*Helviggata,* four

blocks down the main street and two blocks over. Need a hand?"

"*Nei, takk.*"

"Come back at *klokken fem*."

I hesitated. He held up five fingers and winked.

Lillehammer was surrounded by 6,000-foot mountains that sloped to a plain on which the town was set. Below the town lay Lake Mjosa, 60 miles long and a half mile wide. The mountain ridgelines extended to the horizon, rising seamlessly into the clouds so that you didn't know where the mountains stopped and the sky began. The school enrolled forty university students a year for study in the arts.

The main street in Lillehammer, barely wide enough for two cars, had two blocks of stores - a drugstore with racks of magazines and newspapers; a small market with stands of fruit and vegetables; a clothing store displaying everything from tuxedos to fishing boots; and a bakery that scented the air with butter and sugar.

My room was in a white clapboard house on a side street a few blocks from the center. Froken Sorsgaard, my landlady, was in her sixties. She tied her hair back so tightly that her face was as taut as a drum. The room was furnished monastically: four poster bed; knotted cotton rug covering a few feet of a cold wooden floor; boxy metal heater that quivered spasmodically but offered little heat; and an oak dresser I had to pry open. The Last Supper hung over my bed. I was given a brass key for the front door and told to be quiet at night. As I gazed out my window, overlooking a 16th century church, the belfry tolled *klokken fem*. I changed my shirt and ran to school.

The students were gathering in the downstairs rooms as I arrived. I scanned the girls with great expectations. Not all were blonds, but they all looked fit and in their 20's - just like the pictures. I repeated my standard greetings and made my way around the rooms, never staying long enough to exceed my vocabulary while noting the new words: *kunst* (art), Kierkegaard, *filosofi*, *maleri* (painting), *samtale*(discussion), Munch, *fjelds* (mountains), Grieg. At every greeting there was a ripple of surprise that I was from America. Where in the States? Why Norway? Did I have family here? They wanted to know so much that I began to feel exotic. Being a stranger in a strange land was better than being a stranger in my own.

Soon, though, it all became a blur of questions and replies and too many names to remember until I came upon a girl standing in an alcove by herself. Dressed in matronly pants and blouse, she seemed older than the others and had a quiet assurance. My Norwegian vanished when her pale blue eyes stared into mine and she said, "*Jeg heter Elvira*," and offered me her hand.

It was warm and pliant. I blushed as I heard myself say, "Call me Josh."

She bowed, her blond hair spilling over shoulder. "Where do you come from?"

"Boston."

"Boston, where?"

"Massachusetts, America. West of Oslo."

"Everything is west of Oslo," she laughed.

"Where're you from?" I asked.

"Stavangar, east of Boston," she said with a smile. "I have family in America. Are you near Minnesota?"

"Nope. I hear they have a lot of lakes."

"*Ja*. My uncle lives there. You speak Norwegian?"

"*Higgeling a treffer deg*," I said, surprising myself. It was nice to meet her.

"*Det vaer godt*! You learn quick."

Thorlief interrupted the gathering for announcements. "We'll talk more later," she whispered, touching me lightly on the arm.

Thorlief welcomed us to the academy, announcing locations of morning classes and hours for breakfast. There was a brief back and forth about reading lists and as the group disbanded, I went looking for Elvira. I was stopped on the stairs to the second floor by a woman in her thirties. Barely five feet tall and stocky like a teddy bear, she seemed unconcerned about starting a conversation in the middle of a staircase.

"Josh, the American student? I heard you were coming. I'm Emma."

"Oh. What're you studying?"

"I'm not a student," she chuckled. "I'm married to Edvard, the literature teacher. The one with the tweedy jacket and book under his arm."

"Your English is excellent."

"It should be. I lived in England for six years." Her smile ran through me like a warm current.

She told me that she'd arrived in Norway 5 years before and was the only person in Lillehammer who didn't ski. She preferred hot climates like Egypt where she was born. She was so easy to talk to that it felt like I'd known her for a long time.

"How's your Norwegian?" she asked.

"Good, as long as it's about the weather."

"Will you join Edvard and me for dinner tomorrow night? It's been a while since we've talked to anyone new."

Emma and Edvard lived in the foothills in a small brownish bungalow with a view of Lillehammer and the lake. She answered the door with a book in her hand and glasses perched on her nose. There was not a whiff of dinner in the air.

"Enjoy your first day?" she asked.

"I didn't understand much." Typing was coming from behind a closed door down the hallway. "Edvard joining us?"

"Edvard doesn't eat. He works. He's finishing a book review for the morning." She went to the refrigerator and removed butter and eggs. "First days are hard. I could translate his lectures for you."

She put up the water to boil and set the plates on the table. "Why did you come to Norway? Your family here?"

I told her that my father had come from Russia when he was nine and that mother's grandfather was from Germany. German Jews hated Russian Jews but often married them.

"I come from Italian Jews who moved to Cairo and I married a Norwegian."

Another itinerant Jew, I thought, and pulled up a chair. She'd gone to England to study at the University, met Edvard who was on a holiday, and eloped with him three weeks later. It was a hell of a year learning to get along, but she'd wanted to get away from England.

She set out our dinner: cheese, rye bread, and a can of sardines. "By the way, you like sardines?" she asked, then noticed my face. "Don't worry, they're an acquired taste."

She fried me an egg on toast instead. I salted it lightly, cut it in squares, and washed it down with hot peppermint tea.

"Why did you need to get away?" I asked.

"My sister committed suicide," she said, as simply as pass the salt. I skipped a breath. The typing stopped. After a moment or two it started again, filling the room with a halting clatter.

"Another egg, Josh?"

"No. I've had enough."

"We don't have to talk about her." Emma seemed

comfortable with silence.

I took in a breath and let it fill my lungs. "What happened?" I asked.

"Elena was depressed. At first she couldn't hold a job. Then came insomnia, days of walking the streets, drifting away from friends and us. Day and night became the same. We tried to help, but you can't help someone if they don't help themselves." As she talked her voice seemed to grow dimmmer as if she was sliding away. She told me about how they had played together when they were small. Silly games that nobody knew. But something happened when they'd moved to Egypt. Elena lost her way, spent more time by herself, became a person Emma didn't know.

"Your own sister?" I asked.

"Sure. Families can be as hard to know as strangers."

She described Elena's deterioration, never looking you in the eye, heading for unknown destinations in the middle of the night, forgetting to wash or change clothes. It was a vanishing act as flesh and blood became a shadow, a person who could neither hear nor speak. The sky had darkened and a chill entered the house. Emma donned a sweater then scanned the cupboards for sweets. She stayed open and calm as she spiraled through the past, recalling the facts sadly but without blame. I asked questions about the doctors, her mother and father, the medications. Didn't anyone try to help?

We talked until the typing stopped. Edvard appeared briefly to say good night, and Emma and I sat, watching the candles flicker. The sky was covered with stars when I finally went home. At two in the morning I crawled into bed, shivering under a comforter with my electric heater glowing uselessly in the dark.

The birds woke me a few hours later, ferrying from

the vines outside my window to the evergreens by the Church. Fragments of dreams lingered: Elvira's eyes, Paul asleep on my shoulder. But I let them slip back into the night. I put on a shirt and followed the smells of butter and cinnamon to town.

The bakery was closed, but a waitress working in back came to the door, dusting the flower from her clothes. Tall and gangly with dark frizzy hair, she didn't look Nordic at all. Her baggy white uniform hung off her shoulders like a scarecrow's garb. "*Kan jeg hjelper deg?*" She asked.

"*Kan jeg … *"

"Buy some pastry? You're American, *ikke sant*? It's called, *kakedeig.*" She smiled.

I repeated *kakedeig* and entered the store. She pointed to the pastry in the case. "*Mordeig, tertedeig, butterdeig, weinerbrod,* and *vaniljekrem?*" I chose a *vaniljekrem.* It looked like the éclairs that Dad used to hide in the refrigerator; he shared everything until it came to pastry. "Are you studying here?" she asked.

"At Nansen Skolen."

"You're lucky," she said, adding apologetically,"one *kroner.* By the way, we open at eight, but if you come early, knock on the door, *ikke sant*? *Jeg heter Tulla.*" She curtsied.

I bowed. "*Jeg heter, Josh.*"

I didn't understand much of Thorlief's lecture in Art History class, despite his frequent English translations of Kandinsky's transformation. Since Norwegians understood English, it wasn't much of a disruption, but I didn't like being in the spotlight. I became tongue tied and forgot the little Norwegian I knew. The new vocabulary was overwhelming, so I scrutinized the paintings in the textbook, fascinated by the way the realistic landscapes disintegrated into blots of floating colors as Kandinsky grew older. When I tired of the paintings, I studied the students. The youngest, fresh from *gymnasium,* took diligent notes; the older asked more questions and engaged Thorlief in discussion.

Elvira sat by a window at the end of a semi-circle of desks ringing the lectern. She'd fixed her hair in braids that made her look sixteen. But her baggy skirt and dowdy blouse made her seem thirty. She took careful notes on three by five cards. She was mostly silent during discussions , but when she joined she joined with passion, punctuating her opinions with dramatic gestures. I practiced conversational openers for Elvira as Thorlief wrapped up his lecture about Kandinsky's last abstract paintings.

We had lunch in the oak paneled dining room overlooking the lake. I arrived early, but the seats near Elvira were taken.

"Joshua, come sit down," a student invited, sliding a chair from the table. "*Jeg heter Tomas og det heter Anna.* Can we speak English? We never talk to Americans."

Tired from class and afraid to hurt feelings, I agreed.

"You understood Thorlief?" Tomas asked. His sympathetic eyes softened the sharp angles of his high cheekbones. Dressed in a button-down shirt, he seemed in his late twenties.

"Not much," I answered.

He summarized his notes as we ate and told me about his family in the Lofoten Islands above the Arctic Circle who made their living as fishermen.

"You live near the *maelstrom?*" I asked.

"How'd you know about that?"

"Shipwreck stories. My favorite bedtime reading when I was small."

He laughed. "The tides are tough, but don't believe all you read."

With no afternoon classes I borrowed Tomas' notes

84

and picked up a Herald Tribune on my way home. I found a letter from Kristen on my doorstep. She'd enclosed a note from Mother.

It's been only a few months since you left. It's hard to get used to the fact that you will be away for a year. We had such a lovely time this summer and now it's fall, not my favorite time, so cold and dark. Father's been busy at the office and meetings at night. I hardly see him. And sorry to say no news from Paul. I guess he's working on the weekends. I stopped by his apartment to say hello but he wasn't around. Too bad that we all can't be together at Hanukkah. I started my fall courses. Taking a great class on Sartre with Professor Dauphenier. Only two semesters to go! So that's the news. Hope you're getting enough rest. Don't forget the Munch Museum in Oslo. And write! Mother XXOO

After I'd deciphered Tomas' notes, it was too late to eat at school so I headed for the Café. People were finishing their evening meal, sipping coffee and reading *Aftenposten*. I was looking for something hearty and Tulla suggested potato soup.

"You always eat potatoes?" I asked, grabbing a stool at the counter.

"*Nei*, it tastes good," she said. She disappeared with a swish of her uniform and returned with a steaming porridge of potatoes, onions, and leeks. She dallied about the counter, filling sugar bowls while I told her about school. She described her brief stay at Oslo University the year before and why she had to return home when her father had suffered a stroke and was unable to work.

"You staying around here long?" I asked.

"As long as he needs me."

"Am I holding you up?" I noticed I was the last in the café.

"*Nei*." She blushed.

I finished the soup and home made bread. Its creamy texture, thick and peppery, reminded me of Cape Cod chowder. When she returned with the tab I was surprised to see she'd changed into nice fitting jeans, had let her hair down, and brightened her eyes with liner. We stacked the chairs on the tables and closed up. I could barely see her in the twilight when she locked the door.

"What are you up to?" she asked.

"Oh, tonight? Nothing, I mean, reading Kierkegaard."

"Oh. Will you be by tomorrow?"

"*Ja*. I hope so."

"*God natt*, Josh," she said, and left a trail of perfume in the chilly air.

CHAPTER 11

The next few weeks were a fluctuating crossword puzzle. As soon as I'd filled in a few squares with words, new squares appeared. But slowly phrases began to cohere into sentences and some conversations became automatic. The class listened to my fractured grammar and responded politely. It was a simple equation: the more I spoke Norwegian, the less I spoke English. Word by word, I was leaving America behind.

I always sat across from Elvira. I'd become enamored of her dated wardrobes, the way she dangled a shoe off her stockinged foot while she took notes, the singsong inflections in her voice, and the way she said *ja* with a delicate, intake of breath. There were dozens of *ja's*: breathy, exclamatory, hesitating, and teasing. I often practiced the *ja's* as I walked home, repeating the most banal conversations enthusiastically; "Would you like coffee? *Ja, takk*. Did you sleep well? *Ja, sikkert*." I wanted to sing in the language, to stop translating into English and live in Norwegian, wanted the magical *ja* to appear without thinking.

By the end of September summer was spent which left a permanent nip in the air. Lawns had browned, dotted with red and yellow leaves. The sun had shortened its arc across the sky; it hugged the horizon and provided little warmth in the receding light. Only a few leaves clung to the trees in the blustery western winds.

Thorlief chartered a bus in early October for a weekend in Telemark, a mountainous area southwest of the school. We left in the early morning and entered a labyrinth of narrow, steep-sided valleys. It was a forlorn landscape, beautiful but frightening in its solitude. The road followed a stream, nourished by smaller creeks, up to a pass. There the pavement ended and Telemark began. Below lay the town of Rjukan and our hostel for the night. But with the afternoon just beginning, we turned onto a side road into the mountains, winding upward, switchback by switchback, until we crested on the *vidda,* the high country of Norway.

I had seen pictures of the *vidda*, but nothing prepared me for its vastness. Mountain ridges rippled in every direction for hundreds of kilometers, like waves on a petrified sea. I was on the roof of the world, squinting into a harsh light with every detail sharply etched. It was hard to breathe, not because of the altitude, only two thousand meters, but because of its emptiness.

"Shall we walk together?" Tomas asked, slipping a windbreaker over his head as the bus left for the valley. Many students had already started to hike.

"Sure. Where?" The wind sliced through my flapping jacket.

"Rujkan." He pointed to a tiny patchwork of houses a thousand meters below. "Walking's our sport. We hike the mountains in the summer and ski them in the winter. Elvira! Want to join us?" She had just finished braiding her hair and looked ten.

"Where's the trail?" I asked.

"No trail up here," Tomas said, with a wave of his arm. "We just walk. You have food, *ikke sant*?"

"*Ja,* sure." I checked the sandwich in my parka.

He launched himself with long quick strides. Elvira followed, moving easily over the spongy tundra in her tightly fitted stretch pants. For the first time I saw what she looked like under her floppy skirts and was glad of the long hike ahead.

We descended a ridge overlooking the valley. Life was sparse in the high country. Moss and lichen splashed across the rocks like spilled paint. Small bushes hugged the ground sheltered from the prevailing winds. A mist was gathering below on Rujkan Lake, shrouding its shoreline. Tomas paused by a jagged outcropping and picked a small, yellow berry.

"*Molte*," he said. "You like?" Tart like a raspberry, it had a sweet caramel kick.

"Cloudberries, they're called. They only grow in the mountains." He pulled out a pair of binoculars and scanned the horizon, pausing to look at a ridge. "*Reindyr*," he said, handing me the glasses. What looked like a mottled ridge to the naked eye was covered by hundreds of reindeer, grazing a path into the valley. They shifted among the hillocks, pausing to sniff the wind.

"They feed here in the summer and migrate into the valleys for winter. If we're lucky, we'll find some antlers."

After three hours of cross-country walking we began our final descent. The landscape of lichen and mosses changed into grasses and small wind-whipped trees. Flowers no longer clung in bunches close to the ground, but blossomed on tall, waving stems in lush meadows.

Thomas had lingered behind to keep me company as both of their walking paces were faster them my own. He told me he came from a fishing family and was the youngest of six children. His uncle, a fiddler, had hooked him on the cello. He'd come to *Nansen Skolen* to study classical music.

"There wasn't much chance to play Bach in the Lofotens," he said.

"I played the clarinet for years but never really liked it. I switched to the guitar in college."

"Maybe we can play music together. The school has a bunch of recorders that are easy to learn."

The town began to emerge as we descended, a half dozen streets with a *stave* church in the center. As the roofs multiplied so did our hunger. Tomas clambered to the top of a steep boulder and suggested lunch. I followed quickly, but Elvira was unable to reach the handholds. I clambered down, extended my arm, and hauled her up the face of the rock until she stumbled into my arms. Our eyes locked in surprise, then we quickly parted, arriving on top to consume a feast of bread and cheese and vistas.

Waterfalls cascaded down into the valley from lofty ridges, fed by glaciers. White capped mountains lit up in the afternoon sun. We peeled off our parkas and sweaters and drifted through the day in the palm of the rock, lulled by the bells of sheep and cows nibbling the grasses in the high pastures.

As the sun sank toward the horizon, we reluctantly descended, passing through hemlock and red cedar forests. By the time we reached Rjukan, it was almost dinnertime and the shadows were deepening. Tomas continued to the hostel, but Elvira and I paused at the *stave* church, *stavkirke,* as she called it. Built in the 1100's, it had a wood shingled roof, dragons flying from its buttresses, and tiny holes for windows. Carvings and runic inscriptions covered the walls. The roof, supported by twelve, tree-like pillars, disappeared into darkness. We sat on the weathered pews, still in use, and settled into the silence.

After exploring the apse and transept, we wandered out into a burial ground in the back. Ordered by century, most of the gravestones were flat markers aged into illegibility by wind and water. But as we walked into the 1900's, the inscriptions became readable.

"Se du det," Elvira pointed. "He was young."

Erik Carlson, 1930-54, Beloved Brother Of Johann, Lost At Sea.

The granite was shiny, the grave tended with pots of red and white geraniums, so different from our family plots home where Jacob and Dad's only brother, Saul, lay buried. I still remembered the thuds of earth and rocks cascading onto Saul's polished wooden coffin. The terror I felt in my father's arms as he held me at the grave was the same terror I saw in his eyes when he told me about Mother's breakdown.

"My uncle died in his forty's," I said. "He loved to *kibbitz* with my Dad."

"*Kibbitz?*" she asked.

"Yiddish for teasing."

"*Kibbitz,*" she repeated with a singsong inflection. I'd never heard it said more beautifully. "My father likes to *kibbitz*. You *tease* at home?"

I shrugged. "Not lately."

"How come?"

"We've had some troubles."

"*Ja,* I understand. My father was not very happy with me coming to Nansen School." She said that she'd lived on an island her whole life, as her father and grandfather had done. One day, as she was teaching in the same one-room school she'd attended as a child, she realized that all she knew of the world was Fineran. She decided to leave and have a year for herself. But her father thought that at 26 she should get married and have children. She asked me how I knew Yiddish and I told her my father had come from Russia.

"You speak Russian?"

"*Spritzieg fovstorg ry bracht guzucht.*"

"Nice. What's it mean?"

"Nothing. My Dad taught me it when I was a kid. But when I turned fifteen I learned it was gibberish. He was *kibbitzing*. Want to hear more?"

"*Nei*, Josh. Your Russian sounds like your Norwegian," she laughed.

The sun had slipped behind the mountains and a cold wind blew through the graveyard. She shuddered, folding her arms close to her body. I gave her my sweater and she wore it for the rest of the day.

It was hard to return to the classroom after Rjukan. The freedom of walking six hours across the tundra was unlike anything I'd ever done. But when I tired of the lectures or got lost in the lesson, I studied Elvira.

She'd shift in her chair, cross and re-cross her legs, sit on her foot, fiddle with her hair clasp, flick her hair over her shoulders. When fatigue overtook her, she'd stretch her arms above her head, and her breasts would swell her sweater. Sometimes I'd make a smile bloom on her studious face by turning my textbook upside down and and look cross-eyed. She'd try to hide behind her notebook, but the subversive crinkles around her eyes gave her away.

The Wednesday after we'd gotten back, Thorlief was exploring the evolution of modern art from the turn of the 20th century. Elvira and I emerged from class eager to share notes.

"Edvard Munch's strange, *ikke sant*?" Elvira said, flipping through a book of his early paintings on the living room couch where we usually sat. She paused on *The Shriek*. "The waving colors, people watching and avoiding a poor woman. She looks sick."

"I don't think the picture's about the people," I said. "Emotions, maybe. Did Munch have a breakdown?"

"*Ja*. Thorlief said 1908."

"That makes sense. But all those airy landscapes at the end of his life - did he recover?"

"He spent two months in a clinic in 1910." She laughed. "You don't need my notes. You studied the paintings."

"I have to do something in class besides distracting you."

She turned to *Madonna,* a naked woman luxuriating in bed, her head framed by swirling dark hair etched with a red halo. Her eyes were beckoning, the tips of her breasts full and pink.

"Beautiful, isn't she?" Elvira said.

I felt the warmth of Elvira's body beside me, her breath on my n my face. I was afraid people were watching us and wanted to turn the page. "Ja," I mumbled, forgetting her question.

"His women are so solitary. He must have been lonely."

"*Ja,* for sure." I didn't know what I meant or where the conversation was going. The school seemed too quiet for three in the afternoon.

I held my breath when she turned the page. A sunny landscape from the Azores appeared. "1913. You're right, Josh. All those beautiful colors. So *vakert,*" she sighed, rolling a lovely sibilance under 'vakert'.

"*Ja,* nice colors," I said, gazing at the translucent water and transparent colors in the sky.

A raw wind was blowing from the mountains when I left for home, roiling the lake into whitecaps. I stopped for my daily Tribune and on my doorstep found a package of brownies from Ida with a note inside.

Schmen, Happy New Year! You forgot? Rosh O Shonar! They have Jews there for Yom Kippur? Mein Godt, its far! Keep warm. I don't see Pauly. He come no more. Jacob I see tuesdays for kugel. You come home Chanukah? I make hommentashen. Hope you happy. Mine

mother say grandma only as happy as happiest kinder.
Be happy with brownies - no nuts just for you. Ida.

Chapter 12

Although I didn't like the cant of the Day of Atonement, *Yom Kippur*, and hadn't fasted since high school, my family had always observed the High Holy days. I took an early train to Oslo to find the Oslo Synagogue near the University and arrived with an empty stomach and a headache. Built in the 1920's, it was a charming two story stuccoed building with a round tower topped with a Star of David. It more resembled a country chapel than a big city Temple.

People were still settling in when services began; a program that would last the entire day because the congregation was Orthodox. I looked for a place among the men on the first floor while the women were seating themselves in the balcony. Most congregants were old and the Temple was barely half full. Virtually no young families were present. In Boston, *Yom Kippur* was packed with young and old alike. I knew the Jews were deported from Norway during the war, but now understood the full extent of the loss.

As the choir began the slow lament of Kol Nidre, I took a seat on a dark wooden bench. I draped a prayer shawl around my shoulders, a white silk scarf with blue tassels that reminded me of my Grandfather's. Ida used to sit beside me to keep me quiet during the holidays in Boston. I'd rustle the prayer book during meditations and kick the pew bench when I got bored. Although I'd follow her bony finger across the prayers and listen while she chanted in Hebrew, I understood nothing. I stood when she stood, and sat when she sat. When I'd reached my limit, she'd slip me a Schrafts hard candy and whisper the evening dessert in my ear. Paul used to sit between Mother and Dad like a book between bookends.

My stomach began making indiscrete noises after three hours and I left for a stroll. The Temple was in the Jewish section of Oslo with cobblestone streets, crowded apartment buildings, and a few commercial stores - a bakery, deli, and tailor. I knew from Ida's stories that survival in Russia had depended on sticking together. If things had been different, she'd said, I might have grown up in a *shtetl* and attended services with family and friends, instead of living in the woods twenty miles from her dinner table.

I found a bench in a park across from Bruge's Deli. It would open at sundown at the end of the fast. I stared at the salamis that hung in the window, freshly cooked turkeys wrapped in cloth, and jars of pickles hovering in brine. How could I cleanse my soul if I couldn't stop thinking about corned beef and cabbage? I wondered who would be fasting in Quinnipiac and if they were at the Temple. Thanks to the northern latitudes the Oslo services ended at three. I entered Bruge's with the foulest breath I'd had since I'd left the plane.

It was an old fashioned deli with a scattering of tables surrounding a U-shaped counter which was stacked with pastrami, corn beef, herring, fresh breads, and sticky buns. Rotating fans from a tin ceiling dispersed an array of smells. A few families huddled at the tables awaiting their orders. I wanted to join them, but the tables were full. I wedged myself onto a stool at the counter between two stodgy men with dark suits and beards.

The waiter gave me a glass of seltzer and a menu. But I didn't need a menu. I ordered from memory – a triple-decker sandwich that Paul and I used to share at Jack & Marion's. Thick corn beef, pastrami with pepper, and warm turkey right off the bone. Every year we'd shared the same sandwich except when he'd returned from the Peace Corps. Gaunt and restless, he'd gone for a walk midway through the meal, leaving Dad, Mother, and me to finish alone.

I'd lost my appetite: Bruge's sandwich looked too marbled with fat.

"*Vil du ikke spise* sanvich?" the waiter asked, mangling three languages at once.

"*Nei*, not hungry," I said, welcoming his interest.

"*Har du ingen mispoucha*?" he asked.

"*Nei, ikke* family here. *Jeg er en student.*" I took a swig of seltzer and belched.

"*Skal du ta hjem*?"

"*Ja, takk.*" I'll take it home, faithful to the Norwegian custom of not wasting food.

He smiled as he wrapped up the sandwich and asked me if I wanted a *salte*. I said yes, though I didn't know whether *salte* was Norwegian or Yiddish for pickle.

The cold night air calmed my queasiness. With a few hours to spare before the train, I took a trolley to Brad's, half way across the city but close to the railway station.

"I thought you were Greta," Brad said, as he opened the door, dressed in boxers and a T-shirt molded to his chest. "Want some lunch?"

"At six?"

"I'm on a staggered schedule." He set out bologna, peanut butter, and white bread. "What's in the bag?"

I showed him the leftover triple-decker and told him about my visit to Temple. He pushed the bologna aside and examined the layers. "This is Norwegian?"

"I got it in a deli."

"Not like the delis at home."

"Those aren't the real delis. *Goyem* think that corned beef on white bread is a deli sandwich."

"*Goyem*?"

"People who buy retail."

Brad worked his way into the turkey. "How do you finish one of these jobbies?"

"You don't. I usually share it with my brother."

"The one at Harvard? He must be pretty smart."

"Harvard was my parent's idea. He dropped out after his first year, then went back after a short stint in the Peace Corps."

"I can relate to that. My Dad expects me to serve my country, like him." He gave a mock salute.

"Where's he based?"

"He's retired but runs the family like a platoon. He let me go to college as long as I did ROTC."

Brad jumped at a knock on the door. Gretta entered. Her pants were snug and her reddish brown hair reached her waist.

"Remember Josh, my buddy in Lillehammer?"

"A beautiful valley," she said, taking my hand with a soft, firm grasp. "Great skiing. You must be studying at Nansen Skolen. Some of my friends went there." She sat down close to Brad, stuck her finger in the peanut butter, and licked it off. "What are you taking?"

"Philosophy, literature, and art. We're studying Munch."

"A little gloomy, *ikke sant*?" She smiled as she played with Brad's little finger.

"I like his woodcuts, the way they symbolize emotions."

Brad coughed.

"Anyway, I should be going."

"So soon?" asked Greta, rising.

"I have to catch a train. Returning for more angst."

I counted each step as I descended, 8 per landing, 34 including 2 on the stoop. The misty air dampened my hair as I walked under the flickering street lamps. Greta looked foxy in her jeans and turtleneck. I kicked a pebble along the sidewalk until I angled it into a sewer for a goal. The night was quiet; I wondered if everyone had slipped out of town.

I didn't want to return to my room when I got off the train in Lillehammer. I could still feel the moistness of Greta's fingers in my hand. I walked up to Elvira's but her windows were dark so I kept going uphill. The light was on in Emma's living room and, recalling our last late night chat, knocked on her door.

"Josh," she yawned, opening the door in her nightgown. "I wondered who'd be knocking so late."

"Sorry, Emma. The light was on."

"Don't be silly. I leave it on when Edvard's away. I was only reading in bed." She invited me in and put up the water to boil.

"He's in Oslo again?" I asked.

"Ja. Where did you come from?"

"Oslo, too. I went to Yom Kippur."

"That nasty holiday where you atone for bad thoughts about people who deserve them? I gave up Judaism a long time ago. It brought too many troubles. Moving from place to place, looking for somewhere to live."

She placed jam and rye crisp on the table. "You know if you boil raspberries right after they're picked the jam is sweeter?"

"What time is it, Emma?"

"Don't know. Close to ten."

"My mother's probably making dinner."

"In the afternoon?"

"She starts early and waits to see if Dad will come home for dinner."

"Sometimes eating alone is a better idea."

I pictured Mother's birch veneer door with its aluminum knob, firmly closed.

"You look tired, Josh. Want to sleep on the couch tonight?"

"No, I'd just as soon go to my flat."

We sat for a while sipping tea, Emma still with sleep in her eyes. On the way back to my flat I dialed home from a pay phone. I let it ring for a long time before I gave up.

CHAPTER 13

Elvira and I sat on the couch in the living room as she took notes from Gombrich's Story of Art, writing every word in rounded, articulated letters. Her hair had strayed from its pewter clasp and dangled around her neck. *Winterfest* was approaching, the annual school skating party before the winter solstice. She asked if I could skate.

"*Ja*, but in a straight line."

"It doesn't matter. It's just for fun. What are you going to wear?"

"It's a costume party?"

"*Ja*, Josh, for sure. I'm coming as Princess Irena, Queen of Stavanger. And you?"

"How about a troll?"

"*Nei*, Josh," she giggled. "Why not a knight? We'll look for a costume in the thrift store." She dug her pink fingernails into an orange and skinned it off in one piece.

"Nice work," I said.

"It's easy, even for an American." She tossed me one.

I hated oranges. They were messy and sticky. I jabbed my finger into the pulp but the skin came off in fragments.

"You lose," she smirked, popping a section into her mouth.

I'd never been to a thrift store. Mother had bought my clothes at upscale places in Brookline and Boston. Cashmere sweaters, alligator shirts, dress pants - I always looked like I was going out to dinner.

Engle Magasin was in the basement of a Lutheran church. Clothes were strewn around tables and shelves - trousers, shirts, sweaters, and shoes. Elvira chose a white flowing gown, wedding veil, and pink tights from the piles. I thought she was going to be a very cold princess and asked her what a Viking would wear. She told me a helmet, armor, a tartan, and a sword. We sorted through the tools and hardware and settled on a goalie mask, checkered skirt, black tights, and a pitchfork. Elvira thought I looked great. I had my doubts.

Every year Lillehammer flooded their soccer field to create an oval of milky, smooth ice. Kids skated around the track, hoping to become the next Per Ivar Moe, Norway's latest long distance skating champion. I was not a winter sports fan. I'd failed with skiing lessons in the White Mountains and seldom skated on Lake Quinnipiac.

Students arrived at ten as the sun rimmed over the mountains - leprechauns, trolls, giants, dwarfs, monsters, and witches, the Norwegian myths sprung to life. Tomas dressed as a gremlin from Lofoten, Thorlief as a King from Hamar. The school provided hot chocolate and music to skate by. I laced on a pair of racing skates borrowed from Thorlief. The blades were four inches longer than hockey skates so you could glide further, but during the routines we practiced for the dance contest, I often tripped and fell. Elvira skated smoothly, her white veil trailing behind her. Everyone in school had been on skates and skis since they could walk.

We began our program with The Blue Danube, one of Elvira's favorite waltzes. With arms around each other's waists, we circled the oval stride by stride. I was used to hockey's choppy strokes, but after a few minutes, I found my glide. It was hard to get my breath, we skated so quickly. I distracted myself by looking at the white capped mountains and Elvira's cheeks grew redder by the minute. I would have skated till midnight, but the music soon crescendoed into a finale. She spun into my arms and I lowered her to the ice with a flourish I remembered from the Olympics. My heart was pounding so hard, I nearly dropped her.

"*Fint!*" she said, as we skated off to a round of applause. "You skated great."

She let go of my hand when we joined our schoolmates, but stayed by my side till the party ended. I left for my flat oblivious to the streets and stores, trying to hold onto the warmth of her breath.

Later that evening we met at school to review her notes about Eric Fromm's, *The Art Of Loving*, which I'd read in Norwegian. A fire had warmed the living room overlooking expanses of Mjosa Lake.

"I got lost in the stages of love," I said.

"*Ja*, I remember. Love of oneself, love of man, love of God. Loving the self comes first."

"That's a hard place to start."

"*Nei!* Why?"

"Do you like yourself?" I asked.

"*Ja*, for sure."

"But you said you hated your life on Fineran."

"Ambivalent, maybe. Living on an island *forlovet*."

"*Forlovet*?" I asked.

"*Jeg ma gifte seg med Soren i sommeren.*"

The new words were confusing.

"I'm engaged to marry Soren this summer," she said.

I stopped taking notes. My arm felt heavy, my fingers unable to write. I examined the words. *Forlovet,* a derivative of *love*, to promise. And *gifte seg meg*, give yourself to. Very logical antecedents with Germanic roots. I reviewed the spelling, imagined the future tenses.

"My father wants me to marry Soren. I've known him since *gymnast*. But how can I marry when I don't know myself? Soren's a good man. But he's only lived on Fineran and wants me to stay there. I just don't know if his life is for me."

She unpinned her hair which fell on her shoulders. "We got off the point," she said.

The front door burst open, bringing a surge of cold air.

"Hello there!" Tomas said, stomping the dirt off his feet. "I thought everybody had left. What are you up to?"

"Catching up on Erich Fromm," I said.

I walked Elvira to her flat four blocks from the school. Her room was on the top of a three-story house with white lace curtains in her windows. I imagined the rest: a four-poster bed with a patchwork quilt, fluffy pillows, and a folded white nightie on the covers.

"Thanks for a wonderful day. The skating was fun," she said. She was looking my way, but it was hard to see her eyes in the dark.

"*Ja*, fun," I said.

She mounted the stairs and turned on the light in her room. Shadows played on the ceiling as she pulled off her clothes, sliding the blouse over her head and slipping out of her pants and under the covers of her bed. My face had turned numb in the cold by the time she switched off her light. I

turned to go home, kicking a stone down the street
as far as it would go.

CHAPTER 14

Hey Josh, here I am. At least I think I'm here. Not sure where I am. Fucking Harvard. Christ. I hated it before and hate it now. But I have no choice. Manny fired me. What a jerk. And then Mother and Dad told me it's here or nowhere. It's always nowhere for me. Was nowhere in Guatemala, a real nowhere place with nowhere jobs. Like building a fucking school. How the hell do you build a school in the middle of nowhere that nobody wants? Sometimes I got into San Pedro to play with the girls. Pretty faces with big boobs and skinny legs, but I got to like them. I screwed one a month. Elena was the best. Claimed I was her favorite. Came from a poor village and earned her living fucking PC volunteers. I'd dream about her in nowhere land. Great until she copped my wallet when I was sleeping. No more San Pedro after that, fucking cunts. No time for R&R either. Had to finish the school before the rains. Laying a foundation with cinder blocks and building walls. Spent months on the fucker. Christ knows how long. And then it rained. You know what it's like when it rains in Guatemala. Humid so you can't breathe and when it rains, water everywhere, every day, spilling off roofs, mud for roads, rivers rising so you're trapped miles from nowhere. And then one day the walls fell down. The rain washed the fucker away. That's what nowhere's like, a hot stinking shithole where no one speaks your language and days and nights are a sleepless hell. I got sick of telling the fucks at McLean this shit. Christ I got to get out of this fucking room. Miss you buddy. Tammy says hello. She's all I got besides you. Paul

I folded the letter and stowed it with the others under Paul's sweatshirt. A few idle snowflakes drifted by my window. I scanned the gray sky for more. It was ten a.m. but there were only a few hours of daylight left. I still wasn't sure what to do in the dark on weekends. I went for a walk to enjoy the daylight and when I returned I found Brad on my doorstep and Greta's beat up VW bug parked on the street. I threw some things in the back and left for Oslo with his promise to get me back on Sunday.

"Small town for a long winter," Brad said, as we followed the road around the shore. "The lake's pretty. You skate on the damn thing?"

"Great skating. You have the day off?"

"I have the year off. I got expelled. Missed too many stupid classes. I really wasn't into wood carving and folk dancing. Time for a job, I guess."

The sky darkened as patches of fog drifted over the landscape and the winding gravel road. Brad slowed to a crawl.

"How's life by you?" he asked.

"I haven't understood a hell of a lot. Kind of slow-go with the lectures and readings."

"Found anyone interesting?"

"Yeah, her name is Elvira. She's engaged."

"Great," he chortled. "A school full of cuties and you pick one that's hitched. Damn, I can't see a thing." He flicked on his high beams and stuck his head out the window. "That's better. How am I doing over there?"

I rolled down my window. "Sort of okay," I said, noticing the steep drop off to the lake. The mist dampened my face and made me blurry eyed.

"Christ, I should have brought a sleeping bag," Brad said.

It was a long drive past the lake and through the mountains. Even when the fog lifted, the night seemed impossibly dim, forcing us to continue slowly with our heads hanging out the windows. We didn't pull up at Greta's restaurant until after eleven.

"Why so late," she scolded. "I've been waiting for hours."

"We got hung up in the dark," Brad said.

She walked around to the front of the car and stopped. "It might have helped if you'd cleaned off your headlights." She wiped a thick layer of dirt off one of the headlamps.

We go out and finished the job. "Thanks for letting use the car," Brad said.

She drove off in a huff, relegating Brad and me to a trolley ride back to his room. It hadn't changed much in the last month. A new coat tree, a reindeer calendar in the kitchen, a bigger pile of dirty clothes for Greta to wash. The cupboard was still empty except for white bread and Skippy peanut butter.

"I see you've acculturated," I said.

Brad put up water to boil. "I kind of like the idea of not studying now and making some money."

"Dropping out of college? How're you going to find a job if you don't speak Norwegian?"

"I haven't got that far in the plan."

I smeared peanut butter on my bread, scraping the extra on the plate. Brad stuck his knife in the jar and licked off the blade.

"What's the deal with Elvira?"

I explained that she'd been seeing a guy for a while but wasn't sure she wanted to get married.

"Like one of my girlfriends in high school. She wore her boyfriend's ring around her neck, but always checked me out when we passed in the hall. She broke up with him after our first date. Sweet Melinda, with the golden hair."

"You stay together?"

"A semester or two. What's Elvira like?"

"Very studious until she laughs and then she's really fun to be with. I can't figure out if she's 16 or 30 especially when she wears pigtails. But when we're together we really talk. She grew up on a farm on an island near Stavanger in a kind of time warp."

"The whole country's in a time warp." Brad scraped his chair back and dumped his dishes in the sink. "I'll clear a place for you on the couch."

"God, it's cold in here. Does your rent include heat?"

"Heat, Norwegian style. It goes off at nine." He shoved his dirty clothes off the couch. "Can't beat the amenities," he said, tossing me a sleeping bag. "Good to ten below. We'll shower at Greta's. Mine's broke."

I slipped into my bag as he turned out the light. I strained to see something in the dark. "It's like camping out," I said. A car door slammed in the street. I could barely see Brad's bed against the window.

"What are you going to do about your parents and school?"

"I haven't figured that out. My Dad's not exactly flexible. I don't tell my parents everything."

"Like?"

"Drinking, pregnancies. Sound familiar?"

"No."

"How come your brother left the Peace Corps? Knock somebody up?"

"No, he just didn't like it there."

Not soon after, I heard Brad turned over and fall asleep. It got quiet except for the refrigerator that rattled on and off. I blew into the sleeping bag until it got toasty. Then Brad's breathing deepened into a gentle guttural snore that lulled me to sleep.

The knocking radiators woke me early in the morning. Frost had coated the windows. I dressed inside my sleeping bag and slipped out to buy food. Ida used to say that November was a hard month, *nista her nista har* - cold without the beauty of snow. I bought a few breakfast essentials in a small *dagligvareforetning*: instant coffee, bread, cheese, and *syltetoy* (jam), welcome additions to our peanut butter. When I returned, Brad was just waking up.

"Looks like we're re-provisioned," he said, rubbing the sleep from his eyes. I emptied the bag on the counter. "You ought to come more often."

After breakfast, we left for town where we looked over the Christmas trinkets on Karl Johannesgate before taking a *trikken* up to Frognerseteren, the mountaintop overlooking Oslo. Within minutes we'd found a trail and disappeared into the forests that encompassed half of Oslo.

"Done much camping?" Brad asked.

"My Dad isn't the camping type. His idea of a weekend away is a night in a New York hotel." I stopped to tie my shoe and zip up my windbreaker.

"Mine took me camping a lot. We went on a hike once into the Sierra Arida mountains. About half way up we surprised a bear on the trail with her cub. The sucker reared and stared, ready to charge. I was about to scoot, but Dad grabbed my arm and waited until the cub wandered away and the mother followed."

"I'd have pissed in my pants."

"I was tight for sure, but it didn't bother Dad any. Kind of what you had to do."

The trail looped around the mountain through

hemlock forests until we reached a *kafe* with views of the Oslofjord, a patch of blue with a scattering of small wooded islands close to city. We bought salami and cheese sandwiches and settled down at a picnic table. Brad asked me about ideas for jobs in which he didn't have to talk. I suggested washing dishes in restaurants and wondered if he could ask his mother for money.

"She doesn't know I left the folk high school yet, much less dropped out of college. I haven't even told her about Greta."

I opened a Toblerone bar and snapped off a chunk for him.

"I could always fix things in high school. Now, things are hard to figure out. But Greta has a plan. She wants this marriage to work out."

"What marriage?"

He told me Greta was married before, hitched to a sailor always at sea. But now at 29 she wanted to settle down. She didn't look that old to me, but she definitely had more of a plan than Brad.

"But you just met her."

"I'm just saying we're talking about it."

"Why don't you start with finding a job?"

We took the *trikken* to Greta's apartment, a wedding gift from her parents, on the seventh floor of a new building on the outskirts of Oslo. Brad told her that he wanted to check out a band at the University Lounge and Greta went to change. The apartment was sparsely furnished: sofa, teak end tables, reading chair, and small wool scatter rugs - clean and comfortable. Large windows overlooked the woods that had begun to darken.

Brad opened the fridge. "Want a Ringnes?" I shrugged. "You're welcome to stay here tonight. Easier than going back to my flat."

"This place have heat?"

"Yup, it's got everything."

Greta emerged from the bedroom wearing black jeans and a red turtleneck. Her eyes sparkled with intention. She grabbed Brad's hand and led him out the door.

The dance at the University was packed. We wedged ourselves into chairs and ordered beers, listening to a band play covers of the Rolling Stones. The music was loud for conversation, so Brad and Greta went to dance. She draped her arms around his neck and held him tight.

I joined the ring of onlookers, nursing my beer until a slow song came along and I asked someone to dance. Kari was her name and she was pretty. Surprised that I spoke Norwegian, she asked me questions. She'd had a lot to drink. With every exchange, she leaned closer, hanging on my shoulder as if she might fall. I liked her body next to mine, her thigh in my crotch, her hand in mine. But the beer on her breath, the smell of her armpits, made me pull back. She held onto my hand when the song ended. Where was I living, she asked. Lillehammer. Oh, but in Oslo tonight? Yes, with friends. Her hand curled around my fingers. She looked into my eyes. My heart was beating louder than the drums of the Stones. I looked away. She dropped my hand and went to the Ladies Room. I waited for an hour but she didn't come back.

We walked back to Greta's, too tired to talk. Brad gave me a sleeping bag and slipped into the bedroom. I lay quietly on the couch, watching the light under their door. The refrigerator was silent, but the wall clock had a regular pulse. Their voices became muffled when the lights went out. Then came the giggles, guffaws, chatter, bedspring squeaks, random at first and then gathering speed. At first, I laughed, then flushed in the face and pulled a pillow over my head as the bedsprings became frantic. But I couldn't block out the the oo's and ah's, the moans, the stifled yell at the end. Twenty one and still a virgin. What kind of loser was I in the Land of Free Love?

I boarded a train at eleven as the sun broke the horizon. Resting my head against the seat, I waited for Mjosa's welcome. The waters of Quinnipiac had always frozen by November, a sheet of clear ice on which you could skate for miles. You could look into the ice and see its tiny fractures and bubbles embalmed till spring. Mjosa had just received a fresh cover of snow that reflected a blinding light. When I arrived at the Lillehammer station, I stopped at a pay phone.

"Joshua?" Mother said. "What a surprise. Where are you?"

"A phone in Lillehammer."

"Goodness, you'll catch cold."

"It's not that bad. Dad around?"

"Your father's with family today. I didn't feel like chattering about bargains and sales."

"How's Paul?"

"I'm sure he's doing fine."

"He hasn't been over?"

"No one's heard from him. I'm planning to make him a cake for his birthday. Silly, I suppose."

"He likes birthday cake."

"Maybe he'll call on his birthday," she said. "Why don't you come home for the Holidays? We can celebrate both your birthdays."

"I can't."

"I hate winter. The cold. The snow piling around the windows.

Goodness, this must be costing a fortune. Why don't you write a nice letter with all the news."

"Sure," I said, wondering what news she was thinking of.

"I'll tell father you called and look forward to getting your letter. No need to spend money like this."

She hung up and left me with static. I noticed the clock on the church was thirty minutes behind.

CHAPTER 15

"Thanksgiving?" Thorlief looked confused. I'd stopped by his office in late November. The sun was nearing its shortest circuit, rising at 12 and setting at 2. I walked to school under the waning stars and returned home with a rising moon.

"The day the Pilgrims landed," I said.

"Ah, the Pilgrims. If I recall, they didn't land in Norway."

"*Nei*, but it's a wonderful holiday."

"*Ja*. I remember it at my cousin's in Minneapolis. How should we celebrate?"

"With a turkey."

"I've never seen a turkey in Norway. And cranberries," he shrugged. "Let's discuss it in class. Perhaps we'll make it a cross-cultural project."

A few students had heard about Thanksgiving from relatives in the States, but no one knew much about its history. We formed a *Kalkun Komite* (Turkey Committee) to plan the menu, music, and decorations, and then set off to locate the food. A few times my parents had celebrated Thanksgiving with Abe's *mispoucha* who'd emigrated in 1913 - the uncles who'd created the fortunes in hardware, furniture, and construction. But as they got older they'd retired to Florida and we'd left their stories behind.

After a week the *Kalkun Komite* had found three turkeys, a kilo of cranberries, and a couple of pumpkins at a PX on a NATO base near Oslo and had them shipped to Lillehammer by train. Tomas had modified *We Gather Together To Sing The Lord's Blessing* into a trio. I adapted my clarinet fingerings to the soprano recorder and played the melody while Elvira and Tomas added harmonies on an alto recorder and cello. We met early Thanksgiving morning to practice, fumbling through the notes until our disparate parts blended into a richly textured melody that filled the room and created an eerie silence in the house as others listened.

As the day progressed, Anna made paper Pilgrim hats and cut out turkey silhouettes to hang on the walls, Astrid arranged evergreen and holly bouquets for the table, and Elvira prepared the turkeys, massaging butter and paprika into their rubbery bodies and stuffing their insides with bread crumbs. I was assigned to peel 160 potatoes at the dining room table. Not big Idaho's like I had at home, but the smaller, varieties with pock marked faces. I washed and skinned them till they were white. After Elvira had put the turkeys in the oven, she asked if I wanted help.

"*Nei*. I'll be done in a few weeks," I said.

"They don't have to be perfect," she said, wheeling her peeler quickly. "Leave the eyes alone; they won't hurt you." She laughed and tossed a skinned potato into the bowl. It glanced off the rim and rolled under the table. We got on our knees to retrieve it.

"Seven ball in the far pocket," I said, rolling the potato back to her.

"*Nei*, Josh. It'll get dirty," she giggled.

"So we'll have only 159 – that's still 3.9 potatoes per Viking." I pressed the potato into her palm. "With this potato, I thee wed." I leaned over and kissed her. She opened her mouth and darted her tongue into mine. I'd never felt a foreign object there, so soft and eager, but didn't know what to do with it. Her eyes were closed, her hand caressing my cheek.

"Elvira? Josh?" Thorlief called from the hallway. A pair of trousers and shoes approached through a thicket of chair legs. Elvira squeezed my hand till it hurt. Thorlief paused, called again, and left.

We waited till his steps diminished up the stairs into his office. "I guess I should roll out the bread," she said, avoiding my eyes. As we crawled out from the table with dust balls clinging to our pants, her shirt pulled out of her pants, revealing a patch of skin and pink underwear. She quickly rose, put herself back together and left for the kitchen.

I finished the potatoes and dumped them into a humongous pot of boiling water. The kitchen had heated into a sauna filled with the smells of baking turkey, rising bread, boiling cranberries, and cooling pumpkin pies. It wasn't until late afternoon that we all sat down to dinner.

The windows had fogged from the steaming food and candlelight flickered on the walls. I gave a short talk about the Pilgrims, an easy give and take where the Norwegian words flowed without thinking for the first time. I helped myself to a drumstick and dark meat, the portions Paul and I usually shared. Later, we gathered around the fire where we played *We Gather Together To Sing the Lord's Blessing*. As the night deepened we started singing Norwegian folk songs which I accompanied on a borrowed guitar. Elvira sat by my side, trading melodies and harmonies with Tomas. As midnight neared, the coals subsided and the students drifted back to their flats. Elvira and I left together, arm in arm.

"You play well," she said. "How did you learn so much?"

"My Mom. We sang and played a lot, even if we didn't want to."

"She grabbed my hand which I gently rubbed until it warmed.

"It's a lovely night, Josh," she said, pointing to the sky where red and blue colors shimmered above the mountains. "The aurora starts in November and lasts the winter. My father used to tell me that the Vikings followed it across the ocean. Some nights the sky is green, sometimes blue and red. You never know what color will appear."

We reached her home and walked up to her room. For months I had imagined what lay inside. As she opened the door, I studied

every detail: a canopy bed with a blue comforter, yellow pillows piled against an oak head board; a stack of books on a night table next to a small lamp; a blue blouse neatly folded across the back of a stuffed arm chair. I leaned over to pull her close. Her shoulders stiffened.

"Josh, I can't. I have to go home and talk with Soren."

"I'm sorry," I said. "I didn't ask, I mean, if you wanted to."

"I've never known anyone like you. But I've been with Soren for seven years. Can you understand?"

She squeezed my hand as a clock struck twelve. With each stroke, the bed began to shrink until it looked too small for her and me.

"I'll figure things out at Christmas. *Jeg love.*"

Love, to promise, I translated. Another German derivative with Norwegian parallels.

She turned and closed the door. I took sixteen steps to the landing and three to the street. I didn't look back at the window: I could imagine her perfectly, sitting on the edge of her bed, undressing.

Snow started to fall, the first of the season,

large wet flakes that landed on my face and blurred my vision, painting the dark street white. By the time I'd turned the corner, the snow had erased my footsteps.

CHAPTER 16

Snow fell everywhere, sometimes in flurries, sometimes all day. It dusted every surface, piled up in corners and cracks, and eddied in the air until we inhaled it. As the winter vacation neared in late December, the drifts had deepened forcing us to ski to school. We dressed in layers to lessen the bite of the wind - long underwear, flannel shirts, sweaters, scarves, parkas - and unwrapped at school. We hung our layers by the blazing fireplace and exchanged our ski boots for woolen slipper socks in which to shuffle from class to class.

The morning of our winter break, I offered to help Elvira carry her bags to the afternoon train. She was leaving to see her family in Fineran. She'd packed everything for the month-long break; even the mattress was bare. I'd worried about her talk with Soren and slept little the night before.

"You bringing all the bricks?" I said, hoisting her suitcase off the bed.

"*Nei*, Josh. They're presents for my cousins."

"And Soren?"

"He's still with his family. He'll join me Christmas eve."

We gave her bags to a porter and sat down in the

busy station. Elvira handed me a small present, tied with a blue ribbon.

"Should I open it?"

"Not now. I want it to be a surprise." The gift, a few inches square, was padded and wrapped in red tissue paper.tied with a bow.

"Is it a sweet?" I asked.

"It's not for eating," she laughed.

"A troll?"

"It's a memento." She pulled me close.

"Maybe I won't open it then. I'll just keep it on my night table."

"Then you'll never be disappointed."

A horn shrieked in the valley. Elvira zipped up her parka and pulled her hood over her head - only her eyes were visible. The train rumbled into the station amid a hiss of steam. "*Had det bra*," "Have a nice holiday," she said, and quickly boarded.

Car after brightly lit car slipped silently by as if they were sliding downhill. Two red taillights finally disappeared in the flurries.

Most of the students had left for the break when I returned to school. I dropped by the café to have *kafe* and *kakedeig* with Tulla, but she was cleaning the kitchen and about to close. When I got to my room, I found a letter from Paul. I turned on the heater and sat next to the glowing coil.

Happy Hanukkah, Sonny Boy. Only a few days till my break and I get out of this fucking room. Where who knows. I hate holidays where you sit around and try to be nice. Who was nice to me? At least I can get away to the Scupper Bar where people are nice if you tip them enough. My room's as small as the one I had in Guatemala. I started climbing the walls as soon as I got there. Did I ever tell you about my nightmares? They were as bad as yours sonny boy. The walls got closer and closer every night. I stopped sleeping and eating. I laid in my bed listening to screech monkeys. Everything stopped except for the thoughts in my head. I couldn't stop thinking about the rain on the roof, the heat, the bugs, the rashes, the mud, the broken cinder blocks from the school foundation. I hated that I had come to Guatemala, hated that I had nowhere to go. Dr. Tate finally found me and took me to a hospital somewhere in town. At least there are no fucking monkeys in Norway, at least I hope so. XOXO Paul.

I remembered his crumpled face, wordless mouth, and vacant eyes when he flew into Washington DC. He walked in a slow shuffling gait, pausing at street corners not sure where to go. We'd never written to each other much and I didn't know what to say to him or do except to save the letters in my trunk.

I pulled out my duffle for Lier and filled it with a change of clothes and a bunch of laundry knowing Kristen did her weekly wash on Saturdays.

I left for the Bakkens the following day, stopping in Oslo for presents. The buildings and trams were dressed with holiday lights and wreaths. Mother claimed that we never celebrated Christmas, but Paul and I always found holiday presents under an evergreen tree she'd called a *Hanukkah* bush. I wandered down the snowy Oslo sidewalks, looking for gifts. I bought a *Julkake* (holiday cake) for Kristen and a folklore book for Brigitta. Tired from late night reading and a throat sore from the winter cold, I caught the evening train to Lier where Kristen met me.

The farm was covered with three feet of snow, the ruts in the road choked with ice. Brigitta greeted me at the door and pulled me into the living room.

"*Velkommen*, Josh! Come decorate the tree."

"*Nei*, Brigitta," said Kristen, "Give him a moment

to catch his breath."

"No, it's okay. I'd like to help."

I set my bag down and entered the living room. A beautiful Scotch fir, dense and bushy, stretched from floor to ceiling. Brigitta dragged over a chair and a box of weathered handmade ornaments - angels, reindeer, trolls, stars, balls of various shapes and colors, and strings of colored lights. I climbed up on a chair as Brigitta handed me the trinkets. "How long will you be home?"

"Four weeks."

"*Mor* says we can go to the *hytta,* our cabin in the woods. You ski?"

"A little. I took lessons once."

"Lessons?" She giggled.

"How did you learn?"

"By skiing. Put the angel on the tippity top. She's my favorite. Not there. Further up. To the left. *Fantastick.* We're a good team."

Kristin came in from the kitchen and turned out the lamps, leaving the room suffused in a soft, red and blue light. "Sa vakker!" Brigitta said.

And beautiful it was. I was glad to be back. I could smell the foods for our banquet: raspberry jam boiling on the stove; rye bread and snowflake-shaped anise cookies cooling in the pantry; pork and potatoes in the oven; and a marzipan-covered cream cake waiting on the counter.

"Are you all right, Josh?" asked Kristen. "You look pale. Why don't you lie down for a while?"

I went to my room. The floor felt like a sheet of ice. I crawled under the comforter and shivered.

I was still cold a half hour later when Brigitta came into my room and jumped onto the bed. "Dinner's ready. *Mor* says we can go to the movies. Want to see Cinderella, Snow White, Alibaba?"

"*Ja*. All tonight?"

"*Nei*, silly. We have four weeks."

I put on my wool slippers and shuffled down to dinner. Kristen lit the candles as Lars poured the raspberry wine. We began to sing *Silent Night*. On the words of the second verse, *holy night*, the room began to spin as if I were on a carousel. I looked at my hands; I'd never seen them tremble before. The shaking spread to my arms, chest, and legs. The singing stopped and everyone stared. I was shaking as if I had Saint Vitas Dance. Kristin put a hand on my forehead and left the room. Lars covered me with a blanket, but the blanket didn't help because I was still cold and couldn't stop shaking. He put a thermometer in my mouth; Kristin returned and placed a cold cloth on my head. I couldn't understand why she was using a cold cloth when I was so cold. I started to float out of the room. That was the last thing I remembered for what I later learned was two days.

CHAPTER 17

I woke up at sunset, what day I didn't know. Snow blinded my eyes and everything ached: my neck, my head, my chest. I rolled over and coughed, a wrenching cough that left me breathless and clinging to my mattress. I noticed tiny red spots on the sheets. I couldn't understand why Kristin had given me soiled sheets until I realized the spots were wet.

I yelled for help, but a whisper emerged followed by a cough that doubled me over. The room began to spin. No more carousel, I thought. One ride was enough and Paul was not around to help me off. Where was the music, the horses that pumped up and down? I flopped back on my pillow.

Kristin arrived with a pitcher of water. She had dark circles under her eyes. She began to talk, but I couldn't hear her because I loved to hide underwater when Mother came looking for me in the lake, holding my breath as long as I could.

"I'm glad you're awake, Joshua. Don't talk, just listen. You understand?" I waved my hand. She had a nice smile.

"You've had a couple of bad days. The doctor came when you were delirious. We spent most of the time keeping your fever down. You didn't stop shaking until this morning."

I struggled with the sheet, tried to sit up. But it wrapped around me like a snake.

"*Nei*, Joshua. Just rest. You have pneumonia in both lungs, *doble lungebetennelse*. You can't leave your bed for three weeks."

A new phrase, I thought. *Doble lungebetennelse*: double lung inflammation. Two for two. But how could I hold my breath for three weeks? I collapsed on my pillow.

"I'll get you a bedpan and juice. You'll need to drink a lot of fluids."

I tried to spell pneumonia. Did it start with a *p* or *n*?

Kristin returned with an odd-looking dustpan and glass of cider. "You rambled last night about Paul and a carousel and Elvira. Is she a friend from school?" She took my pulse; her hand felt cool and moist. "Anyway, get some rest. Dr. Amundsen will visit tomorrow. If you need me, ring the bell." She held up a tiny sleigh bell. "*Forstar*?"

Ja, I understood. Her footsteps receded into silence. Lying in a skimpy Johnny without clothes and unable to breathe, I wanted her to keep me company. Icicles hung like daggers from my window and the grey clouds forebode a storm. I longed for the warmth of Dad's palm on my forehead.

A pile of red spotted Kleenex littered the floor. I wasn't sure who they belonged to. I breathed in shallow pulses to avoid the coughing spasms that tired me. Kristin entered with a well-dressed, older man, holding a leather satchel with a stethoscope hanging out of the top. I liked the way he parted his wavy white hair in the middle.

"Good morning, Joshua," he said. "I'm Dr. Amundsen. How are you today?"

"Tired," I heard myself say in Norwegian. Words floated in and out without a thought.

"You'll be tired for a while." He took my temperature, examined my ears and eyes. "I put you on penicillin. That should bring your fever down."

The faint odor of ethyl alcohol from his bag made me feel better. He placed a frigid stethoscope on my chest.

"Your congestion will take time to clear. I understand your Father's a doctor. What kind?"

"Eye, ear…" I forgot the rest. My throat was raw. It was hard to swallow.

"Nose and throat? I studied in America in Baltimore, Johns Hopkins. That's near you, *ikke sant*?"

I smiled.

"I'll see you in two days, but you'll get good care with Kristin. She's a nurse, you know. You won't need a hospital. Do you want me to notify your father?"

I looked at his bag of ointments and pills and Kristen's calm face. I told him I was in good hands.

I sat up. I needed to pee. I hated bedpans. I'd already made a terrible mess once and didn't want another. I put my feet on the floor, but the room started to spin. On my hands and knees, I crawled to the bathroom, pulled myself up on the toilet, and leaned against the porcelain sink. But my bladder wouldn't work. The colder I got, the tighter I held on, shivering and waiting for something to function - bladder, mind, I didn't care. I started to slip off the seat and didn't stop until I had glided into a snow bank. Paul was making snow angels, laughing and throwing snow in the air. I lay in the snow, feeling how nice it was to be cold.

A cold compress lay on my aching head and two

blankets on my comforter. It might have been night or day, I couldn't tell. It made no difference in this crazy winter, living between light and dark. Snow eddied back and forth, unable to reach the ground. English and Norwegian were scrambled amid pictures of monkeys in trees, a train disappearing in the snow. Where am I, night and day? And where are my presents? Under the tree, someone said.

I opened my eyes. Kristin was sitting by my bed. "Where's Elvira's present?" I asked.

"On the dresser," she said. "You want me to unwrap it?"

"*Nei, takk.*"

She put it on my night table next to the clock. I fell asleep, staring at the red wrapping paper.

Sunlight flooded the room, giving my eyes no place to hide. Brigitta appeared in the doorway.

"Can I come in?" she whispered. She tiptoed to the foot of my bed. "*Mor* said not to disturb you. You look weird."

I cracked a smile.

"It's boring with you sick." She twisted the comforter's tassels into a knot. "Want to see what I got for Christmas?"

I propped up my head on a pillow.

"A sweater from *Mor,*" she said, spilling a bag of gifts onto the comforter. "A school notebook from Grandfather, a marzipan reindeer from Aunt Hege, chocolate from Uncle Tor." She modeled the sweater and pranced the reindeer over the comforter.

"Can I open your gift?" she asked. "*Mor* said to wait until you're better."

"*Ja,*" I said, hoarsely.

She sprang from the bed and returned with a parcel. My head vibrated like a tuning fork.

"Let me guess," she said, closing her eyes and turning the gift in her hands. "Marzipan? A puzzle?"

"*Nei.*"

"She felt the outlines of the package. "I give up." She tore off the wrapping paper. "*The Golden Bird*? But we haven't finished *The Little Prince.*"

"We'll read them both." I coughed and reached for water. A car's tires crunched in the driveway.

"*Zut!* Mor's home." She threw her gifts into the bag and raced from the room. Kristin entered with a letter and tray of simple food. My face fell when I saw the letter had a U.S. postmark.

"Expecting something from Elvira?" Kristin asked. "Christmas is a busy time, Josh."

I opened the envelope; one dollar bills fluttered onto my bed. Hanukkah *gelt* from Ida, one dollar for each of the eight days. Every year she'd pressed the bills into my palm and kissed my forehead.

Schmen! Happy Hanukkah. So much snow we have. I hate snow. I can go nowhere. So I spend gelt on someone sweet like you. I can't make brownies - too cold. Mine bones ache. Oih! I call Pauly but no answer. Where he living? New Year comes soon. In Russia we had big party. But Jacob will stop and have food. A good son like you. Happy Birthday! Ida.

My birthday already? I hated my birthday being so close to Christmas. I'd only get one present from Mother and Dad.

"What's the news?" Kristin asked bringing me a boiled egg and toast.

"I got a letter from Ida, my *Bestemor*." Best mother in Norwegian.

"She lives nearby?" Kristin asked.

"*Ja*. My Dad talks to her every day."

"We take care of Gunnar's parents. Remember *Bestemor* and *Bestefar* from the summer? They live in the cottage on the hill, like their parents did."

She pointed to a house at the top of the driveway overlooking the farm. "I make them meals and clean their house. One day Lars and I will live there and Brigitta will take care of us. Aren't you hungry?"

I had spread the food around on my plate, but had eaten little. "Would you like to call home? Wish your family a nice New Year?"

"They won't be home yet."

"It's Sunday. You've lost a few days."

I wrapped myself in a bathrobe and walked downstairs. My head bobbed around like a helium balloon, but Kristen held my arm until we reached the kitchen. She placed the call and handed me the phone.

"Joshua? Oh, my goodness!" Mother said. "You're just in time. Father's home. Jacob, Jacob, it's Joshua, long distance."

There was a pause, then Dad picked up in the basement. "Hi, Josh. How are you?"

"Good."

"We got six inches of snow," Mother said. "Believe it or not we're having a white holiday. You have snow?"

"A lot."

"You get our birthday present?"

"No."

"What are you planning to do during the holiday?"

"Go to the bathroom, on my own."

"What do you mean?" Dad asked.

"I got sick."

"What do you have?" His voice changed from Dad to doctor.

"Pneumonia."

Static filled the silence, the twitching of cables thousands of feet underwater.

"When?" he asked.

"A few days ago."

"How high's your fever?"

"High."

"What hospital are you in?"

"I'm staying with Kristin. A doctor is treating me here."

"On a farm? What's he prescribing?"

"Penicillin and chicken soup."

No one laughed. The conversation was tiring. "What's Paul up to?"

"We assume he's fine," Mother said.

"What do you mean?"

"We haven't heard from him since September," she said.

"Son, I'd like to talk to your doctor."

My faced flushed with fever. "He doesn't speak English," I said, unable to remember if Amundsen had spoken to me in English or Norwegian.

"How about coming home to recuperate?"

"No." I snapped the telephone cord against the wall. "Kristin's a nurse."

"I'll send you some money, in case you change your mind."

"I'm tired. Can we talk another time?"

"Of course. When?" Mother asked.

"Soon."

"We'll be thinking of you on your birthday," she said. I hung up.

Kristen came over and sat beside me. "Were your Mother and Father worried?"

I nodded. She put her hand on my head and brushed the hair off my forehead.

CHAPTER 18

After one week, I was tired of reading, meals in bed, four liters of fluids a day, and negotiating the bedpan. The silence was appalling. If I held my breath, I couldn't hear anything: no wind, birds, or footsteps, not even the shush of the rising heat. I looked forward to taking medications so I could hear them gurgle down my throat.

I opened the gift from Elvira, a princess troll carved in wood that fit into the palm of my hand. Her blouse was painted white, her pleated skirt green, and a scarf covering her hair was red. She held a long narrow posthorn to her lips, pointing it high so that the sound would carry across the hills. I tried to imagine the music she was playing. I'd worried about the absence of Elvira's letters, what she would say when I returned. I wasn't much to look at and hated to see myself in the mirror - circles under the eyes, unshaven and unkempt, a person I'd never known. I breathed in rasping gasps and still coughed up blood on my sheets. What would be left when I was better?

Brigitta dropped into my room one sunny afternoon after the New Year and popped a deck of cards on my lap. "Can I teach you a game?" she asked.

"If I don't have to think." My fever had gone but

my clear-headed hours were few.

"*Nei*, it's easy. It's called *Jakte* (Hunt)." She sat on my bed, neatened my blanket, and dealt me a hand. "I'll ask for a card. If you have it, give it to me. If you don't, say, *jakte*. Four of the same makes a book. The most books wins, *ikke sant*?"

I arranged my cards in suits. She eyed me carefully. "Ever play this before?"

"*Nei,*" I answered, though it seemed familiar.

She went first and asked for sevens. I gave her one, then a pair of two's, a jack, a queen, and an ace. I wasn't sure how she knew what was in my hand. When I asked her for a card, she always said, *jakte*. It only took her a few minutes to get thirteen books.

"You played well, Josh," she said, re-shuffling the deck.

"Not as well as you, Brigitta."We played the rest of the day. I began to enjoy predicting how I would lose.

"Mor says you can come down to dinner," she said.

"Tonight?"

"*Ja*, we're having cake. It's your birthday, *ikke sant*?"

"*Ja*, I guess, a few days ago."

Lars helped me down the stairs to dinner, only my second visit to the kitchen. The table was set with candles and roast pork, carrots, cabbage, and potatoes. I liked eating together, though I drifted in and out of the conversations. They lit the candles on the *blotkake,* a cream filled cake with marzipan frosting. Kristin gave me a cardigan sweater which she'd knitted. It was dark brown wool with flecks of white stars. Brigitta had embroidered needlepoint flowers on the velvet cuffs and added pewter hook & eye clasps instead of buttons. It looked like a sweater for royalty and I felt the warmth of generations when I slipped it over my shoulders.

"*Skol,* Josh," they saluted, lifting their glasses high. "What do you wish?" Kristin asked.

" letter from Elvira I thought.

In the next few weeks I taught Brigitta slapjack and hearts and managed to win a few games. We finished The Little Prince and I began to help with chores inside the house. Four weeks after my delirium, Dr. Amundsen cleared me for school.

Brad volunteered to take me to the train. I heard the rumble of his car approaching our snowbound driveway.

"Damn ruts screwed up my muffler," Brad said, skidding Greta's car to a stop. "You look like shit."

"I feel like it."

The cold air pierced my windbreaker and seared my lungs. He threw my bag in the back and we lurched up the driveway.

"Heard you've had a rough time," he said.

"*Ja,* pretty bad."

"Sorry I couldn't get out here to see you. I guess waiting on tables is what I have to do for a while. Dad cut off my cash when I dropped out of school and now I'm broke." He pulled onto the two-lane road to Oslo. "Glad to be heading back to school?"

"*Ja,* it started two weeks ago. What are you up to?"

"Not much. My day off. I kind of miss school. Not the academic stuff but having a direction."

We followed the road as it wound through the hills and descended into the city. "Thanks for the ride, pardnor," I said, as we pulled into the station.

"Yeah, take care." He smiled and grabbed my hand. His rear wheels spun as he skidded toward home.

The thump of his busted muffler kaboomed off the narrow cobblestones streets like sputtering fireworks.

The last time I'd traveled north, the mountains were ablaze with red and yellow birches. Now I journeyed into a white wilderness. The train burrowed through tunnels of snow created by overhanging trees burdened with ice. When we arrived at Lillehammer, the main street had vanished. I didn't want to delay by dropping my bag at home, so I went directly to school. But the walk seemed long and my bag grew heavy. At every corner, I had to stop to catch my breath.

The school's vestibule was a tangle of skis, boots, poles and parkas. I searched for Elvira's blue jacket with its furry gray collar, but I got lightheaded and had to sit in a chair. I clung to its arms, listening to the drone of Thorlief's lecture on the floor above. Seconds dragged into minutes; the hands of the clock twitched toward three.

Suddenly, a chaos of chairs scraped across the ceiling and a clatter of footsteps descended the stairs. Students crowded around, peppering me with greetings and questions. My head spun with Norwegian, the heat in the room, the thump of the door as students left. But still there was no sign of Elvira. Coat by coat, the vestibule emptied, leaving a row of empty hooks. I went searching for Thorlief and found him correcting papers in a classroom.

"Goodness gracious! You're back," he said, gripping my hand in both of his. "We were worried, you know. How do you feel?"

"Okay."

"You came back so soon?"

"I was tired of lying in bed."

"For sure." He bent over to gather his papers.

"I didn't see Elvira."

He stopped and straightened. "She isn't here. She didn't come back."

"Didn't come back?"

"She called after Christmas. She's staying in Fineran. A disappointment, really. She was a lovely person." He took off his glasses and put them in a soft leather case. "I gather you were friends?"

"Yes, friends," I said.

"I'm sorry," he said. He slipped on his coat. "I say, you look rather pale. Can I give you a lift?"

"No, I'm okay."

"Just close up then when you leave." His keys jangled as he walked downstairs and the front door slammed with a thud.

I turned off the lights; it was easier to be alone in the dark. I could see Elvira sitting by the window, filling three by five cards with her delicate letters. She was wearing a pale, yellow blouse that mirrored the birch leaves when we first met and she asked me where I came from. I didn't know all the right words then, but I didn't need them with her.

Snow began falling, tiny needle like particles that sliced through the air, rattling the windowpanes.

CHAPTER 19

When I awoke in the morning I felt in a free fall. Like when Paul and I jumped off the rope swing and sank slowly into the lake unsure how long we could hold our breath.

The snow was falling, the windows frosted, the birds absent from the trees. The sun would not break the horizon until 11:30. I didn't want to walk to school in the dark. I curled around my pillow and recalled glimpses of Elvira's pink underwear and pale skin under the table at Thanksgiving, remembered the soft brush of her breasts on my arm skating at *Winterfest.* I imagined peeling off her layers until all her clothes were gone. I hated that so many months of friendship had come to nothing but fantasies. I quickly dressed and left the room, determined not to return until I could leave my fantasies behind.

I wandered into town, but the short walk drained me. I didn't understand why I got tired walking up stairs, listening to lectures, and reading my textbooks. I thought the days of lying in bed and coughing up blood were over; I was supposed to be well. But though the fever had gone, there wasn't much was left of me. And when the bitter cold stirred pain in my chest and triggered spasms of coughing, I thought the pneumonia had returned. I became afraid that I would never walk without needing to rest, read without headaches, or breathe without hurting. The Arctic night was upon me. I'd always dreaded the dark: now I had it 22 hours a day.

My meandering led to school where I took my place in class. All the chairs filled, one by one, except for Elvira's which would always be empty for me. Thorlief's words on Kierkegaard tumbled by faster than I could catch, *Frykte og Beven, Fear and Trembling, grasping the reality of existence and transfiguring yourself*. My gaze drifted out the window into the misty mountains which remained dependably white.

Class ended. Tomas came over and put an arm around my shoulder. "Welcome back," he said. "We missed you."

"*Ja*, a hard time for sure."

"And harder still?" he asked, attentively.

I shrugged.

"She had a soft spot for you, I could see. And yet traditions are hard in Norway." He opened his book bag. "Want my notes? *Kierkegaard* is hard to read, even for me."

"Nei, takk," I said, feeling the twinge of a headache. I excused myself and went to sit alone. Kierkegaard would have to stew in his own juices. It was noon, the sky was lightening. It was time to walk into town to see where I could spend the rest of the day.

I had few choices. The theater was closed, the church too cold. I had no appetite for the café, and there was no place to sit in the general store. But the laundromat was brightly lit, with picture windows overlooking the street and an odor of cleanliness. The washers and dryers spun in regular cycles with an easy going hum.

I bought myself a Herald Tribune, settled in a

corner, and watched a young woman tend the machines. She sheparded clothes from washer to dryer and folded them into warm piles. There was something hopeful about a laundromat, as if things might change with a clean set of clothes. I studied the basketball standings, assured myself the Celtics were in first, that Sam Jones, Havlichek, and Russell were having good years. The clatter of metal buttons tumbling in the dryers lulled me to sleep, clickety clack in random patterns like falling tacks. When I awoke, daylight had vanished. The laundry girl offered me a comforting smile as she put on her coat and left.

I had hours to fill before I'd let myself return to my room. I gathered my things and walked to the market, passing the well-lighted rink where athletes were training for Norway's long distance skating championships. They glided over the surface bent low to the ice in skin-tight body suits, building speed by swinging their arms the way Elvira had skated in our warm-ups.

I wandered through the foods of the grocery aisles - butter cookies molded in circles and squares, coated with chocolate; Greek olives embalmed in oil; cans of King Olav's sardines wrapped in mauve and gold tissue paper; bins of Spanish oranges, lemons, and limes; hundreds of foods for which I had no hunger. The store closed and I left for the last place open, the Church Of Holy Saints.

Hewed from speckled granite that sparkled in the streetlight, it exuded a medieval breath. I entered the vestry through a broad oak door, carved with angels trumpeting the glory of God, and took a seat on a stern wooden bench. The arches soared into darkness, the stained glass dimmed into the night. I thumbed through the prayer book, frayed more from time than use, to find a story to read. Snared by a passage in Job, *For the thing that I greatly feared has come upon me*, I started reading. When the bell in the tower finally struck nine, the lights went out. I let myself out the back, recalling the couplet, *neither had I rest or quiet.*

The stores were closed, their interiors dark. Even the stained glass windows had turned black. With no place to go and tired from wandering, I traipsed back to my room, hoping I could fall into a peaceful sleep.

But during the night I was jolted awake. Something was grasping my feet. I thrashed at the tentacles coiled around my ankles, pulling me down. Unable to stop my descent and struggling to breathe, I flailed at the blankets and sheets. Too frightened to scream, I leaped into the mine-deep darkness, collided with a dresser, and stumbled into the bathroom, certain the tentacles would slither under the door. The cold stone floor numbed my feet, rippling chills through my body. Unable to see a hand in front of my face, I had no one to call to, no one who'd come. I sat on the porcelain toilet, wrapped a towel around me, shivering. I waited for the darkness to yield to 90 meager minutes of daylight.

The sun was already setting behind the mountains when I awoke back in bed, having slept through my classes and daylight. My mouth was parched and smelled like garbage. Too tired to get out of bed, shower, or shave, I felt as if I'd landed on the bottom of the sea, pressed into the mud under miles of water. Outside, snow fell like a bad habit. It filled the air with fluffy white lichen, burdening the branches till they snapped or hovering until a gust of wind smashed them into my window.

I couldn't decide where to go. Slipping on yesterday's clothes I started to walk, passing the café where Tulla was serving coffee and pastry. The smell of butter and sugar was nauseating, so I continued downhill until I came to the railroad station and claimed a spot on a warm waiting room bench.

It was comforting to sit in a room that offered so many places to go. Posters of mountains and seascapes covered the dark paneled walls. A father cradled two small boys in his lap, telling them stories about the trolls in Andalsnes where they were traveling to. I'd always wanted to visit the western fjords that snaked through the mountains for hundreds of miles. I bought a ticket and followed them onto the train.

Choosing a compartment next to theirs, I looked out the window as we passed through the backyards of Lillehammer's bungalows. I peered into the windows as families gathered in their living rooms for *aftensmat,* their evening meal. Lulled by the rocking car, I watched the mountains dwindle into silhouettes. Their older son peeked in my doorway munching a sandwich. The salami and cheese was tantalizing. Where was I going, he asked. Don't know, I said. That's silly, he replied, and told me about his Sunday plans with Tove, his uncle. Was it Sunday already, I thought?

The train rumbled over a covered bridge and curved westward, leaving the expanses of the lake behind. We sped into a narrow canyon with no signs of slowing down. Where were the towns of Oyer, Tretten, or Hundrup? I went to look for the conductor, passing the family's compartment. The children were asleep on their parent's laps. Their father smiled, offered me a sandwich. We talked in whispers about their trip, the brother they were visiting. I told them I was from America. They volunteered a bed for me in Andahlsnes. Norwegians always had a room for wanderers, but I didn't want to stay overnight.

A street light flashed by as we pulled into a deserted hamlet. Unnerved by the long ride, I waved goodbye to the sleeping children and got off. The village, Favang, looked like a hiker's jump off, a few buildings in the middle of nowhere. I checked the schedule outside the general store. The last train returned at eight PM - I had three hours to myself.

The clouds had parted, the moon was absent, the darkness complete. But every inch of the sky was splattered with stars. I searched for Orion, the face of Venus, the signs of the Pleiades, my companions during the fall. But winter had rotated the constellations into unfamiliar places and I was unable to find the pole star. Trembling with cold, I retreated into the station.

The waiting room was small with few amenities: a dim overhead light, a luke warm radiator that hissed spasmodically, a bulletin board with two announcements, and an empty trash barrel . I sat on a wooden bench facing the tracks. I throbbed with fatigue, longed for my bed, a bite of food, but still wasn't ready to return to my flat. Resigned to the cold, the embrace of the empty station, I closed my eyes and waited for the last train home.

Dawn or dusk, I didn't know which; I was back in bed facing another day. The snow had stopped but the wind had risen, a roar so constant I didn't know whether it was coming from inside or outside of my head. I had run out of places to go but was determined to take a walk.

I chose a path to the lake, cutting through a beltway of evergreens that muffled the din of the storm. Alone with the squeak of my boots and the sigh of my breath, I sat down in a snow bank to rest. The lake was frozen as far as Hamar forty miles to the south and dusted with patches of snow that shifted in the wind. I'd seen the lake's moods before, from ripples to whitecaps, but had never crossed its surface.

I took a few steps on the silvery sheet, unsure of my balance. But the wind billowed my parka and blew me towards the mountains, their tops shrouded in mist. The ice cracked under my footsteps, jolts that sounded like thunder claps that rippled through the depths and shattered against the shore. Still I persisted, step by step, into the heart of the lake.

Huddling in a patch of snow, I paused to get my bearings. A trail of my footsteps led back to town; untrammeled snow led into the dusk. I stared down at the leaves and twigs frozen in the ice till spring. Below them darkness spread to the bottom. I lay down on my back to rest. Paul and I had loved making snow angels during winter storms. We'd lie in the snow until we got cold, then run home and sit by the fire, filling ourselves with cocoa and cookies.

The chill of Mjosa crept into my body, numbing my aches and spreading calm while the mountain's shadow was stealing across the ice. I recalled the kindness in Elvira's eyes at the train as she turned to say goodbye. Just a few minutes more, I thought. A little more rest and a few deep breaths. The sky was dark and beautiful. Strange how the wind could blow hard out of a clear sky. I remembered how my father would put me to bed, how he'd rest his hand on my forehead. Paul was sleeping, he'd say, and Mother, too. It was time for me to sleep as well. There would be no more nightmares if I would just close my eyes.

I started to tremble. First my hand, then my leg. I stuffed my hands in my pocket, pulled my hood tight over my head, but the shaking rippled through my body. I rolled onto my side, tried to stand, but had no sensation in my legs. I got on my knees, braced one leg, and pushed to my feet. The mountains were moving in circles around me. Then I fell, slamming my head on the ice. Something trickled into my eyes, my parka had splotches of red. I screamed for help. Again and again, shocked by how loud it sounded until I ran out of breath.

I spotted a light on a hill and rolled onto my knees. I started to crawl across the ice. My hands and knees were numb, but my heart was pumping hard. I kept my head pointed into the wind humming, *Per Spelman han hadde ein einaste ku*, over and over until my hands, gloveless and bleeding, touched a bank of snow on the edge of the lake.

I wanted to rest but was scared of the tremors. I pulled myself to my feet and blundered forward over fallen trees and through thickets of bushes, up ice-covered roads where I fell repeatedly and through the empty streets of the town until I knocked on a red door with an evergreen wreath. "Oh, Josh!" Emma said. "What happened to you?"

CHAPTER 20

I stumbled into Emma's house and fell on her bed. She piled two comforters on my shivering body and dabbed at the cuts and bruises with a soft cloth. As I started to warm, I started to hurt. Hands and knees and the lump on my head, everything ached. I began to cry, like the time when a baseball hit me in the eye in Little League and I couldn't stop calling for my Dad. I'd watched it fly into the air, a tiny white speck in a clear blue sky, and worried where it would land. It tipped off my webbing and into my eye. My first chance to play in the outfield and I didn't catch the ball. The coach was laughing and saying I was supposed to catch the ball with my mitt not with my face and I'd feel better if I'd stop crying. Paul came to the field and told me I'd be all right, it takes practice to catch a ball and he would show me how.

Emma rubbed my back and let me sob.

"I've never been to bed with anyone, Emma. All I do is stare at crotches and butts."

"Plenty of people haven't had sex at 21. Gunnar was a virgin when I met him. He was 29."

I rolled on my side and pulled the comforters close.

"He liked books more than dating. What happened

to your face?"

"I fell on the lake."

"Oh, dear. Want to take off your coat?"

"No." The trembling stopped but I was soaked with sweat.

"You don't have to. I just don't know whether you're coming or going." She went to the kitchen. Tinkling plates and silverware and the smell of eggs and tea drew me in. I slipped off my coat and sat down at the table.

"I miss Elvira," Emma said. "She was tired of our traditions and searching for something new."

"*Ja*, for sure."

"And you found something together?"

"*Ja*, it was good to talk about our families. She was the first girl I could really talk to. It's all I'm left with now."

"Meaning?"

"My thoughts."

"Your fantasies? What's the big deal, Josh?"

The room grew hot. I unbuttoned my sweater.

"What are they?" She asked so naturally, it was hard not to answer.

"The usual. You know, I mean, like being overcome, suffocating."

"The girl?"

"Ah, the other way around."

"How?"

My mouth felt plugged with Novocaine. I heard myself mumble about legs encircling my head and passing out and was ready for Emma to change the subject.

"Nice. I shared a lot of fantasies with a boyfriend in England."

"But, I'm always on the bottom."

"Top or bottom, everyone has fantasies. Even me." I blushed and went to the refrigerator to look for bread and raspberry jam. I remembered the pictures

Emma had shown me, how thin and attractive she'd been in England. I was glad she was fat now. It was easier to talk with her.

"My mother liked to chat about sex," she said. "Did you talk about it in your family?"

"No."

My mother used to come to my room in her nightgown to tuck me in and say goodnight. She'd lean over and press her body into mine and kiss me. I wanted the kiss on my forehead, but it usually landed on my lips. I'd open the windows after she'd left to let out the smell of her bath cologne but couldn't fall sleep for hours. She'd always said I looked like my father. I had loved to hear it when I was young. But when I turned thirteen I got embarrassed and decided to go to a boarding school the same year Paul left for Harvard.

Emma asked what we spoke about at home and I told her not much because of the fights. I said they were especially bad when Paul and I had come home from school last Thanksgiving. She'd gone to her room to cry and Dad had followed us into the basement to tell us about her episode. My head grew tighter as I spoke but the words were spilling from my mouth.

"Dad said she was lucky to be alive. He started to say, 'If I hadn't come home early' and began to cry and so did we, why I don't know because we hated her. He'd found her lying in bed wrapped around an album of our baby pictures, a half empty bottle of pills next to her hand. He told us to return to the table and never say another word to anyone. Dad took her to a Boston hospital so no one would know in Quinnipiac. She'd stayed for 6 weeks without seeing friends or family and returned at Thanksgiving for dinner. We never said an angry word after that, afraid she would try it again."

153

—

The eggs were congealing on my toast, the tea growing cold, but I wanted to tell it all no matter how long it took. I told her that I went to college as far from home as Dad would let me, 800 miles away in Ohio. But Paul was stuck at ground zero, only 20 minutes away.

"I think the questions got to him. How many pills had she taken, did she want to be found, did we make her try to kill herself? And despite our anger we still had to be nice to her."

"I knew that Harvard wasn't a good place for Paul, but my parents had chosen it. He failed in his classes, got nervous with girls, and was too light to play college football. After a year, he quit. Mother thought he should join the Peace Corps. 'Try to be useful,' she'd said. He was shipped to the jungle in Guatemala which led to his episode."

"You mean breakdown?" Emma asked.

I let the word sink in.

Dad and I flew down to Washington and met Paul in the hospital. A psychiatrist led him into the reception room as if he was on a leash. I'd never seen him like that. His skin was red and blotchy from the sun and insect bites, but it was his eyes that got me. The life had drained away. We sat three feet apart and he wasn't there. He stared at the floor, rubbing his hands over and over. I tried to talk to him while Dad went through the paper work, but he never looked at me once. Dad kept saying Paul would be all right, we'd find the best doctors. But we'd grown up with one of the best doctors and look what happened. They put him in an institution when we got home.

"What's he doing now?"

"Back at Harvard."

I stared into the night. My head was throbbing, my shoulders ached. The teakettle filled the silence with a sighing whistle. I started to feel hungry, as if I hadn't eaten for days.

"Before Elena walked into the ocean, Josh, I couldn't see her because of my classes. She'd been feeling poorly, but picked up when we were together. We'd made a date to meet at Paddinton Station and go to the shore. We loved the ocean. It reminded us of the desert, the way it changed by the hour. But I lost track of time and when I remembered, I'd missed my bus."

"I thought she'd give me a call when she got back. I knew she'd be angry and waited by the phone. When I didn't hear, I started to worry and went to her apartment. The place was a mess - dirty clothes, unwashed plates, garbage everywhere. Not the person I knew."

"I stayed the night, but didn't sleep. In the morning I called the police. They'd found her bag in a cove where we used to picnic. Her lunch was uneaten, her journal a sheaf of empty pages. I think about all the ifs. If I had gotten to the train, returned her calls, seen her when she needed me."

"Funny that we should meet in Norway, coming from Cairo and Quinnipiac," I said.

"We're not so different from most people. Gunnar's family had their troubles and Thorlief lost his son."

"Thorlief?"

"*Ja*, to alcohol and the long winters."

Exhausted, I'd lost track of the hours. Emma re-heated my eggs and tea. There was something nice about breakfast in the middle of the night. She made me a bed on her couch. As soon as my head touched the pillows, I fell into a dreamless sleep.

I awoke in the morning to rattling dishes. My head throbbed and my cheeks were chapped from tears. I was in no mood to move from my spot and stayed at Emma's, watching the sun rise at noon through a slit in the clouds. I knew daylight would last only a few hours, but I had a comfortable couch for a home.

I spent the next few days rooted in my seat, talking about our family fights, the anger that grew until Paul spun out of control, the years of chasing girls with no interest in me, the dinners without my father, and the nightmares that wouldn't let me sleep. Emma listened to it all and matched my stories with hers from Italy, Cairo, and London. At times I felt like we came from the same family and could finish each other's thoughts. When I got hungry, I went to her refrigerator and cupboard, eating flat bread, cheese, eggs, sardines, whatever was in her house.

By Sunday evening, I'd purged everything and told her I was ready to go. She reminded me that her door was always open. She grabbed her paint brushes and smock covered with the drippings of the rainbow as I left to buy a paper. I passed by Elvira's room, the empty rink, and the silent school, and returned to my room. My pants and shirts still hung in the closet, my socks and sweaters filled the dresser in their accustomed drawers.

I postponed Kierkegaard for Monday and started to read *Sinking The Tirpitz*, a German battleship destroyed in World War Two in a Norwegian fjord, hoping I could sleep through the night. But later, I was startled awake, confined in a coffin, hands bound to my side, the satiny lid pressed into my face. I searched for a light, a space to breathe. The coffin tilted, slid into the dark. I clung to the mattress, crammed my head to the side, and caught a glimmer of light under the doorsill. I waited for shapes to appear. A bureau and window emerged, grey in the blackness. I let go of the bed, took a full breath. I would be okay if I waited. In the land of perpetual night, I'd discovered traces of light.

CHAPTER 21

On Monday, I strapped on my gear to ski to school. The snow had stopped and the trucks had piled it in towering embankments that children slid down from morning to dusk. Students gathered around, bombarding me with questions. I told them I'd had a relapse and moved quickly to class where Thorlief discussed the impact of Edvard Munch's depression on his art. He contrasted the somber grays and greens in his paintings during his breakdown with the bright yellows and blues after he'd recovered. After class, he joined me in the living room.

"You better?" he asked. "Illness is strange, *ikke sant*?"

"*Ja,* lots of surprises."

"I have notes from last week about *Vigeland*. You've seen his work in Oslo?"

"I visited his park last summer."

"Wonderful sculptures of families from birth to death, the cycle of renewal. Speaking of that," he said with a smile, "you got a letter from Elvira." He placed an envelope on the coffee table.

Hi Josh!
Thorlief told me you were sick. I hope you get better soon! I felt awful I couldn't return. Soren was very upset at Christmas. I realized I couldn't

turn my back on him after all those years. He's a good man and knows me well. I'll remember our days together and hope you will too. You opened my heart to many things. I only wish we could have had more time. I sent you a picture of Fineran.
Kjaerlig hilsen, Elvira

Kjaerlig hilsen, yes, and loving greetings to you, too. Her snapshot was a picture of a small island in a blue sea with scattered farms ascending a hill. A solitary road wound through the fields and orchards. I wondered which house was hers, whether she'd gone back to teaching children, if she'd marry Magnus soon.

"A beautiful spot," Thorlief said, sucking his pipe. "The western lands are lovely. Maybe you should visit them when school is done?" He waited for me to fold the letter into the envelope, picked up his briefcase and followed me out the door.

"Glorious when it isn't snowing, *ikke sant*?" he said, slipping into his skis.

"*Ja*, I guess."

"The sun is setting later and it's not so cloudy. You cross country ski?"

"Not in the mountains. It's too hard to stop."

"Do a snowplow." He pigeon-toed the tips of his skis together.

"I ski too fast."

"Then fall." He shrugged. "The snow is deep and powdery. And use the herring bone uphill." He splayed his skis at forty-five degree angles. With his long spindly legs, he looked like a praying mantis. He tossed me a roll of ski wax. "No charge for the lesson," he said as he glided down the sidewalk.

I dug my poles into the snow, bent slightly forward at the waist, and slid my feet forward, right then left, until I found a rhythm. I liked the

160

rasping sound of my wooden skis on the granular snow. It had been a while since I'd broken a sweat. I took off my hat to vent the heat and reached home at sunset. Thorlief was right: it was 3:30 and there was still plenty of light.

As the days passed, I adjusted to school, switching seats daily for a different view - the lake, the mountains, or the forests north of town. I studied my classmates: the curly haired Maud with thick glasses who read the books and arrived with prepared statements; the fun loving Bjorn who never opened a text and asked questions like - 'Was Kierkegaard depressed or did he just write that way?'; the urban Harald with a small goatee and black turtleneck who questioned the existence of God and everything Thorlief said; and Freia from Tromso in the Arctic who listened intently but hardly spoke. On weekends, I was smothered by quiet. It wasn't that I couldn't find friends: I didn't want any. But if I panicked, I retreated to Emma's couch from which I came and went freely.

The snow cover began to thin in March, wearing down into dirty piles of slushy ice. One Saturday morning while reading in bed, I heard a rumble approaching my room. I looked out my window and saw Brad climb out of Greta's VW with a laundry bag over his shoulder.

"I see the muffler's fixed," I said, opening the back door.

"What muffler?" He grinned. "Greta went to her parents. Stavanger or some weird place. So I said, what the heck, it's a good day to cross country."

"You ski?"

"Nope, but this is a good place to try." He pulled a pair of skis and poles from the back, explaining they were Greta's.

"Where's your boots?" I asked.

"Damn! Will these do?" He looked at his work boots with thick rubber soles.

"They won't stay in the bindings."

He retrieved a roll of black electrician's tape from under the seat and wound it around the boots and bindings.

"If it works for the muffler, it'll work for the skis," he said.

We shushed across town to the woods where the trail went up to the high county. The students at Nansen School skied forty kilometers every Sunday in the high country and said the snow was pristine.

"Where's the lift?" Brad asked.

"There isn't any. You ski up the hill, into the mountains, and down."

The trail rose 600 meters through dense hemlocks. Brad was an odd sight in his blue jeans and Dodgers baseball hat. As soon as he started uphill he slid back, flailing his poles to get his balance. I showed him the herringbone, imprinting V-shaped angles in the snow to create traction on the path. We lapsed into silence, focused on preserving our rhythm and our breath. After two hours, we crested onto a broad valley rimmed by two thousand meter peaks that spread north in solitary splendor. I'd downhilled in New Hampshire mountain resorts surrounded by lifts and cafes, but had never skied through a snow bowl. Sunlight ricocheted off the tree-less slopes, blinding my eyes. Tracks led in every direction without a signpost or a person in sight.

"Your choice," I said.

"Let's stay on the flats. I don't have any brakes," Brad said.

Although I was feeling better, I was tired after the climb. I was weak in the knees, sweating a lot, and getting the chills. I began to understand why Dad had wanted me to come home. Brad re-taped his

162

boots and we skied into the valley, taking turns cutting a path through the fresh snow. A persistent wind swirled over the slopes, kicking up showers of icy particles that got inside my goggles.

"I wish I had one of your triple deckers," Brad said. I was hungry, too, but had forgotten to bring food. "Where the hell are we?" he asked.

We stopped to get our bearings. "We could retrace our tracks to town," I said, leaning heavily on my poles.

"Which tracks? It's a mess of choices. I got a hunch it's this-a-away." He jabbed a pole towards an escarpment at the valley's end. As we reached the ridge, I noticed a mountain's shadow creeping across the landscape. Below lay endless woods and a sliver of a frozen lake. A single track descended sharply into a grove of dense evergreens. I shivered and tightened my hood.

Brad studied the sun and terrain and pointed. "This has got to be the quickest way to town. Too bad it's downhill." I showed him the snowplow, he notched his ski tips together and shoved off. When the hill steepened, he picked up speed, lost his balance, dragged his poles to slow his speed, and disappeared into the woods in a cloud of spray.

I quickly followed but my legs were rubbery, my clothing damp from sweat. The forest felt like a deep freeze and I wasn't sure where we'd emerge. I strained to see a trace of Brad, trying to avoid the swipes of low-lying branches in the dim light. I cursed myself for not going first or skiing faster. If we lost the track in the deep snow there no going back.

Coming quickly over a rise, I tripped on a log, lost my snow plow, and flew into a hollow out of control, plowing into a lump at the bottom. It was Brad, snared in hip deep snow without his skis. "What the hell happened," he said. Alone I would have freaked, but mishaps seemed normal with Brad. I extended him a pole and pulled him upright, then retrieved his skis among the trees.

"We have to follow the sun," Brad said, observing a glimmer of light through the trees. "We're bound to hit a road, a farm, something to go by. I've tromped around too much with Dad to get lost on a dumb ski trip."

The track, barely visible now, would soon become a memory. At every rise, we'd re-check our direction. After an hour's descent, the hemlocks thinned, giving way to skinny birches and leafless bushes. Then the trail straightened and leveled into a meadow and we left the forest behind.

I don't remember how long we slogged through the flats, but knew my stomach was running on empty. I hummed some Sousa marches that I'd played in high school - Invincible Eagle, El Capitan, Stars & Stripes Forever - repeating the stanzas twice like we did at football rallies. After another hour a lake emerged, a vast sheet of ghostly white that faded into a darkness where a set of headlights flickered among the trees.

Quickening our pace at the sign of a car, we stumbled onto an ice-covered road. We put our skis on our shoulders and started walking, too numb and tired to care if we were heading in the right direction, but hoping someone would give us a ride to town.

Everything was closed when we were dropped off in Lillehammer except the Church and a small grocery. We bought everything edible - spam, pickled herring, peanut butter, beer - and returned to my room.

"Hell of a trip," I said, stripping off my layers of damp, frigid clothes.

Brad popped open a beer. "Yeah. A paradise. By the way, how's Elvira?"

"She didn't come back."

"You serious? She stayed on that dumb little island?" He dug out a spoonful of spam.

"Yup. I felt really stupid."

"Think you're the first who fell for someone engaged? Well, now you know two. Not with Greta, but a bunch before, a habit of mine to keep me single. Now Greta wants me to get a job, find a direction. I don't speak Norwegian and don't have a dime."

"So it was time to ski in the mountains?"

"Yeah, even without boots."

The radiator hissed and expired.

"That's it for the heat? Jeez!" Brad unfurled his sleeping bag on my box spring and tossed his clothes on the floor.

"Heading back in the morning?" I asked, turning off the light.

"I guess. When's school out?" The box spring squeaked as he turned.

"A month." The room was cooling. I could see my breath. "Just to warn you, I might have a screamer tonight. I've had a few nightmares lately."

"I don't scare easy, unless it's someone wanting to marry me," he said.

CHAPTER 22

The next day I got a letter from Paul.

Hi sonny boy. I'm out of here. Can't stand this fucking place, can't study, can't sit in class with preppy snobs like Stanley. They're all from the good schools that Dad didn't want to pay for. Stanley likes to bully, but he's an asshhole like the others. I'm cashing in my chips – heading back to Guatemala. It's cheap and the whores are good – cleaner than Boston. I'll live like a king, eat when I want – no more freezing days for me. Maybe I'll climb Pico Fortuna one of the volcanoes in the jungle that's still rumbling. No more parties, Harvard assholes, Manny crap, shit at the Scupper. Even the bartenders got sick of me and tossed me out cause of a scene with Tammy. She's a cunt. Like mother –she has to get her way. But I'm out of here. land where nobody knows me. Fuck McClean's. I rotted there for 9 months. Those kike shrinks were going to leave me there until I said what they wanted. Love your mother. Fuck that. She would have left me there forever. Did you know SHE never came to visit? And Dad, where is he anyway? Still screwing the nurses. Sorry buddy it's true. I put two and two together a while ago. I'm gone. Don't forget me – you're still my little brother. See you around, I hope. Paul

No wonder Dad was never around, I thought. Not that I was too surprised and I didn't blame him either. But Paul heading back to Guatemala? How much had he been drinking? I thought about calling home, but felt like I was watching my family from the long end of a telescope where things were impossibly small. I put his letter in my bureau and walked out of town, following the rivulets of melting snow through the sodden woods to the lake. The ice was thinning around the edges. I plunged my hand into the water, black and still, and let the cold rise through my body.

With only a month left to school, I was restless with classes and the mountains, though Brad and I had made plans to return in the summer. I went to discuss my *samtale*, my oral presentation, with Thorlief. He suggested I consider Monet, but I had no interest in haystacks drying in the sun. So he recommended the seascapes of Homer, my neck of the woods, as he put it. He pointed to *The Sea At Sunset*.

"One of his last oils. Look at the colors in the waves and the sky."

"I know the painting," I said. It hung on the maroon wall over Paul's bed. I studied the cresting breaker, a seagull hovering inches above its curl, moments before it would hurl itself on the rocks.

I borrowed his books and explored them in the cafe while I had *kaffe* and pastry. I wanted to understand Homer's story in paint as it unfolded year-by-year. I bit into a crusty half moon, scattering flakes like petals on the counter. Tulla's father was cleaning the glass cases, pausing between the trays to wipe his forehead and rest. I wondered why he was working alone, then realized I hadn't seen Tulla since January and spring was soon to begin.

168

Rain was falling on Lillehammer, eroding the ice like acid. Plumes of smoke rose from the smoldering snow from which yellow green tendrils were emerging, soft on top, frozen inside. Mists hung everywhere - at the water's edge and in the treetops. The ice on the lake had dwindled into a few drifting patches and a single slim crescent marooned on the northern shore.

My *samtale* came in the last week of school. Tired of a semester of lectures that spoon-fed information, I arranged Homer's prints and pictures in books on chairs around the living room, a mini-museum culled from the school's library. The paintings spanned from his youthful days in the Adirondacks to his brooding later years at Prouts Neck on the Maine coast. I told the class he was born in 1836 and died in 1910 and to explore his life in the pictures. "Ah, a painter's approach," Thorlief sighed happily, and went to study Homer's Caribbean watercolors created in his 30's. At first confused, even angry, the class finally started to look, and after an hour we talked.

Each student had discovered a favorite painting, but I was drawn to a picture of a small, dismasted sailboat adrift on a stormy sea. A solitary sailor lay on its deck, his clothes in tatters, his spirit broken, as a waterspout neared. Had he given up, was he aware of the circling sharks or a ship on the horizon that might save him? The discussion was lively and when I stumbled in my Norwegian, Thorlief rescued me with translations. At the end of class he came over, excited.

"No more lectures for me," he laughed. He asked me to come to his office where he gave me one of his own paintings, a watercolor of three birches on the shore of Mjosa. "Looks like it's clearing," he said, picking up his beret. I noticed his hair was thinning on top and that he had trouble finding his glasses. He left with his paints and easel with enough time to capture the last rays of light.

I gathered my books and prints and wandered through school. The sun had split the clouds, sending shafts of light through the rooms. But the fireplace hearth was cold, the dining room tables pulled to the side. Pictures of Pilgrims and turkeys still hung on the walls beside Elvira's dried flowers. I left through an entryway of empty coat hooks and headed to Emma's.

She sat in the living room, writing in her journal. I searched through the cinnamon scented cupboard to make a cup of tea and settled on my couch. She was wearing the same baggy pants and floppy turtleneck from when I stumbled through her door in the winter. She wrote with her glasses on the tip of her nose and often looked at the clouds to see how their shadows were falling. Between the sky and her book, nothing seemed to matter, unless I needed to talk. But that day, I didn't have to.

CHAPTER 23

My train pulled into Oslo in early May at eight in the evening. Brigitta was waving from the platform in a throng of anxious faces. I had scarcely dropped my bag at her feet when she began to talk about not knowing which train I was on and how to unspool her new fishing pole. "Have you any presents?" she asked, and grabbed my bag and dragged it away.

"A long winter, *ikke sant*?" Kristen asked. Her warm embrace lasted longer than usual.

"Josh," Brigitta yelled. My bag had snagged in the revolving door.

"It may take months to feel better," Kristen said. "You were sick in both lungs."

We drove south over the mist-shrouded hills largely free of snow and down their driveway, bordered by dark, turned-over fields. Clusters of tiny green leaves clung to the trees in the raw evening air. Winter was leaving but spring hadn't committed. I buttoned my jacket as we pulled up to the brightly lit house.

"We're painting the barn," Brigitta said. "I did the trim. Want to finish the doors tomorrow?"

"Tomorrow Josh might like to sleep," Kristen said."By the way, Brad called. And you have letters from home."

I put them in my pocket and went to my room. Nine thirty and still daylight. I opened the windows to let in the fresh air.

"*Mor* said not to bother you," Brigitta said, popping into my doorway in her pajamas.

"It's okay. I was just having alligator time."

"Alligator what?"

"Time to lie and think."

"About fishing? Let's go tomorrow. Our dory's at the fjord." She settled on my bed. "You won't be leaving soon?"

"I thought I might find you here," Kristin said, entering the room with a plate of cookies and shooing Brigitta to hers.

I opened Ida's letter and put Mother's in a drawer.

*Oih do I ach. You should not get so old. I sit in kitchen and say, what to make when Jacob comes? I hate to sit. What you doing? I found a map. Oih you so far. And cold? Bad for hands and knees. They give no peace. I went to hospital. A little fixing here and there. I have to please my son the Doctor. He plugs me into machines. So much money. I take pink pills with white and blue ones. Schmen, when you home? Passover comes. You go to Seder? Haven't seen Pauly. He didn't come to Hanukkah or my birthday. What gives? Nobody tells me. I love you.
Ida*

Kristin and Lars had started their chores when I awoke in the morning. I sliced some bread and cheese and sampled the *bringebaer* jam from the raspberries I'd picked the previous summer. Brigitta bounced through the front door just as I was finishing up.

"*Mor* says we don't have to paint today! We're free to go," she said, pointing at the fishing rods leaning on the car.

Kristin followed with a handful of fire wood. "Have you eaten? I left a picnic in the pantry. You know how to find the cove?"

"I do," said Brigitta, swiping a handful of shortbreads from the cookie tin.

We loaded the car and drove south through rolling farmlands. The countryside changed after an hour to rocky bluffs covered by scruffy, dwarf pines. By the time we reached the fjord's mouth, a wind had arisen, turning the water into white caps. We found the dory upside down near the tide line and dragged it to what Norwegians call a beach, a pocket of sand in a rocky ledge.

I stowed our gear in the boat and studied the wind. It was blowing into shore which would make rowing seaward a hard job. Still, the day was cloudless and the sea a beautiful bluish green, if a little choppy. I pulled the boat into the water and Brigitta, clutching her doll, jumped in. I slammed my knee on the gunnel as I hopped over the side. Before I could grab the oars, a wave flipped us sideways and back toward the rocks. "So fun!" Brigitta yelled, sweeping away her wet hair. I re-pointed the prow and started to row, but the oars jerked out of their oarlocks on every wave.

"Where should we head?" I yelled.

"*Oyen*," she hollered. She pointed to a treeless island in the middle of the bay.

"Too far," I said, and began to look around for a closer fishing spot. To my shock I noticed that we were already a hundred yards from land. I realized then that a current was pulling us seaward faster than I could row and the ocean was getting rougher in the open water.

Waves began spraying over the bow, soaking us with forty-degree water, the Gulf Stream Arctic style. I wanted to turn around, but was afraid of broaching. Something rammed my ankles - our tackle box floating in two inches of water. Bait, rods, and food were sloshing from stem to stern.

"Brigitta! The water!" I shouted.

Grabbing the side of the boat, she emptied the bait can into the sea and bailed. I searched for an opening in the surf, still pulling hard to keep our bow into the wind as we rode up the crests, bracing as we slid into the troughs. I looked for a pattern in the waves to see if there was a predictable lull, a trick I'd learned from Paul when we'd body surfed on Cape Cod. The magic number of consecutive waves seemed to be six. My hands were blistered, my back ached, but there was no room for fatigue or fear.

Suddenly we slipped into a trough and the wind vanished; a wave loomed over our heads. My breathing stopped. I waited for the shock of water, the chaos of swirling rods and bodies. But somehow we floated over and from the top I spotted a sliver of calm in the shoreline.

I waited for a lull, then leaned hard on the starboard oar and slowly turned the boat toward the inlet, its mouth guarded by rocky ledges bleached white with bird droppings.

With the wind now at my back, we surfed down the waves. The boat became harder to control, veering left and right. The water inside the boat rushed forward on every wave, nearly submerging the bow and capsizing us. I barked at Brigitta, bailing continuously, to get in the back. As she stepped over my seat, a swell smacked us amidships. Brigitta's doll poppod out of her hands and dropped into the sea. She screamed, reached over the side. I lunged to grab her. For a moment her doll floated on its back, its eyes gazing into the sky and its blond hair swaying in the current; then it sank without a trace.

I alternated oars to keep our boat at right

174

angles with the waves, taking brief rests when the sea quieted. The white caps vanished as we rode into the inlet and the waves turned into heavy rollers, smooth on top but packing a lot of water below. The closer we got to the beach, the steeper they grew. I tried to wait for another calm, but a monster snared us in its curl and hurled us toward the beach. Helpless, I watched as it broke, flinging us sideways and snapping the oars from my hands. Filling with water, the boat sank and cast us into the foam where we bobbed like flotsam, our feet dangling in the middle of nowhere.

I grabbed Brigitta around the chest and held her head above water, trying to ride the surges to shore. But for every yard we advanced, the undertow sucked us back. "Breathe," I yelled suddenly, and under we went again, sea and sky spinning as we were somersaulted across the rocky bottom finally to be deposited on the beach in a shallow pool with thousands of pebbles.

My pants were torn, my legs covered with cuts. So many places hurt, I didn't want to move. The smile had gone from Brigitta's face as she tended her bruises. But the sun shone brightly and the wind still swept out of a cloudless sky.

A few yards away, the capsized dory lolled in the surf, battered against the rocks. I waded into the water to pull it to shore; nothing was left - clothing, food, and Brigitta's rod were gone. We hauled the boat across the ledge and left it under the trees. Before we returned to the car, she grabbed my hand and stared at the sea, listening to the waves pounding the shore.

Birds roused me the next morning. I crept downstairs in the early light. The roar of the ocean receded but everything still ached. I wandered through raspberry patches where vines had sprouted, furrowed fields where potato seedlings grew, and orchards where apples and pears flowered. Kristin was kneading the bread in the pantry when I returned.

"*Kaffe*?" she asked.

"Sure." I sat down at the table.

"A difficult time yesterday, *ikke sant*? Brigitta had nightmares."

"I heard them."

"You did well to get back to shore." She put an arm around my shoulder. "You're going to Oslo soon?"

"I'm not sure." I opened the Help Wanted section of *Aftenbladet* and sipped my coffee. With the longer daylight I wanted to find a job where I could work outside and make some money. "What's the *Bestum Idretts Foreling?*"

"A sports center near Oslo."

"And a *vaktmester*?"

"A caretaker," she said, smiling.

CHAPTER 24

Bestum Idretts Foreling lay in a park at the city's
edge, eight clay tennis courts next to meadows and
forests that filled with people on weekends. The
manager, Hans, a tall man neatly turned out in tennis
whites, met me at the clubhouse to show me around.

It was a two-room shack beside the courts with
green moss moldering on its sagging roof. The front
room, an office, had an old wooden desk, candy
counter, vending machine, pay telephone, and bulletin
board spattered with notices. The back room was a
snug little flat with a bed, dresser, shower stall,
and a half refrigerator that hummed intermittently.
Two small windows overlooked the park and were
supplemented by slivers of light through the openings
in the uneven cedar sideboards.

It reminded me of camp, but solitary. I wondered
about the girls who might turn up at the club for
tennis or come to the park on weekends to relax in
the grass. Hans showed me how to sweep, roll, and
water the courts and I told him I'd move in Monday.
We shook hands and I headed to Brad's.

"What's with the red dust, buddy?" Brad asked,
opening the door in his boxers.

"I was sweeping tennis courts. Can I shower?"

"You could if it worked."

I propped my feet on a milk crate and told him

about the club.

"Moving to town? That calls for a ho-down." He pulled out tumblers and a bottle of Wild Turkey. "Here's to sweeping courts and waiting on tables! No quibbling about work these days. Every *kroner* counts." He quaffed his glass in a gulp.

"Every *kroner*?" I asked, my eyes tearing from the whiskey.

"Greta's stopped work."

"What's she going to do?"

"You mean, what are we going to do. She's pregnant." He stiffened in his chair and poured another shot. "She wants a baby. I don't, but it's mine."

"And school?"

"The hell with the academic stuff. I'll settle down and raise a kid."

"Using what for money?"

"I'll figure out something. Greta will work until the baby comes and by then I'll be up to speed. I'd like to build a hotta in the woods."

"A *hytta?* Does your family know?"

Brad shifted in his chair. "That part I haven't figured out. My Dad will kill me."

The refrigerator rattled to a halt. "Damn, Brad," I said, softly.

"Yeah, I know." He stared at his whiskey. "I know what Dad will say. It won't be pretty. I'm even starting to believe it myself. The wedding's in August. Want to come? You'll be the Best Man." He filled his glass and held it high.

"I'll probably be the only man," I said, returning his salute.

I got back to Lier late that night, but night was hardly the right word. The sun set at 11:30 and rose an hour later. I began to miss the blackness, the star filled sky, the moonlight. I crept into the house as the clock chimed one, up the stairs past the creaky third step, and by Brigitta's door, which she'd kept open since our capsizing. She slept on her side, embracing a pillow. Afraid to be left alone during the day, we read books and did chores together. I packed my things and waited for sleep to come.

Kristin drove me to Bestum in the morning. I set up my flat, putting Kristin's *bringebaer* jam in my refrigerator, a newly baked bread on the table, and a Bakken comforter on my bed.

The courts had already been cleaned, so I decided to practice some strokes. It had been nearly a year since I'd picked up a racket. I began to hit against the backboard, switching from backhand to forehand and listening to the dull thud of the ball against the green plywood. After 20 minutes I was breathing hard, but had no ache in my chest or fatigue. When I finished, I drew the stubby bristle broom over the red clay and pressed out the bumps with a rusty iron roller that squeaked when I turned the corners. Gathering my laundry, I left to find a laundromat at the University in Blindern.

The center of the campus was a quadrangle of modern brick buildings with connecting paths that overlooked Oslo and thronged with students. The laundromat, deserted in the afternoon, was in the basement of the student center. After slipping two *kroner* into the washing machine, I scanned the bulletin boards, looking for information about films and theater, jazz and folk dances, roommates wanted and rooms to let, and then buried my head in the Tribune sports pages.

"Josh," someone yelled from across the room.

I jerked my head out of the stat lines and there was Tulla dumping her clothes on the sorting table. "What are you doing here?" She asked.

"I got a job in Oslo And you?"

"*My FATHER* decided I needed to finish my degree. What happened to you this winter? Lose your sweet tooth?"

"I had pneumonia." Her eyes were prettier than I'd remembered.

"You better now?"

"Now? Well, I'm better. Did you cut your hair or something?"

Her face brightened. "*Ja*, it always falls in my face. You like it?"

"Nice," I said. Her short hair revealed a beautifully slender neck. She looked prettier out of her cafe uniform.

"*Takk*," she said, and spilt her soap on the floor. "*Zut!* I don't have change to buy more."

"I have. You can repay me with pastry." I pulled my clothes from the dryer, hot and soft, and joined her at the folding table.

"I'm working at the *Bestum Idretts Foreling*."

"Nice. Can I have a tennis lesson?"

"Sure," I said. A pair of my underwear fell at her feet. She quietly retrieved them.

"*Takk*," I said, blushing.

"How about a movie?" she said. "You can leave your laundry in my room and we'll see what's playing in town."

We took the *trikken* to *Karl Joahnnesgate*, passing tourists disembarking from buses in the center. The choices were few - Julie Andrews and Christopher Plummer in *The Sound of Music*, Jack Lemmon and Tony Curtis in *The Great Race*, and Sean Connery in *Thunderball*.

"Jack Lemmon's a funny guy," Tulla said.

"How about James Bond?" I said. He was one of Paul's heroes. "Okay," she shrugged.

We entered a cold, dank theater full of rows of German tourists with cameras strapped to their sides. Tulla shivered, wrapped her arms around her shoulders and leaned against me. From the opening shot I fell into the story, from the Bahamas to the Alps, snacking on popcorn and coke. When the lights appeared, Tulla was asleep.

"Tulla," I nudged. " It's over. When did you doze off?"

"During a chase."

"Which chase?"

"A boat near an island with palm trees."

"That was the beginning." I reprised the movie country by country as we emerged from the theater. "You look tired," I said, "Want to go home?"

"*Ja*. Let's walk."

"To Blindern? It's kind of far."

"Too far for Mr. Bond?" she asked, slyly. "I like to walk after school."

"You have a lot homework work to finish?"

"It's not the work," she sighed. "It's being away from home."

She told me her mother had died two years before. Her parents, married 40 years, had worked in the cafe their whole lives. He'd lost his way without her so Tulla had to help out.

"I hope I didn't spoil things tonight," she said as we came to her dorm, "gabbing about sad things."

"Not at all."

"I liked John Bond," she added. Her fingers touched mine, just the tips, soft in the cold night air. I let them steal into my sweating palms. She leaned into my chest, her breath swelling with mine. My neck stiffened - I remembered I had to get my laundry out of her room.

We walked up two flights, paused at her door. "Come in," she said, turning on a light beside her bed. She sat down, gazed into my eyes. I looked at her, then glanced at my clothes.

"Oh", she said, her eyes blinking. "Your laundry?

I guess I owe you change, *ikke sant*?" She went to her desk, opened a drawer, and sighed. "Looks like I have to go to the bank."

"That's okay," I said. "Another time."

"Yes." She smiled. "Another time will be better."

I slung my bag over my shoulder and left, wondering what I would do when we went out again.

I walked back to the trolley briskly, trying to keep the cold at bay. Even in spring, winter was lurking. The sun had finally set by the time I got home. The pay phone was ringing like an alarm.

"*God dag*," I answered.

"You speak English?"

"*Ja*," I said, then realized it was Mother.

"I'm trying to reach Joshua Volken, V.O.L.K.E.N."

I paused. "I'll take a message," I said in Norwegian accented English.

"Thank you. I do appreciate it. Please tell Joshua that his Mother called and would like to speak to him. He never writes. I do hope you get all this down."

"Of course."

"My goodness, it must be late there."

"Quite late."

"I hope the weather's warming."

"*Ja*, for sure."

"It's funny, you sound young yourself. Are you a friend of his?"

"*Ja*."

"He's a wonderful boy."

"*Ja*, he is."

"His older brother lives nearby but I never see him. What is your name, if I may ask?"

"Erik."

"With a 'c' or a 'k'?"

"K."

"So Scandinavian. What does Josh do in Oslo?"

"Sweeps tennis courts."

"Oh."

"And he's well?"

"Very well. Very busy."

"He's always busy. It's so nice to chat. Kristin was kind enough to give me his number. How do you say good night in Norwegian. I'm a French speaker myself."

"Gud natt."

"Sounds like good night. So many cognates. Well, tell him to call." She hung up. I took a full breath.

CHAPTER 25

The days in May grew long and warmer. Pink and white magnolias burst in bunches, cherry blossoms hovered in midair on fine spun branches. When the colors faded at twilight, the smells of vibernum and lilac lingered in my room.

I often made my way to Tulla's after work. I'd sprawl on her couch, reading Sigrid Undset novels while she prepared for class. She'd lie on her bed, shifting from side to side, and then turn on her stomach, twirling her pen through her fingers like a majorette's baton. In the winter I thought she wasn't my type, but as the afternoons passed, I noticed that her breasts, though small, protruded nicely and her legs, a little thin below the knees, swelled attractively in the thighs. I began to wonder - could I get in bed with a girl I liked to be with?

One morning after I'd cleaned the courts, Brad stopped by on a Lambretta, very excited. He'd borrowed the scooter from Greta's brother and wanted to go for a ride. As we lurched into traffic I grabbed his waist, scared as we darted around the cars. When he cranked it into fourth gear on the open road with the traffic behind us we were humming. I settled back in my seat and enjoyed the wind in my face.

"Good deal, huh?" he yelled. "I can get to work in ten minutes. No more *trikken* for me."

We sped up Holmenkollen Mountain, banking through the curves as our boots scraped the ground. Houses disappeared and forests began. Soon Oslo spread below like a Lionel train set.

"Hey, that's a hell of a ski jump," Brad said, stopping at Frognerseteren, a massive slide 70 meters high that arched into the sky. "Must be cool to land in front of a thirty thousand people."

"If you like suicide," I said.

"Speaking of dire events, seems like my folks are coming to town. I got a letter from my sister."

"You're kidding! They picked a weird time. What if they arrive near the wedding? Does your sister know?"

"Not much. I figure Mom's put two and two together and is mending fences."

"Does she know how many fences?" I asked.

"Can't think that far ahead." He looked over the fjord that spread its fingers through the mountains and flung a stone into the trees.

Tulla came for a tennis lesson the following weekend. The courts were hot in the noonday sun.

"Keep your eye on the ball," I said. Her shorts were snug and her tank top revealed her lovely shoulders. She missed the first few balls I served, so I hopped over the net to give her some pointers.

"This is the forehand position," I said, placing her hand on the top of the grip so that it lay between her thumb and forefinger. "The backhand's a half turn to the right." Her hand was moist, her fingers slender.

I lobbed her a few more balls. She stroked them decisively, muttering "*zut!*" when the shots landed in the meadow.

"Hit the ball in front of your hips. That will keep your stroke level." I zipped a shot into a corner to demonstrate.

"*Det er fantastisk*! How do you do a game?"

"You start with a serve." I jumped back to her court. Placing my hand on her waist, I positioned her arm, willowy but strong, over her head. "Now arch your back, toss the ball above your shoulder, and swing."

The swing was perfect, she just didn't hit the ball.

"You have good *stengelse*," I said.

"You mean *fortengelse*," she giggled. "You said, 'I have a good body.' I think you meant form?"

The heat from the courts flared in my head.

"Let's do the game," she said.

I offered a slow serve and kept the ball in play with easy placements. She ran and hit with abandon. Sometimes her hits landed in the court, sometimes on the roof of the clubhouse. But she was determined and soon was hitting decent forehands and backhands. After an hour our shirts were soaked with sweat.

"I'm tired," she said. "Want to picnic?"

"I haven't much food."

"Whatever you have is fine."

We packed our rackets and balls in our gym bags. As soon as we entered my flat, I could smell her perspiration.

"What a neat place. These look familiar," she said, running her fingers over the Bond paperbacks I'd recently bought at the English bookstore in Oslo. "And a cute refrigerator, too." She squatted and opened the door. "So many cookies," she laughed. "Hey, you have some cheese. It's so cozy, let's eat here."

I opened a window to let in more air. "How about eating in the meadow?"

"Oh, okay," she said, dropping her bag on my bed

as we left. We picked up rye crisp, a small salami, and fruit in the market and spread out our lunch in the park.

"May is my favorite month," Tulla said, slicing thick chunks of salami with my Swiss Army knife. "Have you seen the lupines along the road in Lillehammer? A meter high. We always picnicked on Sundays when we went hiking."

"Has your family always lived in Lillehammer?"

"*Ja*, and for generations before. It's such an American question," she smiled. "Americans are always asking where you're from, as if you're never from where you are." She pulled out a plum. "Want a bite?"

"Sure." I bit into the taut smooth skin, which squirted a bright purple blotch on my shirt.

"Oops," she giggled, and tried to clean it with a napkin. "*Nei*, it's not working. Just take your shirt off."

I pulled it over my head and folded my arms over my chest to hide my hairless body. I was never a match for Paul's physique.

"Want suntan lotion?" she asked, humming as she worked. "You're looking a little pinkish."

Before I could say no, she'd squeezed a dollop on my back and started tracing something in the lotion. "Can you guess the letter I'm writing?"

"I don't know. An I?"

"*Nei*, silly. It's a T. Are you ticklish?"

I said no, but jumped when she added more letters.

"Can you guess the word?"

"Trail?"

"*Akkurat*. Want to go for a walk next weekend?"

There was nobody on the courts Sunday night after Tulla left, so I took the *trikken* to town. Its wooden benches and regular clacking reminded me of the nights when Paul and I escaped on the trolley to Fenway and filled up on food which we didn't have at home: hot dogs, popcorn, and crackerjacks. When I got to Oslo, I picked up a Bislett soccer schedule and walked to Brad's café.

A few tourists were dining in the sun, but inside it was dark and empty. Brad emerged from the kitchen bearing a tray of food.

"Nice place," I said, settling onto a stool at the bar and admiring the mahogany decor.

"If you like *fish cakes*. Personally, a burger would do me fine. Have a beer on me."

I took a drag on a cold Ringnes and told him about the upcoming soccer games. Brad hated soccer: watching the long buildup to scoring a goal wasn't his style. He'd preferred football in high school until he tore up his knee. I told him Paul had played linebacker despite weighing 160 pounds.

"He must have had guts. The fullbacks are moose."

"He was usually the last man between them and the goal. But he often played with a bum ankle when he was captain. I hated to see him tackle someone when he could barely run."

"Ankles are tough," Brad said with a grimace. "Did he play college ball?"

"Never made it that far. Too many problems with decisions, like whether to take a penalty or the down. He'd panic, couldn't decide, until a buddy who someone came over to make it with him."

I told Brad about Harvard and the Peace Corps, how Paul came home a wreck. "He even stole booze from my father's liquor cabinet. I discovered the empty bottles under his neatly folded Harvard T-shirt in his drawers when I went looking for a pair of socks."

"Damn," Brad gulped.

We talked until the manager signaled for help from the kitchen and Brad signed off.

"See you around, *amigo*," he said.

The sun disappeared behind the clouds, springing a cold wind across the fjord. I decided to clean up the court early Monday and took the 6:10 to Lier for a surprise visit. I walked from the Lier station down the valley road amid the scent of ripening fruit and turned onto the Bakken's driveway. Brigitta, working in the raspberry patch, darted across the field and dragged me over to Kristen.

"*Velkommen*, Josh," Kristin said. "We'll finish the weeding and then eat. How's work?"

"Not bad. Slow on the weekends."

"*Ja*, people go to their cabins in summer. Would you like to come to our *hytta* one weekend?"

I told her about Tulla and how I'd met her in a pastry shop in Lillehammer.

"Why don't you invite her?"

I thanked her, then wondered if we'd have to share a room? Norwegians were very open about letting you decide.

The pantry was stacked with cartons of berries, the stove bubbling with *saft*, an extract from raspberries that Kristen turned into juice and liqueur. Lars talked about fixing his broken tractor. He still spoke too fast in his Trondelag accent for me to understand much.

After dinner I curled into the couch with Brigitta to read *The Princess Who Was Afraid of the Dark*. When I finished, she asked me to read it again. With each page her eyes got heavier until she joined the princess in the darkened room. There was something peaceful about her head in my lap, I picked her up and carried her to her room.

Kristin offered to take me to the station and gave me bottles of *saft* and liqueur. As we rumbled up the rutted road onto the highway, she said. "You are *helhjertet,* Josh."

"*Helhjertet*?" I asked, puzzled by a new word.

"A warm heart. You're a good brother. *Forstar du*?"

A good brother, *ja*, I understood

"Are you starting to think about home?"

"*Nei*, not much." Returning was months away and I wasn't looking forward to it.

CHAPTER 26

I awoke early the next day and got on a bus to meet Tulla.

She was waiting at the Blindern *trikken* station wearing blue shorts, a cute yellow halter, and a daypack. The trolley glided past a warren of shops and apartments, ringing its bell to clear a path, until the incline steepened, houses thinned, and forests filled in. cold air greeted us at the top. She set off through the trees, moving quickly over the logs and rocks overgrown with lichen and moss. It was hard to get my bearings in the dense woods. I couldn't make up my mind about inviting Tulla to the *hytta*. I had visions of ending up in bed and not knowing what to do and not to do. I didn't even know if I wanted to do anything.

After an hour we emerged on a cliff, buffeted by gusty winds. "There it is," Tulla said, pointing down to a dark blue deserted pond barely 50 yards across. It sat in a col between cliffs, ringed by evergreens and low lying bushes. Breezes ruffled the water into mottled textures.

I followed her down the switchbacks to a ledge. Swallows veered over the pond at startling speeds while dark speckled fish stalked water striders darting over the surface. Tulla removed her boots and dipped her feet in the water.

"Cold?" I asked.

"*Nei,*" she replied. "It's nice."

The surface began to splatter from a passing cloudburst. I zipped up my parka, pulling the hood snugly over my head. But Tulla slipped out of her top and shorts and dived in. I startled at the sight of her tight little buttocks in miniscule red underwear as she disappeared in the water. Ripples spread across the pond which was dark and deep. Like Lake Quinnipiac at night, tempting but forbidden. She popped to the surface, her hair matted against her head, her eyes brown and luminous.

"*Kom,* Josh. The water is fine," she said, her pale legs and arms undulating in the water amidst the raindrops.

"Oh, sure," I said. I waited until she'd turned her head, then stripped to my boxers, folded my T-shirt in half, and balled my socks into my sneakers. I edged down the slimy ledge, clinging to mossy handholds, and dipped my foot in. It was freezing. As I inched deeper the water crept into my boxers and up my spine. A curious fish nibbled my kneecap and I lost my handhold, teetered in space, and fell in. The vice-like cold pressed the air out of my lungs and popped me to the surface. I churned toward Tulla, waiting for me a few feet away.

"You swim well," she said.

"I don't like hypothermia."

"It's not that cold," she said, then did a graceful somersault. "Can you do it?"

"Ah, ok." I tucked my head, rolled over, and came up butt first.

"*Nei,* Josh." She threw her arm across my shoulders. "We'll do it together," she giggled. We rolled over and came up with mouthfuls of water, entwined in each other's arms. "Let's swim to the point," she said, pointing to a spit dotted with boulders and fallen trees.

We lay down on a rock as the sun emerged from the clouds. Her panties clung to her bum, drying pink in the heat. Rivulets wandered down the sides of her bra-less breasts. I rested, waiting for the sun to warm me.

"A penny for your thoughts," she asked, rolling onto her side.

"I'm cloud spotting. The big one looks like a goat. See the horns and the snout?"

"*Nei*. It's a bird flying," she said, tracing the shape of the wings with her fingers. "But that one looks like a cow."

"Moooo," I bellowed.

"You silly," she laughed, her hand falling into mine.

"Josh, do you like me?"

"*Ja, sikkert*."

"I mean, as a friend, or more?"

"I like you a lot, but don't know how."

"*Jeg forstar*. I like you as a friend, and more." She let our hands lie together and dozed, surrendering to the warmth of the rock for the few minutes the sun decided to shine. I watched as she slept, her mouth open, her chest rising and falling, and felt a spark of desire. Surprised, I wanted to pull her body next to mine. But the rock was small with too many edges so I went back to spotting clouds.

We swam back to the ledge in the late afternoon. As I helped her out of the water, she stumbled into me. She pressed her lips onto mine. They were warm and tender, not like Sonia's kisses at our high school prom where her lips felt like a muscle. "You're so sweet," Tulla whispered.

"*Zut!*" she sighed, as a shadow fell over us. A shower began and within seconds, the pond's surface was shattered by raindrops. We gathered our things and huddled under her poncho.

"Beautiful the way rain falls, *ikke sant*?" she said.

"*Ja, vakkert.*"

"But I think our sun is gone for the day."

We walked back through the pitter patter of falling rain on the forest canopy. As the trolley descended the lights of Oslo began to glimmer. The storm intensified after I left her at the University and returned to Bestum. It pounded my roof and shook the rafters, keeping me restless through the night as I replayed the sight of Tulla's legs swaying in the water, wondering why I only wanted her when she was asleep.

The courts were muddy and spotted with puddles when Brad arrived in the morning.

"Shitty day," he grumbled. He flipped through *Aftenposeten* while munching on a Toblerone from the vending machine.

"You're reading newspapers?" I said.

"Nope. Looking for ads on suits." He told me his parents had cancelled their trip. A plane had crashed in the mountains and his Dad was bound to the base. "What were you up to yesterday?"

"Hiking."

"Who'd you go with?"

"A girl at the university."

"Really." He set the paper aside.

"I knew her in Lillehammer, Tulla."

"The cutie in the café? Where'd you go?"

"Into the hills."

"To?"

"A pond."

"And?"

"Swam."

"A man of few words. I hope she's nicer than Greta." He washed his chcolate bar down with a gulp of *Solo*, Norwegian soda.

"She's really on my case, hassling me about the wedding and what to wear. I don't even have a tie or a jacket and this newspaper is useless." He tossed it in the trash.

"You won't find ads in the news section. Let's go to Karlson's on Hausmannsgata. I've seen some snappy suits in their windows."

We set off through the park to the *trikken* station. He told me that Greta wanted to get married quick and at city hall. Being five months pregnant, she didn't want to make a fuss. He remembered that his Mom had once spoken about a church wedding with family and friends and their pastor, Alvin, doing the vows. "In a way, I wish they could be here. It wouldn't be great with Dad, but I don't really want a wedding with no one." He belted a stray soccer ball back onto the field.

"Where's the wedding?"

"At City Hall with a Justice of the Peace. Then a weekend in the mountains at a borrowed cabin and back to Oslo." He shrugged.

"Sounds great. You might have to do some cramming with Norwegian to get through the vows." I gave him a punch in the arm.

"How long you sticking around?" he asked.

"I'm working through July and then off to the mountains. If we're going to hike in the *Jotenheimen*, we'd better get there before the snow does."

"Yeah, we don't want another ski to nowhere scene," he chuckled.

The trolley arrived with a swish and clanging bells. We took a seat in the back.

"I like places in the middle of nowhere," Brad said, staring at the landscape blurring past our window. "Tulla kind of reminds me of my first girl."

Brad said he'd met her when he was a senior. She was a freshman and had a crush on him and invited him to a drive-in double bill. Afraid to ask his Dad for the car, he'd borrowed one from a friend.

"I didn't know much," he said, shaking his head, "but she sure helped me through it on the back seat. She liked me a whole lot and I never figured out why. Maybe it's harder to like someone when they're available. How about Tulla?"

"She was available."

"At the pond?"

"Yeah."

"And you?"

"Wasn't the right time."

"Because?"

"I don't know." I could hear the murmur of voices at the front, the doors open and shut, the trolley picking up speed.

"How about putting an arm around her, see what happens."

"I'm not good at seeing what happens."

"Maybe she's good at it. You don't have to know much."

"You were a senior when you did it?" I asked.

"Yup." He gazed at me for a few beats.

"Still working on it," I said, expecting a laugh.

"I figured that. Probably makes sense taking your time. I got going in high school and, well… "

"I thought everyone was doing it then."

"Everyone talks a good game."

The trolley jerked to a stop at Carlson's, a two story clothing store with rows of suits and sports jackets on the first floor and casual and dress shirts on the second. We tried a dozen combinations, all of which looked strange with Brad's plaid Bermuda shorts. He got flustered going up and down the stairs, trying to match a shirt with a jacket or a tie with a shirt. But my Filenes' excursions with Dad came in handy. After an hour I had sorted his wardrobe out. The tailor, talking a mix of Italian and Norwegian, promised to shorten the pants before the wedding the following week.

"Thanks, pardner," Brad said, as we left. "I was a goner without you."

CHAPTER 27

The sun blazed through my window in the morning, singeing the dew soddened chairs till they smoldered. I finished my morning routines early and left for Oslo on a new route. I'd long since abandoned street maps on my travels, preferring surprises. I'd stumbled on forts in parks, museums in the woods, tiny cafes in city cul de sacs, and mountain overlooks of a city that was mostly forest. Their way of life had bitten deep. I was content with one toothpaste, one airline, and one channel of television, which I hardly watched. The lack of choices had freed me, left me unencumbered by options that didn't matter.

This morning roaming led me to the eastern part of the city where I stopped by *Den Norske Turisteforening,* Norway's national hiking store. Crammed with maps, sleeping bags, and hiking paraphernalia, it fueled my intent to return to the mountains. I loved their topographic maps with their dotted trail lines wandering over passes and streams and ending at mountain huts where you could sleep and share a hot meal with other wayfarers.

Curious for details about the *Jotenheimen,* I approached a young woman with rugged good looks, as if she swam in the forty degree fjords for fun, who showed me the trail maps.

"*Liker du* cross country or peaks?" she asked, running her fingers through her cropped, dark hair.

"Mountains for sure," I said.

"Climb Galdhopiggen then. The views are great, if the weather's good. There's an easy ascent over a glacier from the south, but stay out of the middle of the glacier. It has many crevasses. Or join a guided group from Spiterstulen. Done much climbing?"

"Sure," I said, counting a few hills near Boston.

"Start at Gjendesheim, hike over the Besseggen Ridge to Gjendabu, then through the valleys to Spiterstulen and up Galdopiggen. Three days. Bring warm clothes and rain gear."

"How do I get there?"

"Two buses and a ferry," she said, consulting a book of timetables. "About two days, if you make the connections. It's pretty deserted up there."

I became a card carrying member on the spot, bought a sleeping sheet and compass, and left with a postcard of Galdhopiggen with its top in the clouds. As I stepped off the curb, a motor scooter nearly ran me over and gave me an idea for a travel option.

The sidewalk of the Lambretta dealer was littered with scooters in bright primary colors with price tags fluttering from their brake cables. They smelled of grease and oil and the shiny plastic that covered their leather seats. Gripping the handlebars, I climbed aboard one of their sleek 150 Series.

"Nice bike," an older man said, strolling out from the store. He had thinning gray hair and a pastel sports shirt with a Lambretta insignia on the pocket."

"*Ja*, for sure," I said. "What does it cost?"

"8400 *kroner*."

I shook my head. "Too much for me."

"You're not from Norway, *ikke sant*?"

"The U.S. - Boston."

His face lit up. It turned out he had a sister living in Brookline Village, the only Norwegian not living in Minnesota, he claimed. "Helga Svenson, teaches at BU. You know her?"

"I go to school in Ohio."

"She had a *wanderlust* for American life but I stayed at home. I'm Herman. You speak *Norsk* well." He shook my hand as if greeting an old friend. His hand was rough from working on engines I assumed. I told him about school and the *Bestum Idretts Forelling* and asked if he had a cheaper model. He led me into the repair shop out back. A light blue Lambretta with plenty of scrapes on its sides sat in a corner. Its seat was frayed, the tires bald, and the brake cable duck-taped to the handlebar.

"Not much to look at, but the engine's good," he said. "Only three years old. 1400 *kroner.*"

I'd never bought my own T shirts, let alone a $200 scooter.

He wheeled it into the street and jumpstarted the engine. "See what I mean?" He yelled. He steadied the bike and I climbed aboard. It sounded great.

"This is the throttle and that's the clutch. Ever drive one?"

"Sure," I said, figuring my ride with Brad would count for something.

"It's not a big deal," he said, stepping out of harm's way.

"Like riding a bike, just faster."

I eased up on the clutch and opened the throttle, excited by the roar of the engine between my legs. Exhaust smoke billowed around me like a moon launch.

"Don't forget the brakes are on the floorboard and the handlebar!" Herman hollered.

I jerked into first, rocketed down the sidewalk barely missing a street lamp, and bounced over the curb into the street. My foot was tap-dancing around floor, feeling for the brake. "Damn!" I muttered as the cobblestones rattled my teeth.

Since I couldn't figure out how to stop without stalling, I whizzed through the first stoplight and followed the road wherever it went. Cobblestones smoothed into macadam, homes on small plots morphed into farms. Surging forward at 100 kilometers an hour, my jacket billowed like a spinnaker. I leaned into the curves till I found the best angle that kept me moving without the wheels sliding out beneath me. I down-shifted, up-shifted, banked right and left. Herman was right: the scooter was a bicycle at heart.

The road turned north to Honefoss, bending through forests and straightening through farmlands where the odor of fresh manure hung heavy. I came over a ridge where clusters of villages spread below me bounded by the extensive waters of the Tyrifjord. My heart was beating so hard, I stopped to rest. Later, I glided down the mountain and ran out of fuel. A couple of students stopped and siphoned gas from their tank into my mine. I finally returned to Herman's in the late afternoon.

"I should charge you a rental," he said, as I pulled onto the sidewalk. "You like it? I figured you would. What did we say? 1200 *kroner*?"

"1400."

"1200's enough. Just sign the papers and give me a check.

He asked me if I was planning a trip and I said the *Jotenheimen*. He told me to stop by for a free tune-up before I left. On the way home, I dropped by Brad's. By then, I'd mastered stopping without stalling and pulled up on his curb.

"Shit man. You friggin bought it," he said, sliding his hand over the taped together seat.

"Got plenty of pop, 200 cc's. But the body's bunged up."

"Badge of honor. Neat little buggy for the mountains."

"About a day's ride, I figure. You coming along?"

"I plan to."

"It'll be a great trip before I go home."

"Home?" Brad said, under his breath. "Jeez, I kind of forgot. Doesn't it feel like a foreign country?"

"Yeah, for sure. But I kind of have to go, I mean, to school."

"That's what gets me. Go back to what? I can't fill in the blanks. You like the name, Lief?"

"Sounds like a guy in a saga."

"Greta wants to name him after an uncle. Last week it was Thor."

"You might think about a girl's name, for the hell of it."

"Christ, I have enough trouble with Lief. I got the graveyard shift tonight. Gad, they have terrible food. How can you always eat boiled potatoes and fish?"

I got back to Bestum later that night, parked the scooter outside my door and covered it with a tarp. The ride had only taken ten minutes on the deserted streets. When I entered my room, I found a note from Ida. Dad had gone to Paul's apartment after his rounds at midnight and nobody had answered the door. *What's happened to mine kinder*, she wrote.

When I was eight, I went to summer camp for the first time because Paul was a counselor there. He stayed close to me the first few weeks, but one day I realized I hadn't seen him in a while. The next day I saw Mom and Dad's green Oldsmobile parked outside the infirmary. At first, I was excited to see them, but then they emerged with Paul with their arms around his shoulders. He walked with a shuffle, like he'd just woken up. They slipped into the car

and after a short goodbye, left without a chance to
have ice cream cones in Hyannis. I waited for them
to return, but the hours passed and evening came. In
the morning I went to his tent. His clothes and
trunk were gone, his bed stripped down to a black
and white mattress. A few days later a post card
arrived from Mother – *Paul's off to prep school.
Enjoy the rest of the summer. See you in August* – it
was a pretty card with flowers on the front from the
Museum of Fine Arts.

CHAPTER 28

I stopped at Tulla's dorm in the morning and gave her a ride through the forests near the University. At first, she held onto the seat. But after the first curve, she wrapped her arms around my waist. My breathing tightened, but I steadied my eyes on the road and we leaned into the curves together. I routed us back through Vigeland Park with its shoulder high lupines and fountains sparkling in the sun. She said she loved the ride and I asked if she'd like to visit my family in Lier after classes.

The day had clouded over by the time we left. We stopped before the pass to put on sweaters and then descended into the valley. Kristin and Brigitta greeted us from the porch. "Goodness, what do we have here?" Kristen asked, wiping her hands on her apron.

"My wheels to the mountains," I said, introducing Tulla.

"*Mor*, can I go for a ride, please?" Brigitta asked.

Kristin agreed and invited Tulla in for coffee.

Brigitta and I lurched up the dirt road behind the barn to the cliffs. She clung closely as we bounced over the ruts, but her skinny body felt light as a feather on my back. We dangled our feet over the escarpment, watching the shadows slide over the land. I'd often recalled the view when I was sick in Lillehammer, a comforting sight because I'd known there was always a place for me to go. It wasn't the most striking view - Norway had plenty of those. But there was something peaceful about the way the farm plots fit together.

"We went up to the cliff in seconds, *Mor*," Brigitta said, running into the kitchen. "You should go!"

Kristin laughed. "I'm too old for that. Tulla and I've been having a good chat. Would you two like to join us at the *hytta*? We're leaving at 6:00 and returning tomorrow."

"I'll ride with Josh," Brigitta said.

"You'll ride with me," Kristin said.

"I'd love to go," Tulla said.

"Oh, sure," I said, trying to recall the size of the beds.

I packed the car while Kristen and Tulla gathered the food and helped Brigitta collect her things. Lars rarely took time off in the summer, using the daylight hours to finish repairing the barn and sheds for the winter. We drove north for two hours, arriving near sunset at a weathered cabin in the woods without another *hytta* in sight. Brigitta sprinted down the path with her new pole and tackle box. Tulla and I followed, emerging onto a swampy pond bordered by six foot eel grass, a haven compared to our last fishing trip.

"Josh, over here," Brigitta shouted from a rocky point where two trees had fallen into the water. I sat down to reconnoiter the fish, but she quickly snagged her line. I took off my sneakers, rolled up my pants, and waded in. The bottom was covered by rocks and ankle deep slime. I kept my balance by holding her line. But when I tugged on the hook, the line snapped and I fell in.

"Do it again," Brigitta laughed.

"Again?" I said, shivering in hip deep water. I splashed her with a dose of the pond.

"Nei," Brigitta yelled, scrambling into the grass.

Tulla draped her coat around my shoulders and we headed home. A fire was crackling in the hearth, the table set with bread and cheese.

"Josh had a nice swim," Brigitta smirked, as we entered the kitchen.

"You must be cold," Kristin said. "I'll get you some clothes."

She retrieved a pair of gray woolen trousers and a green flannel shirt from Lars' trunk and showed me to a bedroom. It had a small double bed with no space for a dresser or night table. Was there another bedroom for Tulla, I wondered? I watched the clock tick toward bedtime as I put on dry clothes and went to the kitchen.

"I haven't seen those clothes in years," Kristen said, adjusting my collar. "You look nice."

I flushed, buttoned my sleeves and squared the shirt on my shoulders.

We joined Tulla and Brigitta, playing cards by the fire. Kristin's eyes had softened. I'd rarely seen her take time for herself. I was used to her in motion, from pantry to kitchen, barn to field. From six in the morning till ten at night. Tonight, she cradled a cup of tea in a worn out chair, looking set for the evening. Her dark brown hair, flecked with grey, fell over her shoulders. In spite of the years of wear and tear, she was pretty.

"We used to come to the cabin on Sundays when we got married," she said. "Lars liked to get away, to have a day to fish by himself. I bought him that shirt for his twenty first birthday."

"When did you meet?" I asked.

"We were 18. I was studying in Drammen and met

him at a neighbor's. We finished *gymnast* and got married, just like that. For a while we came here a lot, but his father got sick and we had no help. Day by day the work got harder, until we barely had time to sleep. I began to wonder if we could have children. But one day I woke up and I was pregnant. I loved that shirt on Lars. But he only wore it here." She shook her head. "Here I am blabbing on. You must be hungry?" She started to rise.

"That's okay, Kristin," Tulla said. "I'll finish dinner."

"We only played three hands," cried Brigitta.

"Shuffle the cards while I make the eggs." Tulla left for the kitchen. She seemed right at home with the Bakkens. Kristen asked how we met and I told her about the bakery. She laughed. "Well, she's sweet, too."

We gathered at the table and bowed our heads, immersed in the smells of sizzling eggs and oven baked bread. The silence deepened into reflection which we didn't disturb, so different from the silence in Quinnipiac. After dinner Brigitta asked me to read her a book.

"Maybe Josh's tired," Kristin said.

"It's okay," I said, smearing my bread with jam. We settled on the couch and I read her *The Troll In the Sea*. I liked the foggy sound of her voice when she got tired.

"Okay, little one. Time for bed," Kristin said, escorting Brigitta to her room.

The logs had collapsed on the coals, pulsing heat into the room. Tulla rested her head on my shoulder and cradled my fingers in her palm. I'd wanted to hold more than her hand since the scooter ride. But now that she was close, those thoughts disappeared. We were jut two bodies in the dark.

I poked at the logs, re-balancing the pile. I felt her eyes looking my way.

"Josh?"

"Yuh?"

"I was thinking."

"Just a second." A log slipped from my fire iron and scattered the coals. "Damn! It's hot in here."

"Shall I open a window?"

"Nah, I'm okay."

"Want to turn in?"

"Yeah, I guess."

She doused the candles and we walked down the hall, pausing in front of her room. Her face looked beautiful in the flickering gas light, pale and shadowy. Her breath was warm and heavy, like her breath at the pond when she kissed me.

"*Er du trett?*" she asked, studying my face.

"Yeah, I'm tired," I blundered in English, the first English I'd spoken in months.

She closed her door and I entered my room and turned off my light. I could hear her moving through the thin, knotty pine wallboards. Opening her dresser, removing her clothes, and lying down on her bed. The light from her lamp spilled through the cracks in the wallboards, offering me fragments of a nightgown and flesh. She opened a book, turned through its pages. I wondered - what it would be like to lie together? Would the bed be too narrow ? She closed her book, leaned close to the wall, and whispered sweetly, "*Sov godt*, Josh." Sleep well.

CHAPTER 29

The morning of Brad's wedding, I dressed in trousers and a dress shirt from Karlson's, the first classy outfit I'd ever bought for myself, and went to his flat with a bouquet of flowers. Although I was the only person at Brad's wedding, I liked being the Best Man. He came to the door in boxers and dress shirt, a bowtie dangling from his fingers.

"Thank God you're here," he said, sticking the flowers in the sink. "Can you knot this sucker?"

I climbed on a chair, put my arms around his neck from the back, and tried to remember how to knot a bowtie.

"I was supposed to bring flowers and do the dinner reservations," he said. Perspiration trickled down his forehead. "Let's get a move on! She's acoming quick."

"I haven't done it in a while," I said. My fingers fumbled with the memory of Dad weaving the tie up and over, down and through, until it snagged in a knot.

"Jesus! What're you doing?"

"It's coming. Where're you going after the wedding?"

"Sjellig Hostel, if I can find the damn telephone number."

I tested the knot. It held. He hurried to shave

and find his pants. Reclaiming my flowers, I looked in the cupboard for a festive container. The doorbell ding-a-linged. Brad flew out of the bathroom, pleading silently that I answer the door while he searched for his shoes. I re-arranged the flowers in a milk bottle and ushered Greta in, dressed in a simple, white wedding gown that bulged in the center.

"What took you so long?" she said, looking pale and distracted.

"Just getting things ready," I said.

"Nice suit," Greta said, as Brad appeared from the kitchen.

"Karlson's," he said, holding himself erect like he was on parade duty. "Like the stripes?"

"*Ja*, nice," Greta said.

"Great!" I agreed. "This is my first wedding."

"Ours, too," Greta said, resting on the edge of the couch and breathing heavily. Brad looked pained, as if his shoes were too small for his feet.

"It'll work out," I said, presenting my flowers to Greta.

"Pretty, Josh. Lupine's my favorite." She planted a kiss on my forehead. "What time is it? We have to be there at 11:00."

"Egad!" Brad said. "Let's get a move on!" As he turned to leave, I pointed at his ring finger.

"Ah, give me a second, Greta." He hurried to the kitchen and returned with a look of relief.

We drove to the City Hall in an old yellow Volvo borrowed from a friend with a bumper tied on with piano wire. The *Radhus* was a large brick building facing the harbor. Entering a side door on the first floor, we emerged into a white, high ceiling chamber where rows of couples in suits and gowns sat on hard wooden benches awaiting their turn. A justice of the peace, stooped and graying, presided from an elevated dais. We took our place. The lazy rotation of ceiling fans propelled gentle breezes through the stifling room.

A clerk punctuated the tittering quiet with a roll call: Berkman, Sven and Tulason, Ingrid. Two people bolted to their feet and strode down the aisle with tight lipped smiles. There was a murmur of voices, rings were exchanged followed by an embrace, and Berkman, Sven and Tulason, Ingrid slipped out of the room, their eyes moist and hair awry. As new names were called, the benches emptied and re-filled, like the comings and goings at the Greyhound Bus station in Boston.

Brad fidgeted with his keys. The Brylcreem had smoothed his hair, but a tuft in back stood on end. Greta sat quietly on the bench, her skin milky in the morning light, adjusting her back for comfort and smoothing the pleats over the hump in her dress.

"Anderson, Brad, and Larson, Greta," the clerk announced. They shuffled to the dais, inches apart, her head barely reaching his shoulder. The Justice began the vows that allowed them to enter a new country. "Will you love and honor… be faithful through good and bad… until death parts you?" I realized that Brad didn't understand much of what he was agreeing to. Greta prompted him with *ja's*, one word he could speak and would now fully understand.

"Repeat after me," the Justice said. "With this ring, I thee wed,"

"With this wing I thee wed," Brad stumbled. The Justice repeated it slowly, but it took Brad a few tries to get it right. Greta held out her hand, trembling. Brad fumbled in his pocket for the ring and slipped it on her finger. She buried her head in his chest as the Justice pronounced them, *ektemann og kone*.

We left by the door that we entered, emerging onto a sidewalk where the married couples had gathered to celebrate. Dazed and relieved, they were surrounded by family and friends, snapping pictures and showering them with flowers. Greta kissed me with soft, rubbery lips that left a red smudge on my cheek. Brad threw his arms around me and held on for a longer time than I expected.

When all was said and done, they climbed into their car and lurched into traffic. I scattered handfuls of rice that clattered on their windshield like hail from heaven. It was the longest day of the year and they were off on their first married weekend.

I returned to Bestum to re-surface the courts and picked up Tulla to celebrate the solstice at Helgeseteren, a modest mountain south of the city. We hiked up from the parking lot through a forest until we reached the top where people had made bonfires three meters high. Plumes of smoke drifted into the sky from hilltops across the countryside.

They gathered in folk costumes from their homelands - Kristiansand, Bergen, Tronderlag, Lofoton, Narvik, Tromso, and Trondheim. Black knit vests, embroidered white shirts, hand knit sweaters with decorated cuffs, and caps with tassels like medieval jesters - costumes worn by their parents and grandparents from solstices past. Tulla had come in Gudbrandsdahlen garb capped with a lovely white scarf.

We gathered around a Hardanger fiddler in his 70's with stooped shoulders, weathered face, white shirt, and knickers. He began playing a lively jig. With four strings for melody and four below for overtones, it sounded like he was playing two fiddles at once. He played with his eyes closed, head cocked to one side, weaving different harmonies into the melody, a scratchy, lonely sound that carried across the tundra.

"This is simple," Tulla said excitedly, pulling me into the dancing circle. "It's a *springar* dance. I learned it in Lillehammer."

I followed her lead by watching her feet. Two steps forward, two back, skip to the right, skip to the left, spin together. She was light on her feet as we twirled, impossible to pull close or let go. So I held on, staring at her radiant face against a whirling background. Her eyes sparkled with a touch of blue and a smidgen of dark on her lashes.

I stumbled through the first few songs, stepping on toes and colliding with dancers. She laughed and pulled me along, her hand firmly around my waist. After a few songs I knew the steps and became part of the dance. Song followed song, the circle grew bigger, the bonfire brighter, spewing embers into the sky. It seemed like a dream to be drifting toward midnight under a full sun. I could see forever in the light and breathed it like oxygen.

"Only a few minutes to sunset," Tulla said, gazing at the horizon. Perspiration had darkened her armpits and matted her hair. "You followed well."

"You dance often?"

"In the summer, *ja*," she said, with a lovely lilt in her breath.

"Say that again?"

"Say what?"

"*Ja*. It sounded beautiful."

"You're so funny."

The crowd quieted to watch the sun dip below the horizon. The sky darkened into a purplish bruise and a line of grey clouds appeared over the hills. Summoned by the solstice magic, birds began to sing, marking the earth's summer pivot. No longer spinning toward light, we'd begun our journey toward winter. A sliver of moon emerged through the trees, delicately balanced with the sun, one orb rising as the other fell, their light mutually exclusive. And then the sky lightened; a glimmer of sun pierced the horizon banishing the low lying clouds. Our four-minute night was done.

"Shall we walk?" Tulla asked, pulling me away from the crowd.

"Sure," I said. A chill swept through my tired body.

"Let's go to the fjord. It's pretty by the sea."

We walked along a ridge that broadened into a meadow sloping to the water.

"Let's roll," she said, taking my hand.

We rolled together, sky and meadow revolving like a Ferris wheel, until we landed on top of each other at the bottom. She pulled me toward her and before I knew it, her lips were on mine, urgent and desiring, her tongue invading my mouth with flickering thrusts. I parried and stopped. It felt like I was kissing my sister.

"Josh?" she asked.

"*Ja?*"

"Something wrong?"

"You're a tease," I blurted.

"Tease?" she asked, her face deflating.

"I'm sorry. I mean, I don't know."

"Tease?" she repeated, trying to understand. She rolled into a ball while I twisted strands of grass into a knot.

"I wanted to make love," she said, quietly.

"Love?" I heard myself say, unsure she was talking to me.

"*Ja*. What were you thinking?"

"I was just, fooling around." My voice seemed far away.

"I wasn't." She looked at me, her face puffy with tears. "I guess I misunderstood."

I reached out to touch her.

"Don't," she said, like a rifle shot. "Maybe I should be getting home."

She tucked in her shirt and walked up the meadow without looking back. I tried to think of something to say, but my sadness was tinged with relief.

I hiked back to the hill top. The crowd had dispersed and the fire was a pile of ashes. I discovered her white scarf lying in a clump of flowers where we had rested between dances. I returned to the parking lot only to find I'd lost the ignition key. I started to walk, keeping the fjord on my left. After an hour, fatigue claimed me. I stumbled into a bed of ferns and slept.

When I arrived at Bestum. The courts were full, the club house jammed. Hans waved me brusquely into the office and closed the door.

"Where were you?" he asked so quietly I thought the room would explode.

"Celebrating, the solstice," I said, tucking my shirt into my pants.

"Till three in the afternoon?"

"It's three?"

He looked away in disgust. "You didn't remember *Sommerfest*? Our annual picnic?"

I blinked, recalling the flyer on the bulletin board. "*Nei.*"

"And you didn't remember to prepare the courts, clean the clubhouse, cut the grass, and pick up the food?"

"*Nei.*"

"Where did you sleep? In a gutter?"

"No, a meadow." I brushed the dust off my pants.

"So, what are we to do?" My seventh grade music teacher posed questions like that when we didn't sing to her beat.

I worked hard on the courts and kept the club clean while Hans pondered my fate. I tried to reach Tulla, but her phone rang without an answer. I was angry that she wouldn't pick up the phone. With Brad gone through the weekend, I read Bond and listened to soccer on the radio. Oslo had filled with so many tourists that it seemed like a city I didn't know.

CHAPTER 30

It took a while to patch things up with Hans and he made a point of looking over my shoulder. After Herman made me a new ignition key, I rode out to Lier on the weekend to help the Bakkens with the haymaking. There was a sweetness in the bloom of the valley in mid-July. Vines burgeoned with berries and grapes, orchards with pears and peaches. Acres of hay yellowed in the sun, awaiting the scythe. Even the smells of the animals and manure were welcoming.

We started in the morning to cut and rake the hay into piles three meters tall with the help of neighboring families. Then we pitchforked the piles into a wagon and hauled it into the barn. The pasture was the size of several soccer fields and by noon my muscles ached from lifting fifteen kilo loads. We gathered under an apple tree for lunch, sandwiches and *saft* made from the berries of last year's harvest.

I got back to Bestum at six, swept the courts, and tidied the office. But no matter how many piles I neatened, things seemed in disarray. I hopped on my scooter and headed north.

"Joshua!" Emma said, as she opened her door. "I wondered about you." She put up the water to boil and we went into the living room.

"I'm glad you stopped in. I was tired of painting

and getting stir crazy." She told me that Gunnar was in Oslo researching a book on Ibsen and would be away two months.

"A long time," I said.

"All he did here was work. Maybe living apart will tell us what we miss. How've you been?" She smiled and waited while I fidgeted with the tassels on her afghan.

"Tulla wanted to make love," I said, blushing.

"Who?"

"The girl I met at the cafe in Lillehammer." I told her about meeting Tulla in Oslo and the confusion in the meadow.

"Why did you stop, Josh?"

"I thought she was crazy to make love."

"Why wouldn't she want you?"

"But I didn't feel anything. I mean, I did in the dance, but then I didn't. Who'd want that? " My voice sounded like it was coming from another room.

"Tulla does. That's a good thing."

I thought she was siding with Tulla. "She won't even answer the phone," I said.

"She's hurt."

"But, we're only friends. Do you have to pick everything apart?"

"But that's what friends are supposed to do."

"What do you know? Gunnar's in Oslo." Her smile flickered and vanished. She got up and went to the kitchen.

I stared at the rug, listening to the kettle whistle. She turned off the stove, put the cups away, and went to her room. The house filled with sounds, a few birds making the rounds, a dog on the hill barking at the twilight. I curled up on the couch and watched the clouds disappear over the mountains.

Emma came over in her pajamas at sunrise and sat beside me.

"You heading home soon?"

"Yeah, a few weeks." I looked in her eyes, but all I saw was kindness.

"Sorry for last night," I said.

"I've heard worse."

She wished me a good trip and gave me a book of Rumi poems, for the moments when nothing makes sense, she said.

I left soon after. Not wanting to break the spell of the early light, I slipped the scooter into neutral and coasted silently downhill, past the ice rink and *Nansen Skolen* in summer hibernation and away from the lake. I ignited my engine when I hit the open road.

I got to Bestum mid-morning and discovered that Hans had watered the courts. He'd left a message that Brad had called. I drove to his apartment. The room was piled with boxes, neatly labeled and stacked to one side. He was moving in with Greta, he said.

"Already?"

"We did get married."

Hungry, I checked the refrigerator. A half bottle of Wild Turkey, two Danish with mold, and peanut butter. I sat down beside a mound of laundry. "Need a hand?"

"I'll do it at Greta's. I hope I don't mess up your hiking in the mountains, but I can't get away. Things got out of hand with the kid and the job. Greta says people often walk in the mountains alone."

"They're Norwegians."

"How about September after I settle in?"

"My boat leaves in August."

He looked at his overstuffed laundry bag and half packed boxes. "Sorry, pardner."

"Are you taking these along?" I asked, pointing at the cinder block couch and orange crate night table that were my bedroom furniture.

"Nope. Going to the dump. Greta's got real furniture. God, I need a picker upper," he said, retrieving the whiskey from the kitchen. "Drinking's not going to be the same without you. Nobody gets plastered on two beers like you. Well, my wife's acalling. How do you say wife?"

"*Kone,*" I said.

"Thanks, buddy." He stuffed a grubby pair of black socks into a bursting laundry bag and tossed me a roll of electrical tape. "Something for your memento bag. You never know when it'll come in handy."

When I returned to Bestum I found a barely legible letter from Paul on my bed.

"*Burning up no time now not enough time too much to say what's up too far away no money home where is home…*"

I called home and let it ring while I watched Hans roll the courts.

CHAPTER 31

Kristin invited me to dinner in mid-August and offered to take me to the boat. The vines were barren of fruit and the hay fields plowed over when I arrived. But the house was brightly lit and a roast pork was in the oven. I was surprised to see the table set with a holiday tablecloth and pewter candelabras. A celebration, Kristin explained. "You're homeward bound."

"Like Christmas," I said.

"*Not* Christmas, please," Kristin said. "No more sickness for you. Did Tulla reach you?"

"Tulla?"

"She tried you at Bestum. She didn't know you were leaving next week." She looked at a loss for words.

Kristen said grace and wished me a joyful reunion with my family. We talked as we ate. The fences needed mending, the tool shed a floor, the barn new siding. I savored the food, even the bitter *rips* berries that needed a heap of sugar. Brigitta slumped in her chair, toying with her potatoes. When dinner ended, Kristen brought me a gift and a cake, sparkling with candles. My present, a grey Bergen daypack, was a trademark of Norwegian hikers I'd longed to possess. I ran my hands over the coarse canvas and black iron frame that steadied it on your back no matter how heavy the load.

"Something to remember us by and bring you back," she smiled.

I dug into the dark chocolate cake, frosted with dense marzipan and layered with a tart raspberry filling. We ate in the silence that a good dessert deserved. As Kristin cleared the table, Brigitta slipped into the living room. I soon followed.

"Cat got your tongue?" I asked. I grabbed a few books from a shelf and sat beside her.

"*Nei*," she sighed.

"I heard a funny thing about fish. You know they swim around at night till they're sleepy?" I rested my head on the sofa and snored.

"Fish don't snore." She pushed the books aside.

"They keep me awake at home. Want to check it out at the pond?"

"Now?" Her eyes widened.

We stumbled down the path behind the tool shed until we reached a stream Gunnar had dammed into a pond, a dark hole of water under a gray sky.

"I don't hear anything," Brigitta whispered, running her hand
through the water. "*Zut!*" She grabbed my shirt and pointed to a swirling phosphorescence.

"Algae. They glow in the water. They're tiny."

"So pretty," she beamed, staring at the ghostly wake.

"I saw them in the ocean one night with my brother. We were swimming with millions of them."

"They live in a pond, too?"

"*Ja*. Some things you only see in the dark."

She twirled her fingers through the water. "Josh, will you come back?"

"*Ja*, soon, I hope. I'll write you letters about the things I'm doing."

Her hand crept into mine. "I like your stories."

I hadn't intended to stay the night, but after

tucking Brigitta into bed, I wanted to sleep under my eiderdown again. The night was still light by the end of August but, day by day, the sky was darkening.

I drove to the university the next morning. The campus was empty with only a smattering of students walking the paths. I stopped by Tulla's room. Her daypack hung in the closet next to the poncho that had sheltered us from the rain. Clothes were strewn over the bed and floor. I felt like an intruder, but I felt safer to be in her room without her. A student dropped by the doorway.

"Looking for Tulla?" she asked. "She's home for the break. She'll be back in a few days." She hoisted a pack on her back and left. I scribbled Tulla a note about wanting to see her before I sailed and left for Harold's.

He was working on the display floor when I deposited my Lambretta on his sidewalk. I told him the trip to the *Jotenheimen* was off.

"Too bad. A beautiful place, not that I know much about mountains." He pushed his papers aside. "Still need a tune up?"

"No, I'm leaving."

"You're bringing it back for good? I don't normally take them," he said, revving the engine. "But it still sounds good. How about 1,000 kroner? Where're you heading?"

"Home."

"I'll keep the bike in the back, just in case," he laughed, peeling off a roll of bills. "Here's my sister's number in Boston. You can practice Norwegian until you come back."

With a crowded trikken and many stops, it was a long trip to Bestum. I was stuck in my room with a bag of laundry and a trunk to pack. I left for the laundromat and put two kroner in the washer, determined to come home with clean clothes.

The night of my departure, packing was simple. I'd come with two bags and was returning with one. Nothing remained of my Quinnipiac clothing which I'd given to the Salvation Army. The alligator shirts, cashmere sweaters, and leather loafers had been replaced by hand knitted sweaters, flannel shirts, and hiking boots. I layered my keepsakes between the clothing: Brigitta's troll she'd made me in school, Brad's electrical tape for the unforeseen, unopened Bond books for lonely evenings, and the scarf Tulla had worn at the solstice.

The Bakkens arrived at noon. Brigitta and I sat in the back, her head on my shoulder. Kristin stared silently out the window.

"Excited to go home?" Lars asked, peering into the rear view mirror. He'd taken the day off, his first of the summer.

"*Ja,* excited."

"When does the boat sail?"

"Eighteen hundred hours."

"I like traveling by boat. Kristin, remember our trip to the North Cape?"

"*Ja,*" she said.

"Seven days through the fjords in the north. What a trip! Josh, would you like to go to a place like that? The sun never sets up there."

"I saw enough of the sun at the solstice."

"Hey, that's good," he chortled, slapping the wheel. "Seeing   too much of the sun. Now you really sound like a Norwegian. We like our winters, you know. Is it cold in Boston?"

"Ja, cold," I answered, as we passed city hall. A wedding party emerged, throwing bouquets and laughing.

"I'd like to go to America. Did you know I have cousins in Minnesota?"

"*Nei,* I didn't know," I said, uneasily. It was

the longest conversation I'd had with Lars all year.

"*Ja*, cousins on my father's side, Kjell, Sven, Ingrid, and Rolf. And lots of children, 17 if I remember. They left a long time ago to find land. And they found it, by golly. Land for hundreds of miles with soil a meter deep. Rich enough for hundreds of acres of wheat. You won't find that in Norway."

"Very true," I said. As we crested a ridge before descending to the quay, I glanced back at the hills surrounding Oslo, bathed in a midday sun that threw no shadows.

"We all have choices to make," he said. "Some of us have miles of farm land and others a few acres on which they were born, stuffed between a hill and a river."

Kristen placed her hand on his shoulder. It was a long time since I'd seen them touch.

"Am I talking too much, Kristen?" he asked.

"*Nei*," she replied. "I'm just not used to you talking," she smiled.

"Who has time to talk?" he said, shaking his head. "One day I'll come to America, Josh. When the work slows down. We'll visit my cousins and see you in Boston. Would you like that, Kristen?"

"*Ja*, it would be nice, but let's start with a trip to the *hytta*," she said, gently.

"How about you back there, Brigitta? You're still as a mouse."

"What?" she asked.

"Would you like to travel to America? See cousin Kjell and visit Josh?"

"*Ja, Father*," she said.

"Good," he said, "We'll come. It's settled." He tightened his hands on the wheel and turned onto the pier.

I'd never seen a ship as big as the Waterman, a corroding black hull eight hundred feet long, streaked with reddish trailings from rusted bolts and gunnels with bilge water pouring from its side like a wound. It was well known to students because of its cheap Atlantic fares. A red smokestack rose amidships from its gleaming white topside, emitting a thin stream of smoke. It looked ready to sail, certainly more ready than I.

"What a ship!" Lars said, awed at the mammoth hawser that tethered the ship. "A lot nicer than the ferry we took to the North Cape, don't you think, Kristin?"

"A fine ship," Kristin agreed.

"Maybe we'll sail to America on the Waterman," he said. He grabbed my trunk and hauled it to the gangway, Brigitta and I trailing behind.

"I wonder how many people it holds," he said, presenting the trunk to a porter. We lingered in silence as he examined my ticket as people embraced and boarded. Kristen waited with bowed head, her arm encircling Brigitta's shoulders, keeping her close. Lars studied the hull as if he were counting the rivets. A blast of the horn interrupted our inertia.

"Josh, we hope you come back," Kristin said. Tears had pooled behind her glasses which she hurriedly wiped on her arm.

"*Ja*, I will," I said, putting an arm around Brigitta. "Remember the algae, Brigitta."

Lars clamped my hand in an iron grip, bowed politely, and that was that.

I walked up a metallic gangway that swayed and rattled with every step. I didn't look back until I was inside the ship. The air in the dimly lit hallway was stale and smelled of mildew. I dumped my backpack in a windowless room with five double-decker beds and fled to the deck. A crowd had gathered by the rail, waving and snapping pictures. I wormed my way to the front and spotted the Bakkens, barely discernible, in the densely packed crowd.

The ship gave a blast of the horn and dropped its hawsers. A slip of black water opened between us. I gripped the railing, tense and rigid. It didn't feel like we were moving, but the gap in the water was growing. Kristin waved and the crowd began to dissolve into blots of color as the icy currents pulled us backwards. We paused in the middle of the harbor. Then bells clanged, the ship shuddered and vented a blast of white steam. We churned into the fjord, leaving an empty pier littered with confetti.

We meandered south, passing Helgeseteren where I'd spent the longest day of the year. After a few hours the fjord widened and as we greeted the ocean and gradually turned west, a chilling breeze ruffled my hair. Clouds had gathered on the western horizon, promising an early sunset. There was no sense of momentum, only the lazy roll of the ship in the swell. I stood on the stern, watching the continent disappear in the dwindling light until darkness descended and the last views of the mountains had vanished.

CHAPTER 32

I spent the first eight days reading on deck and fending off nausea when the sea grew rough, I went to the bow watching the hull split oncoming waves. Towards evening of the ninth day, a fog descended and the swell subsided and the boat slowed to a painful crawl sounding its horn in staccato bursts. In the morning, we entered New York Harbor. Two stubby Moran tugboats met us in the Hudson, prodding us through the currents into a slip of water floating with garbage. The closer we drew to the pier, the more the river churned around us releasing an odor of decay. Amid the clinging of bells we shuddered to a halt.

I spotted Mother and Dad on the pier by the gangway, Dad was smaller than I'd remembered, his face pale and creased with age. Mother looked dressed for a *bon voyage* party, a light gray dress topped with a flowery cravat. I maneuvered through the crowd, approaching them from behind.

"*Quelle surprise!*" Mother squealed. "My goodness, what's on your back?"

"A backpack."

"What on earth for? You're not going hiking in Quinnipiac, are you?"

"You never know when a pack comes in handy," I said.

Twelfth Avenue throbbed with tension. Heavy traffic
thundered
   overhead on the elevated highway. Cars, jammed at
the pier, blared their horns. Garbage trucks roamed
the streets, swallowing refuse with a piercing
hydraulic whine.

"You'll strain your back, Jacob," Mother said, as
Dad bent over to help me lift my trunk into the car.

"My back's fine, Mira."

"You should have parked in the garage. We'll be
here for hours."

"I parked to get the bags."

I got in the back with my pack. Dad turned on the
radio, listening to bits of disc jockeys, music, and
commercials while we waited for the traffic to
clear.

"How was the voyage?" Mother asked, adjusting her
cravat.

"Boring. Ten days of nothing."

"No shipboard activities?"

"Eating and sleeping. It wasn't the Cunard line."

"What are you doing, Jacob?" Mother asked, as he
jerked onto 54th Street and headed cross-town.

"I'm going to the Stage."

"The traffic's terrible."

"I'm hungry. How about you, Josh?" He looked at
me in the rear view mirror.

"Sounds good," I said.

"I planned for dinner at home," Mother said.

"That's four hours away, Mira." Dad came to a
halt behind a garbage truck.

"57th is wider," Mother said.

"The Stage is at 54th. This will clear out soon,
he said gazing at the tenements. The traffic leaned
on their horns and a garbage man replied with a
finger.

"Good Lord, Jacob! They have delis in Boston. We don't have to go to Stage every time," Mother said.

"Boston delis are not the same, Mira."

"Just because your father…"

"My father has nothing to do with it."

"Your family has everything to do with it."

"Mira! I'm hungry. I like the Stage." He punched the radio button off. Mother adjusted her hat.

"They always come first," she said, quietly.

"Will you shut up?!" His hands had turned white on the wheel. Mother sat without moving a muscle.

"A fine thing for Joshua's homecoming." She pulled out a tiny, white, handkerchief scented with Channel #5. Her hands were trembling. as she dabbed her eyes, careful not to smudge her mascara. I pulled a Bond book out of my pack. There always was something that tripped us up on the road. Wrong directions, finding a clean bathroom in a gas station, choosing a restaurant when we got hungry.

Dad pulled onto Seventh Avenue and double parked by the Stage. Leaning in my window, he asked. "What do you want?"

I started to say a Hymie triple decker out of habit, but the thought of pastrami and tongue nauseated me after a year of fish and cheese. Dad hung in the window, jangling his keys.

"What are you having?" I asked.

"A Bertie triple decker."

"How about turkey on rye, no cole slaw."

"You're not hungry? How about you, Mira?"

"A cup of soup, chicken soup, Jacob," she said in almost a whisper.

He left us on Seventh Avenue with our lights flashing and cars whizzing by.

"Now we're set," he said, returning fifteen minutes later with a bag of food stained with grease. He bit off half a pickle. I could smell the garlic in the back. He settled himself with his

Bertie and headed north on Broadway. "Want your soup, Mira?" he asked.

"No, thank you." She slipped her handkerchief up a sleeve. "Have you heard from Paul, Joshua?" she asked, taking advantage of the lull.

"Ah, not for a while." My stomach knotted. I put my sandwich aside.

"He's been incommunicado with us, too," she said. "Father stopped by his apartment a while ago."

I looked at Dad, but he kept his eyes on the road.

"Tell him what you found, Father."

"Mira, he just came home."

"What did you find, Dad?"

"Nothing." He looked at me in the mirror. The color had drained from his face.

"Tell him the whole story, Father. He's home now."

"I couldn't get in his apartment. The super said he hadn't seen him for months."

"He hasn't been at school, hasn't been anywhere we know," Mother said. "He's disappeared."

"You didn't get a card from Guatemala?" I asked.

"Guatemala? I thought Manny said he saw him in Boston, Father."

"We don't know who Manny saw," Dad said. "You know Manny after a *schnapps*. It could have been anyone."

"We think it was Paul," Mother added.

"Oh," I said, confused. As we passed the GW Bridge, I turned to catch a glimpse of the Waterman. The pier obscured the ship, except for a thin plume of smoke that rose from its funnel into the empty sky.

"Your soup will get cold, Mira."

"I'm not hungry. Could we stop for a minute?" she asked.

"Sure, Love," he said. I hadn't heard Love from

Dad in a while. He pulled into a gas station and Mother went to the ladies room.

"You gotta go?" Dad asked, looking in the mirror.

"No, I'm fine."

He tapped on the wheel while he pried rye seeds out of his teeth. "How's the turkey?"

"Good."

"What do they eat in Norway?"

"A lot of fish." He'd lost more hair and his *yarmulke* didn't cover all of his bald spot.

"Had a good year?"

"A really good year."

"Good to hear. You gained weight."

"Too many potatoes. How's Ida?"

"Same aches and pains." He pulled on his fingers until they cracked. When I was young, I thought he was making them longer. "When do you go back to school?"

"Four weeks. Dad, what did Manny see?"

"Manny's *forslugenah*."

"But what did he think he saw?"

"A drunk that looked like Paul. He was hurrying home in the North End. By the time he turned around, he was lost in the crowd. So, he doesn't know what he saw. You got cards from Guatemala?"

"I thought I did, but now I don't know."

"Nobody knows a damn thing."

The whites of his eyes were streaked with red. I wanted to put an arm across his shoulders, but I was sitting in the back.

Mother returned. She opened her soup. It must have been cold but she drank it. I kept my eyes on the dotted white lines darting under the car, clickety clack every few seconds, as we continued north on the concrete highway.

CHAPTER 33

We arrived in Quinnipiac in the late afternoon. Clouds had thickened, threatening rain. The possibility that Paul had written from Boston was more upsetting than the letters. I dragged my trunk into my bedroom, musty from a year of closed windows. It felt like a kid's room - bed too small, lamp too dim, and curtains imprinted with barnyard animals. I didn't want to unpack. I wandered into Paul's room and flicked on his wooden table lamp which he'd made in junior high shop. On the wall were his high school football pictures. He stood between the goal posts in a bright red and blue uniform, holding his helmet by his side and looking proud. I sat on his bed and re-read his letters to Norway, searching for clues.

Mother began making dinner while Dad listened to his messages. I took the sports section and went to the kitchen.

"I can't skip a meal like you boys," Mother said, stuffing garlic into a roast. "It's good to see you, Joshua. You haven't changed a bit!"

"Save the roast for Sunday, Mira," Dad said, as he stopped in to down a *schnapps*. "I have to go to the hospital." He handed me five twenties and left the kitchen. I wondered which nurse he might be seeing after his patients.

Still full from my deli sandwich, I threw a poncho in my pack and drove to the North End. I missed the wind in my face, the agility of my scooter on the road. Although a Thursday night, Hanover Street was busy. I walked by the overflowing bars and streetside cafes, where Paul used to hang out, staring at hundreds of faces. I started home on Commonwealth Avenue but swerved into Kinross. It was ten, but Ida's lights were on. I jabbed her buzzer.

"Hello, who goes?"

"Me, Joshua."

"*Oih vase mere*," she said. "You back!"

She was waiting on the stairwell wrapped in a bathrobe and wearing a hairnet.

"Hi, Ma." I waved, taking the steps two at a time.

"Shush," she answered. "People sleep." She grasped me close. It was hard to breathe.

"You smell like a brisket," I said. "Yah, brisket. Hungry?"

"I'll take what you got."

She pinched my cheek. "You always eat what I got. Good thing. Too much in icebox."

I sat down in the kitchen. She deposited cole slaw, herring, borsht, and beets on the table and pulled up a chair. "So when you come back?"

"Today. How come you're up?" I asked.

"Who sleeps?" She drummed her fingers on the table. "Maybe I talk to Abe too much. He asks, how was you day? You taking care? So we talk. Sometimes I sleep, sometimes *nyet*." She checked on the brisket in the oven and set my place with her Sunday china. "You want drink?"

"Sure, Ma."

"Dr. Brown?" she asked, knowing the answer. "The only doctor I like, except for your father." Probably because he let her eat ice cream and ignore her cholesterol.

I took a sip of a cream soda, savoring the vanilla. "Ma, do you know if Manny saw Paul?"

"He knows nothing, I know nothing, Jacob knows, who knows what? I too old to look. Where is he, *Schmen*?"

"I don't know, Ma. Don't worry."

"Worry? All my children I worry." She rubbed her swollen knuckles. "You, Paul, Jacob, Dorothy, Manny, Natasha, Bess. And their *kinder,* I worry."

"I know, Ma."

"Manny said he saw a ghost. I ask, ghost? Manny said, he wandered here and there and then Paul is gone. Pauly mine first *leipshen!* I hold him when he born and when I hold him, *tsores, pogroms,* Odessa, money, go away. You *forstain*?"

"I see." A charred odor began to fill the room.

"*Oih vase mere,*" Ida yelled, snatching a blackened hunk from the oven.

"I'm not that hungry, Ma."

"*Oih, oih, oih,*" she lamented, picking over the burnt meat as if it was her pet. "What to do? You want *kreplah*? *Homentashen*? *Kugel*?"

"Ma, I'm fine."

She put the brisket on the counter and slumped in her chair.

"It's late, Ma," I said.

"Ya, maybe I sleep, too," she said, untying her apron. "Maybe Abe give me peace."

I passed her bedroom as I left. Her sheets and blankets were strewn around the bed. Abe had died in his sleep, passing quietly in the night without a warning, without a complaint. She still slept on one side of the bed.

"I hope you sleep," I said.

"I will now, *leipshen*. You are home."

I walked into the night. Hot and humid, the last of Indian Summer. Trees sighed in the breezes. Boston was quiet, six hundred thousand people without a soul on the street.

    I slipped past Mother's closed door and opened the Rumi book from Emma. I fell asleep as I began to read, *Welcome all strangers in your house.*

CHAPTER 34

I left For Paul's apartment the next morning. It was four blocks from Central Square on a run down street of tenements, bodegas, and laundromats - 37 Pleasant Street. He'd moved there from Brookline after returning to school. I left before Mother awoke and parked in front of his building, its small front yard overgrown with weeds. Walking into a foyer, I found six, nameless call buttons under the mailboxes. One said, Super. I rang it and was buzzed in.

I shoved my way into a dimly lit hall and knocked on the Super's door. A security porthole stared back. Above it was a name, Ramirez. A short man with a T-shirt and gold neck chain cracked open the door.

"What do you want?"

"I'm looking for Paul Volken."

"He ain't here."

"I'm his brother." A dog whined behind the door. Ramirez unhooked the chain and a large black lab jumped up on my chest, licking my fingers.

"Jenny," yelled Ramirez. "Bad dog." He scowled and pointed to the corner. "That's your brother's dog," he said, yanking her away.

"You mean, Molly?"

"Molly? No wonder she don't mind."

"Nice of you to care for her."

"I have to. She barks all the time in your brother's place, drives everyone crazy. Be nice if he showed up."

"How long's he been gone?"

He screwed up his eyes to the ceiling. "Don't know. A while. If he don't come back soon, she's going to the pound."

"Can I see his apartment?"

"Not much to see."

He bolted two locks on his door and led me upstairs on worn linoleum risers that creaked with every step. The moment he opened the door to Paul's apartment, I was stifled by the smell of chloroform. Dry dog shit lay on the floor on yellowed, curling newspaper. A single light bulb dangled over a bare table in the kitchen.

"Jesus!" Ramirez said, throwing open a window. "People've been complaining about this place. I'm going to toss him if he don't show." I could hear Molly's howl from the floor below.

"You have something to clean up with?" I asked.

"Maybe," he answered and left.

I walked into the bedroom. The shades were drawn and the room was dark. A stripped down mattress lay on the floor next to a foam cushion covered with dog hair. On the dresser was a toiletry bag from Filenes with nothing in it. I snapped open the shades, but the room look emptier in the light.

"Rent's up," Ramirez said, returning with a spatula and paper towels. He dropped them on the floor.

"I'll talk with my Dad," I said. I scraped up the dog turds and threw out the soured milk and moldy cheese from the fridge. The trash was already full of vodka and gin bottles. I tossed two bags of trash into the dumpster and sat down on the front stoop. It was hard to think in the clinging humidity. I decided to walk over to Harvard Yard.

I stopped on the steps of Widener Library. Students were playing touch football in bare feet on the yellowing grass. Bodies collided: a spiraling football spun through the air into the fingers of a player running across the lawn.

I walked into Wigglesworth, his last dorm, and wandered down the hallway, eyeing the vacant beds, empty bookcases, and stained pizza cartons from the semester break. Distant guitar strumming mingled with the traffic from the Square. I remembered Paul doing one-handed pushups, stripped to his boxers, gasping for breath. I returned to the yard and saw one of Paul's friends biking across the grass. I hollered and he stopped.

"Stanley, I'm Paul's brother. We met in the Rusty Scupper in the Fall," I said.

"Ah, yes. The one beer brother."

"Yup. Have you seen him?"

"Not for a while, now that you mention it. Hope he didn't go off the deep end."

"What do you mean?"

"It wasn't smooth sailing for him," he said, running his fingers through his stringy blond hair. "He studied a lot but only pulled C's. I couldn't figure out what he was doing at Harvard." He slumped against the ivy encrusted wall. "Weren't you trekking in Lapland somewhere?"

"Norway."

"Oh, yes! Did you partake of the region's free love?"

"Sure. Lots. When did you see him?"

"Let's see. Sometime last spring in the Yard, but I did trip over him later in a few watering holes. No offense, but he spent more time with a bottle than a book." He swung his leg over his bike and pedaled away.

I left for Boston and searched through the narrow, twisting streets, checking out the dim interiors of waterfront bars, finally ending at the Rusty Scupper in the late afternoon. The place was empty and reeked of cigarettes. A broad shouldered bartender, more linebacker than server, swabbed shot glasses behind a mahogany bar polyurethaned into glass.

"You don't look like your brother," he said, when I introduced myself.

I shrugged. "That's what everyone says."

He set the glasses in the drain, watching me carefully. "He's been around. Hung out with Tammy, sort of. Smart fella. Harvard, right?"

I nodded. "You're Phil?"

"Yeah, how did you know?"

"We met last fall."

"I meet a lot of people. I gave him his drinks, that's all. But Tammy didn't give him the time of day. Want a Bud?"

"Sure." I said, reaching for my wallet.

"It's on me. You his kid brother? I have a brother like him. Problems with broads. Landed in jail for assault and battery. I didn't expect to see Paul after Tammy quit a couple of months ago. It was ugly at the end. She chewed him out real bad. Had a nasty temper. You know her?"

"I met her once."

"I feel bad for your brother. So many broads. Why did he pick her? Take what you can get and leave the others alone. Know what I mean?"

"Sure. If you see him, tell him I'm home."

I went and sat on a bench by the harbor and watched planes soar into the sky. I began to think about checking with the police.

CHAPTER 35

I parked my car on New Sudbury Street in Boston the next day and entered the First Precinct. Ivy grew up the worn cast iron façade and hung over the arches of the ten foot gothic windows. The mint green walls with flaking paint and gun metal furniture reminded me of the hospital in Washington. I walked up to an officer with a shock of white hair and rumpled blue shirt sitting at the reception desk and told him I was looking for someone who was missing.

"And who might that be?" he asked, looking up from his sports pages.

"My brother."

"Does he have a name?" He pulled a file from a drawer.

"Volken, Paul Volken."

"How do you spell it?"

"V-O-L-K-E-N." I began to wish my father could have joined me. He had no patience for people full of themselves.

"Don't have him on file. When did he disappear?"

"I don't know. Months ago."

"Did you just notice?" He shook his head. "File a report." He slid a form across the desk. "Most people turn up, if they want to." I retired to a desk and filled in the blanks. Paul Volken, Oak Knoll Road's End, Quinnipiac, five feet eight inches, 160 pounds, blue eyes, last seen in Brighton. The officer studied the report while he tapped his pen on the blotter.

"From Quinnipiac, huh? Home of the Champions. Isn't that what they say?"

"It's our football motto."

"Governor Dummer Prep School, Harvard, Peace Corps. Smart guy. What happened? Shacked up with a broad probably."

"I doubt it." I stared at the black and white mug shots on wanted posters and realized a picture would be a good idea.

"Well, I don't know what to tell you. There's a cop who handles this stuff but his file is full. Worse than the dogcatcher. I'll pass it along." He slid the form into a pile.

"When will you call?"

"Us call? I don't think so. You call us. Maybe he's short on dough and staying at the Governors Inn. You know the place on Pine Street?"

I thought a hotel was a possibility if he wasn't living in Central Square. We'd had fun at hotels in New York when we'd visited Dad's cousins. We'd watch the traffic on Seventh Avenue from forty stories high, run through the Metropolitan Museum to see who could get through the galleries first, slip nickels and dimes into the Automat's slots for our favorite desserts. I sat on the steps outside the police station and then decided to have a donut at the Metro Diner.

A young waitress with lots of freckles and auburn hair tucked under her cap came over and leaned on the counter, pencil and pad ready. After admiring the donuts under a glass globe, I ordered one with a thick layer of chocolate and a cup of coffee.

"Chocolate's my favorite, too," she said. "I always hide one for later. The boss's kind of strict." She looked over her shoulder. "I'll make you a fresh pot of coffee."

I spun around on my stool, inhaling the smell of percolating coffee. Dad liked to make a full pot on the weekends so there was plenty for both of us. He wasn't a cook, wasn't even comfortable in the kitchen. But he made great coffee, deli sandwiches, and sundaes. "You got no *Baaston* accent," she said, with a Midwestern twang. She gave me the coffee and I added two sugars and a lot of cream. "Where're you from?" she asked.

"Oslo," I said.

"Oslo?" She leaned on the counter. "In western Mass?"

"No, Norway."

"You speak good English. You don't look the Nordic type."

"Not all Norwegians are blond."

"Yeah, I suppose so. Sonja Henie? Remember her? She was special. Wish I could skate like that. I'd fall on my butt, pardon my French. So what brings you here?"

"Looking for someone I haven't seen in a while."

"Isn't that nice. Staying long?"

"I hope not."

"Don't like the weather? I tell my family, the weather is bad here. Muggy in the summer, little snow in the winter, at least compared to Montana. But three years later here I am. Maybe I'll get back. I miss the mountains, but I like the ocean. How about you?"

"Do I have to chose?"

Her full throated laugh made me smile. "Yup. Like Jeopardy. Ever seen it?

"Never heard of it."

"Of course. Just a dumb quiz show. Do much sightseeing in Norway? I bet it's pretty."

"*Ja*, it's beautiful."

"It must be great to live in a place like that. I grew up three hours from the mountains. Every summer we'd make the drive, Dad's two week vacation. He'd bring his rod and settle down in a stream for the day. At dinner he'd bring home a load of trout, bass, pike, whatever was running, and fry it on the fire. But here I am blabbing your ear off." She straightened up. Her body filled out her uniform nicely. I ordered another donut.

"Say something in Norwegian, like how are you?"

"*Hvordan star det til*?"

"Neat. Say your name."

"*Jeg heter Lief Bakken.*"

"Lief? Like the guy who sailed around the world? I like that. Very positive."

"*Ja*," I said, with a slight intake of breath.

"How long you here?" Her eyes fixed on mine.

"A few weeks. Maybe longer."

"Well, if you're down this way again, stop in." She handed me my bill. Her hand was warm, slightly sweaty, and loitered in my palm. "Hope you find who you're looking for," she said.

I drove to the Governors Inn, a dark brick four story building on a dead end street across from a shoe factory in South Boston. It didn't have a doorman or waiting cabs, just a plain front door that opened into a poorly lit lobby with two worn-out sofas. I walked up to the desk clerk, a man in his fifties with sideburns and tattoos on his arms, and asked if Paul was staying there.

"He don't ring a bell," he said. "They come and go. What's he look like?"

"My height, a little heavier, light skin, short reddish brown hair."

"Clean cut, huh? Not our type."

I looked around the empty lobby. "Where is everybody?"

"People can't stay here during the day. They're out at nine and back at six. We're a shelter."

I heard myself say, 'Oh', though it was barely audible, and steadied myself on the desk.

"You okay? Most families don't know about this place. Want to look around?"

I entered a high ceiling dormitory with peeling paint, hissing radiators, and the pervasive odor of urine and Lysol. Bunk beds were stacked to the ceiling next to boarded up windows. I moved down the aisles, staring at tattered blankets, natty rucksacks, and clothing strewn on the floor. Under a bed I spotted a maroon sweatshirt with a monogrammed H on the front, big enough to be Paul's but too dirty to examine. No other signs confirmed or denied that he lived there and I left.

"Try tomorrow, son," the clerk said. "He could have been here. Where are you from?" He set his ledger aside.

"Quinnipiac."

"No kidding. I'm from Norton. We played you in football."

"My brother was a linebacker."

"Is that who you're looking for?" He let out a low whistle. "When did he play?"

"'58."

"Son of a gun. After my time," he said, patting his girth. "You can check out the shelter in the North End or look in the Common. They hang out there during the day."

I left for Beacon Hill and the Public Garden. A few older Brahmins sat on the benches, feeding the pigeons next to the duck pond. As I passed down the walkways under ageless trees, the sun played on my face. Men in overcoats and briefcases hurried by the vagrants. One had a torn jacket and sipped something from a Brigham's paper bag. Another, wrapped in a blanket, slept under a tree while his companion, a

251

woman or man I couldn't tell which, went through the garbage. All smelled bad, even from a distance, and none of them looked like Paul.

After searching for several hours, I walked to the Charles. It made little sound, despite how much water was flowing by. Except for places where it snagged on rocks under the surface, the water was tranquil. A breeze brushed my face, warm and humid, carrying its muddy smells. I lay down to rest under a weeping willow, its soft branches dangling into the river.

CHAPTER 36

I returned to the parks and bars for another week, but there were so many places to search in the North End, Sculley Square, the South End, and the Waterfront. Like Manny, I wasn't sure after a week who I'd seen. I began to worry about cold weather. Already, leaves were starting to turn.

My stomach was growling when I got home Wednesday night. Mother had left a note about meeting at her sister's, Hilda, for dinner. But I was too tired to drive to Newton and looked in the fridge. I'd unwrapped the leftover asparagus and stuffed chicken when the phone rang.

"Mr. Kaufman?" her voice was tense.

"You mean Dr. Kaufman?" I asked.

"Yeah, the doctor. Is he there?"

"He's not home. Call his office, 653 8382."

"Shit!" She was breathing hard.

"I'll take a message. He'll call you back."

"That won't work. Who am I speaking to?"

"His son."

"Josh? Oh, God. He talked about you." She began to sob.

"Who's this?"

"Tammy."

My breathing stopped. I could hear traffic in the background.

"I can't leave him here," she said.

"Who?"

"Paul. Phil said you were looking for him."

"Where is he?"

"On the street."

"Is he all right?"

"No."

"Where are you?"

"A phone at Hanover and Tileston. The North End."

"Don't leave. I'm coming."

I called Dad's office, but he was operating. When I called Hilda's, mother had gone.

I tried to keep a clear head, but got lost in the maze of downtown streets and tall buildings. Stuck at a stoplight behind a line of traffic, I slammed my fist into the horn. It jammed, helping to clear a path to the North End. Hanover was easy to find, but Tileston was nowhere to be seen. Eventually, I saw a police car, its red light blinking, a block from the harbor. I looked for a place to pull over. A crowd had gathered and a policeman was standing by.

The red light was flashing over a drunk who lay against a brick wall, his feet splayed wide, his eyes half open, a bottle of liquor hemorrhaging beside him. Blood oozed from a gash in his forehead, soiling a beard that obscured his face. His sweater was caked with dirt and shredded at the elbows, his trousers beltless and ripped in the knees, his loafers shorn of their soles, his sockless ankles ringed with dirt. I squatted down, afraid to touch him, reeling from the stench of alcohol and vomit. Studying his features, I spotted a scar on his wrist where my brother had cut himself filleting fish on Cape Cod.

"Paul," I said. His eyes fluttered open. He tried to speak but nothing emerged.

"Don't talk," I said. I staunched the blood with my handkerchief. A small smile curled on his lips when I touched him. A woman approached, young and pretty.

"Josh?" she asked. "I'm Tammy. I was walking my dog and saw him lying there. I haven't seen him for months. I couldn't believe it was him." She hesitated to get too close. The police officer came over.

"You know this fella?"

"My brother."

"Oh, Lord. Sorry," he said. He stuffed his pen and pad in his pocket and looked down in confusion as his radio crackled with emergencies. "What do you want to do? Your folks around?"

"Yes."

"Give them a call. I'll wait."

I couldn't reach Dad at the hospital but Mother picked up the phone at home.

"Where have you been?" she asked. "Hilda was disappointed."

"I found Paul."

"Oh, God. Where in the world?"

"The North End."

"Does he want to come home?"

"Not yet."

"What do you mean?"

"He's been drinking. He should go to a hospital."

I could hear her thinking. "Did you call Father?"

"He's operating. Where should I take him?"

"The Beth Israel."

"Boston? Why not Quinnipiac?"

"I don't want to make a scene."

"A scene? He's a wreck. He's been wandering all over the place. What difference does it make now."

"I was thinking of our family."

"If you'd been thinking of our family he wouldn't be here."

"Don't' be upset, Joshua. I don't know what to say. Where is Father when we need him?"

The policeman and I grabbed Paul under his arms and legs and carried him to the car. His sweater slid up his body, revealing sores on his bloated belly. "What a load," the cop said, wedging him into the back seat. Tammy thrust her head in the window. Her green eyes were beautiful in the dusk.

"I'm so sorry. Is there anything I can do?" She held her Pekinese close in her arms, stroking his head.

"You found him. That's enough."

"I'm at the Sail Loft now." Her face turned ashen. "I'm sorry it ended bad. Your brother was a good guy. I never realized he'd gotten like this."

"That makes two of us."

The cop pulled up beside me. "Want an escort?" He flicked on his siren and wheeled through the traffic, over Beacon Hill and down Brookline Avenue, scattering cars like pigeons. Paul was always being taken places - private school, Harvard, McLean's Hospital, and now the emergency ward.

The cruiser pulled up to the entrance. Two young orderlies dressed in whites rolled out a gurney and strapped Paul down. His shoes fell off, exposing the dirt caked between his toes. I held his hand hanging off the gurney. His fingers were bruised and he'd bitten his fingernails to the nubbins. I followed them into the emergency room and answered their questions about his medical history.

The room was hot and stifling, full of groans from behind white curtains. I wrapped my fingers around the seat of my chair and held tight. An hour later a doctor in his thirties appeared and sat beside me. He wore the look of an all nighter.

"You his family?" he asked, scanning the reports.

I nodded.

"Your brother's sick. His blood alcohol's high,

his liver function borderline. A few more weeks on the street might have finished him." He put aside his reports and looked at the curtain separating us from Paul. "Has he been in treatment?"

"At McLean's, a while ago. Not any more."

"What do you want to do? We could pink paper him into the psych unit and dry him out. It's your call." He handed me a card. "See Claire in Social Service, third floor. She'll get the paperwork going."

"I'll wait for my father. How long would you keep him?"

"Ten days. We'll detox him. After that…" he shrugged.

I brushed aside the curtain and stood beside Paul, robed in a light blue johnny, the color of his eyes. An IV dribbled saline water into his vein, replacing the Johnny Walker. His personal effects lay in a clear plastic bag - a few crumpled bills, a driver's license, and a gold graduation ring from prep school. His shredded clothes were stashed in a garbage bag sealed with duct tape.

Dad arrived at nine. He listened intently as the doctor filled him in, asked a few questions, and reviewed the test results. When he went to visit Paul behind the curtain, he crumpled into a chair with his face in his hands. I put my hand on his shoulder. The wool blend suit felt rough and warm.

Dad filled out the paperwork and we left Paul to his sleep, his ravaged face resting on a clean white pillow. We drove down Beacon Street, not saying much. When we got to Brookline, we pulled into Jack & Marion's, looking for a reason to eat. The aroma of smoked meat and fish provided it. Mel, the owner, came over with menus and water.

"Hi Doc. Been a while. How's the family?"

"Fine. How's Rachael and Rebecca?"

"Good memory. Couldn't be better. Is this one of

your boys?"

"My youngest, Josh."

I tried to smile.

"Your father's a great man," he said. "He'd never tell you, but I will. Whenever my kids had a problem, he was there, day or night. Studying to be a doctor, Josh?"

"I don't know."

"Medicine will never let you down. Am I right, Doc?"

Dad cleared his throat. "It's a good profession."

"That's what I mean. The deli business has its ups and downs, but people are always sick. Your other boy? I forgot his name."

"Paul," Dad said.

"Two fine boys, Doc. I hope my girls can find guys like yours. By the way, the pastrami is *vunderlech*! Know what that means, Josh?"

"Wonderful," I answered. Same in Norwegian, *vidunderlig*."

"Norwegian?" he asked.

"I was living there."

"You have a son born to wander, Doc."

"I have a son who finds his own way."

We ordered triple decker sandwiches and lapsed into silence. There were just a few people in the Deli having a late snack, *noshing,* as Ida would say.

"When do you go back?" Dad asked.

"A couple of weeks."

"Have enough money?"

"You gave me some yesterday."

"Oh," he answered, jiggling the change in his pocket. "Chosen your courses?"

"I haven't thought about it. I've been looking for Paul." It came out sharper than I meant.

He looked away, put his glasses in his lapel pocket."I know I've screwed things up."

"I didn't mean it that way, Dad."

"No, I've screwed it up. Never around day or night."

"But,"

"No buts, son." His voice cracked and he stopped. I was at a loss for words.

Mel arrived with our food and left after a look at our faces. Dad took one bite, then gazed down at his plate.

"I'm sorry for all of this and you in the middle trying to help."

"I wanted to, Dad."

"I thought you would. I never thought it would come to this."

"Neither did I."

Our eyes locked. I heard the scrape of chairs as waiters began to clean up. Dad bit off a hunk of his sandwich that left part of it hanging from his mouth. I removed the top layer of bread and munched on the turkey. We finished our meal with seltzer and belches. Then he blew his nose so loudly into a napkin. It was embarrassing.

When we got home Mother came out from the living room, stopping us on the stairs. She was still wearing her apron and looked disheveled. "My goodness, it's late," she said and yawned. "I must have dozed off."

"I'm sorry, Mira. We should have called," Dad said.

"That's all right. I kept the roast in the oven."

"I don't think we're hungry," Dad said, gently.

"Okay. I'll put things away." She untied her apron. "They didn't release him yet?"

"It wasn't a check up, Mira." Dad whipped his tie through the collar. "I signed papers to commit him. He was drunk."

"At six in the afternoon?"

"At six in the afternoon and all day long. There

was more alcohol in his veins than blood."

"How long till he comes home, Father?"

"Ten days. Then we'll see."

"See what?"

"I wish I knew."

Caught between Mother standing by the kitchen door and Dad half way to his bedroom, I didn't know whether to go up or down the stairs. "I'll have a bite," I volunteered, and followed her to the table, set for four with candles burned down to snippets.

"I was hoping that Paul would be all right," she said as she prepared a plate of roast beef and potatoes. "The doctors do such marvelous things, don't you think?"

"Sure, Mother."

Dad came down to the liquor cabinet, loosened his shirt, and poured a *schnapps*. "Won't you join us, Father?"

"I'm tired, Mira," he said, downing a shot of whiskey.

"Maybe Paul could visit Josh in the fall."

"Josh has his own life to live."

The candles flickered in the evening breeze and blew out. I carved my meat into tiny pieces, hoping to find a crevice in my stomach to put them. Dad looked out at the lake, opaque and still.

CHAPTER 37

A few days later we went back to see Paul. Without a police escort it took a while. He'd been moved to the seventh floor annex. The door was locked and a sign read, Blumenthal Psychiatric Wing. Dad looked through the wire mesh window and rang for an attendant. We were escorted into a hallway where patients wandered in bathrobes or were strapped in chairs, their faces worn smooth by medications. I'd never visited Paul at McLean's. I stared straight ahead, afraid to look into their eyes.

Paul shared a room with two other patients, his bed wedged tightly against a window overlooking a vacant lot. They had stitched up his forehead with black thread but left him unshaven. His cheeks were swollen, his eyes clammed shut, his forearm marked with yellow-brown bruises from IV needles and purple contusions from restraints binding him to the bed. We gathered around unsure whether he was awake or asleep. Mother wore a full length black dress, Dad had on a blue striped suit. Both looked as if they were going to a funeral.

"How're you feeling?" I asked Paul. It sounded stupid as soon as I said it and he didn't respond. I was listening to the twing of the heart monitors when Ida limped into the room and went to his bedside. Dad turned ashen the moment he saw her.

"So, Pauly, you found," she said, stroking his forehead like he was a child. He turned his head and mumbled a few words. "*Nyet, leipshen*. No speak now," she said, then turned to Dad. "So, Jacob, this you cannot tell me?"

She put an arm around Dad's shoulder and he began to cry. I cried, too. Despite the sadness, it felt good. Mother sat by Paul, smoothing out his rumpled sheet, her cheeks puffy with feelings. I wondered if the Blumenthal wing had been the hospital where she'd been admitted and who would be hospitalized next.

A nurse arrived to tell us visiting hours were over. Dad dried his tears and propped his handkerchief in his lapel pocket while Mother powdered her face.

"When you small, troubles are small," Ida said, rubbing her knuckles. "When big, troubles are big."

"You didn't have to come to the hospital, Ida," Mother said. "I wished they'd comb his hair. He'd look more like himself."

When we said goodbye to Paul, he was staring at the red and green lights flickering on the monitors. Mother and Dad left for home and work and I took Ida to her apartment. We didn't talk much in the car, but when we entered her living room, she slumped on the couch. "Manny right. Pauly a ghost."

"Dad said they'll detox and clean him up."

"Clean, ya. But can they fix *kopen*?" she said, tapping her head.

"How come I hear nothing?"

"I guess Dad didn't want to tell you."

"And you, you know Pauly gone? I have eyes. I can look."

"Ma, you can barely walk."

She pulled an afghan around her. I snitched a butterscotch candy from the coffee table jar.

"Why Pauly not come here? I cook for him."

"He would have liked that."

"Have clean clothes."

"He needed them for sure."

"So now he lives with *mashugenahs* in hospital."

I cracked open a walnut, scattering the shells on her polished tabletop. Abe used to open them with his bare hands.

"You hungry? I have *knish*. I make this week." She left for the kitchen. It was nice to hear the dishes rattling and I joined her. She took a pan of knishes out of the refrigerator, jabbed at them with a spatula, then stopped, sighing heavily.

"*Knish* is *kaput*," she said, tossing them in the garbage.

I looked at the other leftovers, removing a platter of roast chicken. "This looks good."

"Just like your father," she said, shaking her head, "Always ready to eat."

As I lay on my sheets in the heat later that night, I wondered how Paul could fall sleep with his hands tied to the bed. When I was young and couldn't sleep, I used to wait up for Mother and Dad, listening for the crunch of their tires coming down the gravel driveway. But tonight, Mother was already in bed and I had no idea when Dad would be home. Now that summer was turning to fall, the night was completely silent.

The next morning I sorted through my trunk, deciding which of my Norwegian clothes and keepsakes to take to school. It would be the end of the raspberry harvest in Lier now. Soon all of the hay would be in the barn and Lars would plow over the potato field. I thought about the flat bread with goat cheese, sardines swimming in olive oil, bread smeared with jam , and butter cookies late at night. I missed the screenless windows open to the night air, staring at the summer light from under my comforter, the roosters crowing from across the valley as day broke. Everything sounded close in the early morning if the wind was blowing right.

I went to see Paul in the afternoon as visiting time ended. A patient stopped me in the hallway, checking to ask who I was. His breath stank and his glance shifted uneasily. I said I was a doctor doing my rounds and proceeded to Paul's room quickly. He had two new roommates, but it hardly mattered since both were sedated. He rested in bed, smiling in his sleep, oblivious to the stitches etched in his forehead.

"He was up all night, honey, fighting the restraints," a nurse said, checking his IV. "Don't worry. We won't wake him. The doctor gave him a shot. Are you a friend or family?"

"Family," I said.

"His brother?"

I nodded yes.

"It'll be tough for a while. Do you want us to shave him? He didn't have a beard on his driving license. He was good looking."

The past tense gave me a jolt.

"DT's are the worst. You feel like you're coming apart. You from around here?"

"Quinnipiac."

She stopped and stared. "The Volkens from Quinnipiac, the doctor's sons?" she asked.

"Yes. I'm Josh." I was afraid I'd revealed too much. Don was supposed to be a family secret.

"And this is your brother, the one who went to Harvard? I'm sorry, I didn't know what had happened."

She changed the dressing on his arm and tidied up around his bed. "I worked with your Dad at the Beth Israel and the Eye & Ear. He's a good doctor, always on the ward. Well, at least your brother's in the right place."

"I hope so."

"He'll be out of here soon." She paused and smiled. "Anyone said you look like your father?"

"Yes." I put my hands in my pockets.

"A spitting image. We were at Tufts together. Classes in the day, working at night. He helped in his father's tailor's shop, if I remember. He was always worried about money, afraid he'd fail an exam, let his family down. He had a lot on his mind."

"Were you…"I blushed.

"Good friends," she said. I wondered if she was one of Dad's late night appointments.

She looked at Paul. "Your father worked too hard for this." She moistened a cloth and wiped his swollen face, dabbing around his closed eyes.

"In a few days," she said, "I'll give him a shave." She took his pulse, tucked in his sheet.

I stopped by Dad's office on the way home. Stellina said he was still at the hospital. Her perfume created a mixture of alarm and allure. I thanked her and left. The house was dark except for a light in the living room. I opened the front door quietly, hoping to sneak into the TV room.

"Father?" Mother called, hoarsely.

"No, Josh," I said. I went into the living room. She was sitting on the couch, a textbook propped on her lap.

"I was hoping it was Father. Where were you?"

"The hospital."

"I called. They said he was sleeping. He always needed a good night's sleep. How did he look?"

"Tired."

"But well?"

"Yes."

"Good. I'll plan a visit when he's himself. Maybe we'll all visit Sunday. And then where did you go?"

"Dad's office. He wasn't around."

"Oh. You should telephone first. You don't want to surprise him."

"What do you mean?"

"He likes me to call. He has a busy practice." She set her book on the marble tabletop. "I did your laundry."

"But I haven't unpacked."

"I thought it would be nice to have clean clothes."

"My clothes are fine." I turned to leave.

"Sit, Joshua. I haven't seen you today, please?"

I stayed, perched on the edge of the couch.

"I'm reading about Margaret Mead in Samoa. She was always ahead of her time living the life she wanted in far away places. Maybe Father and I will take a cruise to the South Pacific."

"Dad? He thinks New York City's a long trip."

"He's too tied to his family. I never realized it until after I married him. I had hopes we'd have more privacy after we moved to Quinnipiac."

"But his family likes being together."

"I suppose, in their way." There were wrinkles under her chin and wisps of gray in her hair. "Summer courses are so demanding. Miss one class and you miss a lot. I hope I can graduate this spring. Well, I won't keep you longer and I have a chapter to finish. "

I left for the TV room. I hadn't watched much television in Norway and didn't care what I saw now, just wanted to be by myself. The den was a musty room on the ground floor, cold in the winter, humid in the summer, but I liked its moldy chairs and ratty shag rug. It was full of our trophies and camp pictures and our heights were etched on a closet door from ages five to thirteen. A museum of Paul and me.

James Arness was hunting down bad guys on

Gunsmoke when I heard Mother make her way up the stairs and across to her room. The phone rang a few minutes later.

"*Snakker du norsk*, pardner?"

It took a moment to ring a bell. "Brad! When did you learn Norwegian?"

"In my free time in Idaho."

"Idaho? What the hell are you doing there?"

Brad said his Mom had made a surprise visit to Oslo and discovered that her grandchild was on the way. To avoid trouble with his Dad, she'd found a place for them to live with her sister in Idaho. Marge had a good place to stay, just dry and dusty.

"What time is it anyway?" he asked.

"Eleven."

"Son of a gun! I thought it was dinner time. Did I bother anyone?"

I laughed. "No one to bother. Mom's asleep. Dad's not home." I turned off the TV and told him about Paul.

"Jeez, a hell of a homecoming. What're you going to do?"

"Don't know. And you?"

"Beats me. The kid's a'coming. I might build a place on a parcel of land Marge has on a creek. I could float logs down it and put up a log cabin. A $100 forest permit buys a lot of trees in Idaho. Give me a buzz at the Chupas in Obsidian when you figure things out."

I couldn't find Obsidian on a map. It was great to hear his voice and I celebrated with a chocolate sundae. Dad rolled in a few minutes later, his tie slack and dark shadows under his eyes.

"Looks good," he said, opening the freezer. He scraped out the last bits of chocolate and settled beside me.

"I went to the hospital," I said. "Paul was sleeping."

"I stopped by to see him after dinner. Kronstein says he can come home the day after tomorrow."

"Great. By the way, I met someone there who says hello."

"Oh?" he said.

"A nurse who knew you at Tufts, Mary somebody?"

"Mary O'Callahan?" he said, under his breath. "How did you run into her?"

"She's taking care of Paul."

He set his spoon down.

"We were talking. She likes to gab."

"That she does. I didn't know she was at the B.I."

"How do you know her?"

"A friend from medical school." He got up and dumped the rest of his sundae in the sink. That was the end of the conversation. We heard the soft padding of slippers on the stairs. Mother appeared in the doorway, pale and tired, her hair in a tangle over her shoulders."What are you doing up, Mira?" Dad asked.

"I couldn't sleep. You're home early, Father." She looked at the clock. It said twelve. "What are you boys talking about?"

"Not much. Just Paul," Dad answered. "He's coming home this weekend. But don't get your hopes up."

"What do you mean?" She rubbed her eyes.

"He's not doing well," he said.

Feeling tired, I rose and put the chocolate sauce in the cupboard.

"Turning in?" she asked.

"Yeah," I said.

"Did you remember my medicine, Father?"

"Are you out already?"

"I have a few pills, but I feel better when there are extras." She went to the sink and filled a glass with water.

"How many pills are you taking, Mira?" Dad asked,

watching her.

"Jacob! I have to sleep. I can't be alone every night."

Dad stiffened, then walked past and up to his bedroom. She inserted two tiny pills in her mouth and closed her eyes.

CHAPTER 38

Paul was waiting in a chair in his room, holding a
laundry bag of personal effects tagged with a yellow
label that said, Volken. They had shaved his beard
and given him a buzz cut that reminded me of
haircuts at camp. He wore a wrinkled white shirt,
baggy brown khakis, and loose fitting loafers
without socks. He almost looked like my brother
again, except for the look in his eyes and the scar
on his forehead.

"Hi son," Dad said, nervously putting a hand on
his shoulder. Paul answered with a pained smile,
breathing in halting gasps. He stood and waited to
be led away.

"Hungry?" Dad asked.

Paul shrugged and slung the bag over his back.

"I bet you're sick of hospital food. I know detox
is lousy. But you'll snap out of it." He put an arm
around his waist and guided him out of the room.

They walked down the hallway, arm in arm, past
the patients in the common room staring at the TV.
They made an odd pair - Dad in his Brooks Brothers
suit, Paul with his shirt hanging out of his pants.
Dad kept up a steady chatter in the car until we
turned into our driveway.

"Paul Volken!" Mother said, as we came in the
door. She put her hands in her pockets to stop them

from trembling. We sat down in the living room surrounded by books, unable to find a word to say. Paul dropped his bag and studied the Persian rug.

"Well," Dad said, and then left to call his answering service. Mother went back to the kitchen. I followed Paul to his room. He lay down on his bed.

"Want to throw the football around?" I asked.

"Nope."

"How about after dinner? The Giants and Browns are playing at eight, the first game of the season."

"Maybe," he said, hoarsely. He went to the bathroom and splashed water in his face, studying the scar in the mirror."How'd I do that?" He poked at the stitches.

"I don't know," I answered. "They hurt?"

"A little."

"Maybe you fell?"

"When?"

"I don't know." We went to the den and took our usual places, Paul in the recliner and me on the sofa.

"Cleveland's good this year," I said, as Jim Brown darted through the line and sprang into the clear. A defender pursued, catching him just before the goal line, only to be dragged into the end zone.

"Damn! He ran through the Giants like they were stuck in mud." I looked at Paul, but he was biting his nails, chewed down to puffy pink stubs. Dad joined me on the couch.

"Who's winning?" he asked.

"Cleveland," I said. "Jim Brown had an 80 yard touchdown."

"Which are the Browns?"

"The guys in white."

"Want me to get some Patriot tickets?"

"Sure, Dad," I said. September had always been my favorite month for sports because football and baseball had so many games to watch.

272

Mother called that dinner was ready. I turned off the TV and shuffled upstairs. Bowls of steaming chowder were sitting on our plates, thick with chunks of clams and potatoes. Paul nibbled at the edges, then, while reaching for the ice water, tipped over his soup. The puddle oozed across the table toward his lap. "Paul!" Mother shouted. Dad rushed over with napkins, Mother ran for a dish towel. Paul just sat there and watched the chowder spill onto his pants.

I stuck around the next day, waiting for Paul to come out of his room. He lay in bed with the shades drawn, smoking cigarettes and coughing. He picked at food when no one was around and left the dishes on the table. By the following day, Mother and Dad had decided to take him back to McLean. They talked it over at dinner, telling him it was a chance to work with the best doctors, that this time the hospital would do him wonders. As Mother packed his leather suitcase embossed with his initials, Paul grew fidgety, started pacing the halls. I suggested we take a walk.

The night was mellow and moonless, but we knew the way to the lake. We sat on the dock beneath the limbs of our swinging tree, an old pitch pine with half its roots exposed to the encroaching water. The knotted rope still hung over the lake. Paul sat near me not saying much, his feet dangling over the pier, his restless hands peeling bark off a stick.

When I came down to breakfast in the morning, he was on his way to the hospital. He was wearing his blue and red football jacket from high school. While Mother assembled a basket of food, Dad finished his calls. Still groggy from sleep, I gave him a hug, told him I would see him at the holidays. As they drove away, he looked out the back seat window, his face a mixture of sadness and confusion.

I showered quickly and left for Ida's, then remembered it was Friday and she'd be at *Shul*. It was good to get away from the house. I entered the dank Temple and looked for her black hat and veil. A few people were scattered around the sanctuary, mostly older, mostly alone, *dovening* and mumbling portions of the Torah.

"*Schmen*," Ida hissed, waving her hand. I slid onto the bench and followed her finger as they read the Kaddish, the prayer for the dead. Grasping my arm at the end of the service, she staggered to her feet.

"Hurting, Ma?"

"*Nein*. Just mine back. Abe's birthday today, so I come to *Shul*."

"His birthday was September 28th?"

"The Hebrew day, seventh of *Elul*. *Goyska* day, who knows?"

She leaned on my arm as we went down the steps and crossed the trolley tracks onto Kinross Road.

"I told Abe about Pauly," she said. "Abe say, finally he come home. I say, home? Oy! Know what Abe say?"

"No."

"Of course you don't. He was talking to me. He say, Jacob will fix his son."

We made our way up the stairs, step by step, and entered her apartment."So *Schmen,* you going? You know, every day you gone in the *forsluggana* country mine heart was heavy. But Pauly's back." She eyed me carefully. "You home, but not really home?"

"*Ja*, I gucss."

"You do nothing for Pauly now. Go your own way."

"No matter where?"

She smiled. "You *raizender. Forstain*?"

"*Ja*, traveler. Same in Norwegian, *reisende*."

"*Hoih*! At least Norway good for learning Yiddish," she laughed. She went to the refrigerator and pulled out her coffee rolls laced with cinnamon and nuts. I could have eaten the platter. "Take and come back Hanukkah, *yah*?"

I munched on the coffee rolls as I drove home, stopping by Liberty Travel to pick up my ticket for Dayton that Mother had ordered. I was packing my trunk when Mother came in with the last of my laundry. She hovered around my desk, admiring the Schaeffer pen and pencil set Ida had given me for my Bar Mitzvah.

"A beautiful gift, isn't it," she said. "I don't know how she afforded it. Did you know this was my grandmother's desk?"

"No, I didn't." Small and dark with age, it barely had room for a lamp and a writing pad.

"She'd sit up at night and write to her brother. They were close in Germany but he settled in Wisconsin after the war. Funny how people lose touch. You got a letter from Norway by the way." She put it on the desk and left for her bedroom.

Norway seemed a distant country by now and my language was fading. *Dear Josh*, it began.

I passed the courts last week. The nets were gone and the clubhouse closed. Getting ready for winter I guess.

I felt awful for walking away, not giving us a second chance. Remember when we met at the café, eating kakedeig at the counter? I didn't think you liked me then, but that sort of changed.

I don't know what happened at the Solstice. I guess I got caught by surprise. But let's find a way, to be together.

Loving you,

Tulla

P.S. I came to the boat but couldn't find you!

P.S.S. Can you understand my Norwegian?

Love for the guy who ran away, who'd returned

from the land of free love empty-handed? But apparently not empty for her. Maybe I'd visit at Christmas. Meet in Oslo. Borrow the keys and go to the hytta. I put her letter in my pocket.

Dad came home shortly after. I found him rummaging through the refrigerator.

"You're home early," I said.

"I figured it was your last week, we'd do something together.

Coffee rolls gone already?"

"They're behind the chowder."

"I got two tickets for the Patriots this weekend. I thought we'd grab a steak at Ken's, have a night out."

"I fly back Thursday."

"Oh." He stopped, closed the refrigerator door. "Want to hit some golf balls tonight?"

"Sure." I couldn't even remember the last time we'd been to the driving range together.

We drove to Tillie & Sam's on Route 9, a favorite haunt when we were kids. On a hot summer night, we'd go there with Dad and top it off with a cone at Brighams.

Only a handful of people were hitting late. We got two buckets of balls and drivers. Dressed in his plaid Bermuda shorts and a striped Ara's dress shirt, he hardly fit in with the T-shirts and jeans crowd. His strokes were like a Pitch 'n Putt player, short choppy swings that dribbled balls off the tee in every direction. But I got a kick out of his trying. I drove my shots deep until they became tiny white specks sailing into the trees. I wasn't usually the heavy hitter. Paul use to deliver the balls so far into the night that I never saw where they landed.

CHAPTER 39

Mother dropped me at the airport the next morning. It teemed with travelers scattering to far away cities. Paris, Helsinki, Rome, Istanbul, Barcelona – many of the places I'd read about in National Geographics. The Dayton gate was in a sparsely inhabited cul-de-sac. I sat down on a hard plastic bench, dreading the semester of pre-med classes. I hated the odor of formaldehyde, the pictures of anatomical deformations, the ghostly creatures floating in specimen jars.

The PA began to announce departures gates and times. When I heard Boise, something snapped. I walked down the hall to the Idaho gate, fingering Dad's new roll of twenties.

"Boise, please," I said.

"Any bags, sir?"

"One. Is Boise near Obsidian?"

"Is that your final destination?" Her fingers rattled over the keyboard. "We can get you a connection to Twin Falls. Is that close enough?"

"Sure," I said, wherever that was.

I presented my Dayton ticket and semester's spending money. She gave me three dollars back. I gave her my stub to reclaim my bag from the Dayton flight and walked up the gangway in a daze.

"Hi there, son. Where're you headed?" The bus driver asked outside the Twin Falls airport which was not much more than a shack. He was an older gent dressed in jeans and a cap that said Prairie Trailways. I told him Obsidian.

"Hefty bag you got there," he chuckled.

"I was headed to college," I said.

"Stow it below. I'll bust my gut lifting that thing into the bus. Where's your school?"

"Ohio."

"Whoa. Quite a detour."

"Yes-a-ree," I agreed. It didn't look like too many people were going to Obsidian, or anywhere for that matter.

"Take a seat. In fact, take as many as you like," he laughed.

I sat behind him with a view of the road. He ground into first and headed north on a two-laner. The land was flat in every direction with contorted cacti dotting the countryside.

"You get the southern tour today. Sixty second stops in towns you never heard of. What brings you to Obsidian?"

"The Chupas."

"Marge Chupa? Great gal. I live in Stanley, a few miles north. How long you here for?"

"Not sure."

"It's a pretty part of the country."

I looked at the miles of desert and thought he needed a vacation.

"Plenty of fishing, hunting, and hiking in the mountains."

"Mountains?"

"Not here. Up in Stanley." He pointed north out the driver's window, streaked with grime and dust. "The Sawtooth Mountains. You didn't know Idaho is mountain country?"

"Not really. A friend said it was flat and dry."

"A lot of it is. But over in Obsidian we got salmon in the rivers and elk in the forests. By the by, I'm Clarence." He stuck a cigarette between his parched lips and lit up.

We drove up the dry plateau, pulling into small towns where he picked up packages and gossip, and moved on. With each new mile the incline steepened until the tips of white-capped mountains began to rise from the plain. He downshifted into S curves for the final climb to Galena Pass. My ears were popping and my head was about to burst when we arrived at the summit.

Below unfolded the Sawtooth Valley, stretching a hundred miles north and bordered by jagged 12,000 foot peaks. A thin blue river snaked through its bottom, watering ranches and meadows. Forests cloaked the mountains from river to snow line. My heart was beating hard - it looked like the *Jotenheimen*.

"I never tire of this valley. Kind of like homesteading," he said, and coasted into the valley, stopping at the Obsidian general store.

"Enjoy your stay, son." He helped offload my trunk and gave me Marge's number. It rang a while before a breathless woman answered.

"Hello, my golly, hello! Had to run clear across the yard. Anybody there?" Marge asked.

"Yes. Is Brad around?"

"Oh, no. He's at the cabin site. Be back tonight. Who's calling?"

"Josh, a friend."

"Josh, his Norway pal? How do you do! Can I give him a message?"

"Tell him I'm at the bus stop."

"Where?"

"Obsidian."

"Well, golly! Brad know you here?"

"Not exactly. It was sort of last minute."

279

"He knows a lot about that. Tell you what, I'll be there in a snatch. I'll be driving a blue Chevy Blazer with a cracked window."

I heard the Blazer before I saw it. It lurched into the parking lot and jerked to a halt, motor throbbing.

"Hop aboard, son. Can't stop the engine, it'll stall. Throw your bags in the back seat."

The seat was covered with a torn blanket, broken tools, bags of fertilizer, and a rooster perched on top.

"Don't worry about him, hon. He likes to go for a ride. He'll keep an eye on your things."

I squeezed my bags onto the seat and climbed into the front.

"So you're Josh," she said, lurching into the road. "Brad said you were headed back to school."

I told her about my sudden change of plan.

Marge cackled and slapped the wheel. "Like some of my best decisions, including my husband. And most of Brad's. His Mom and Dad are fit to be tied."

We arrived at the Chupa's at six, a modest ranch house surrounded by sheds, a garden, and blueberry bushes. Chickens, roosters, and goats ambled through the yard presided over by a fat angora cat sleeping on the porch. A scruffy dog with patches of missing fur poked his head in my crotch.

"That's Leftovers," Marge said. "He wouldn't harm a flea and he has a lot of them." I patted Leftovers gingerly while Marge shooed the rooster out of the back.

Grabbing my bags, I entered the kitchen, a small room strewn with dirty dishes and bowls of various pet food. Marge fixed me a cup of coffee, black and strong, and started cleaning. A few minutes later a pick up truck drove in.

"Hey, Brad, you got company," Marge yelled.

Brad entered, carrying a tool box and four foot level. "Son of a gun," he said, doing a jig across the room.

"He's on a detour," Marge chuckled. "You're setting a great example. Anyone else headed this way?"

Greta trailed through the door, settling heavily in a chair. "You're just in time," Brad said. "I'm losing my help and can use a hand."

"Look guys, I've got a mess to do, so why don't you handle the dishes while I work on the grub. Throw your bags in the back bedroom, Josh, and stay as long as you want."

Greta stood up to help.

"Not you, honey. Just sit and rest. My husband will be home in a snatch."

Marge went to the porch to skin potatoes while Brad filled the sink with sudsy water. I gathered the pots, pans, and plates in piles.

"Looks like dishes get done once a week."

"Not even then." Brad laughed. "It's always been that way with Marge."

I filled Brad in about Paul and my decision to head west. He told me his Mom had already snuck in a visit. She'd arrived with home baked cookies, mumbled about Christmas plans, and went to the orchard and cried. He handed me the last pot and pulled the plug on the drain.

"Any day now there's going to be three of us and I'm a short order cook with a borrowed car, homesick wife, and no roof over my head." He stared at the scuzzy water slurping down the drain. "What are you up for tomorrow?" he asked.

"Whatever."

"How about floating logs down a creek and raising a wall?"

"I don't know much about building."

"That makes two of us. Hey, I've got a level and

a saw."

Marge swung through the backdoor with a pot of peeled potatoes. "Much obliged, boys. Now scoot and let a girl do her work." We joined Greta on the porch where crickets were announcing the dusk.

"God, I could go for a soak," Brad said.

"*Ja,* my back really hurts," Greta said, adjusting herself on the edge of the sofa. Her breathy *ja* made me smile.

"Why don't we head to the hot springs after everyone's asleep?" Brad said.

We ate beef stew and greens from Marge's garden and boiled potatoes that tasted great. After Marge and Ed turned in, we glided silently out of the yard, waiting for the road to open the throttle. The road's dotted white lines flew out of the darkness, guiding us through the valley.

After a few miles, we turned onto a dirt road that zigzagged through a meadow damp with dew. We parked by a barbed wire fence and walked across the grass. A redwood tub, several yards across, stood out in the distance, its sulphurous fumes luring us forward. We stripped off our dusty clothes and lowered ourselves into the water, our pale bodies barely visible. A heavy mist lingered in the cold night air. With the tips of our faces barely above the surface, we gazed at the parapet of the mountains.

"He's kicking," Greta said.

Brad put his hand on her stomach. "I guess he likes warm water. Want to feel, Josh?" Timidly, I touched her stomach, stretched as tight as a drum.

"*Nei*, Josh, *ikke der*," Greta whispered, guiding my hand to a palpitating bulge. It kicked a few times then went still.

The sky was filled with stars, millions of them in the moonless night. I wondered if the Aurora was blooming for Tulla. I'd write her a letter in the next few weeks and see if we could meet in Oslo.

Tomorrow Brad and I would drive to the meadow and start on the cabin. We'd float logs down Alturas Lake Creek and raise the foundation, chinking the spaces between the logs to keep out the cold, and splitting the brushwood for fire and light.